The Half of It
of
It

Theresa Christine

Identifiers: Ebook ASIN B0DT4XVX5W | ISBN 979-8-9924257-0-3

Contents

Content Warnings

The Half of It is a spicy slow-burn contemporary romance that tackles some emotional topics before ending in a Happy Ever After. Listed below is the content that may be triggering for some readers. Some of this content may be minor spoilers for what's ahead, so proceed at your own discretion.

Mentioned but not shown on page: childhood neglect, parent battling addiction in the past, death of a parent in the past, relative with dementia, emotional cheating by a former partner, building collapse in the past resulting in casualties, death of a sibling in the past, drunk driving, grief, parents separating

Shown on page: passive-aggressive remarks from a family member to an LGBTQIA+ character, covert sexist remarks in a work setting

A Note on Ballygrá, Ireland

When deciding on the setting for *The Half of It*, I chose to create a town in County Kerry. I wanted to represent Ireland in an honest and respectful way when writing this book. Dreaming up Ballygrá, a fictional town rooted in reality, gave me room for certain details, like train times and neighborhood haunts, to align for *The Half of It*. This town, which I hope you come to love as much as I do, is an amalgamation of the places I have visited in Ireland.

Chapter One

Juniper

During the three-hour ride, I focus on the raindrops forming tiny tributaries on the train windows. The lush countryside zips by in blurred lines of emerald, and I zone out. Flying over an entire ocean worked up my nerves so much that I couldn't close my eyes on the plane, let alone rest. Watching scenery pass by at ground level feels therapeutic, and this is the most at ease I've been since getting the results two weeks ago.

A garbled announcement jerks me back to reality, and my body tenses.

"Next stop, Ballygrá."

A stout ticket inspector walks by and nods toward the silver train door as a reminder to depart. "S'your station, miss." The man has a sing-songy accent, which

I barely understand, and cheery, twinkling eyes. "On holiday?"

"Um, yeah."

"Don't get many tourists stoppin' off here. What brings you to the South-West of Ireland?"

"Work. And family." That word tastes foreign on my tongue. *Family.*

"Business and pleasure."

I match his excitement with a weak smile, because I'd describe this trip differently. Stressful. Anxiety-inducing. The pleasure will happen in a couple weeks when I'm back in the office, filing my article.

We lurch to a halt, and I ungracefully take my leave, throwing on my jacket in such a rush that I knock someone sitting by the aisle. I apologize in a hurry, tugging my phone from its charger and crumpling my notebook into my backpack.

"Here, I can grab this for you," the oblivious train inspector offers as he reaches for my worn-in canvas duffel. He means well, but my hand swoops in before the offer leaves his mouth.

"No, I've got it. Thank you."

Growing up in homes that never felt like homes helped me master the art of packing everything important to me in a single bag. I prefer to carry the weight on my own.

He nods and leads me over to the doors as they open. A brisk October chill greets me, and two other people exit onto the damp, empty platform. What a stark contrast from the crowded subways on my daily commutes. The train screeches away and fills the atmosphere with the excruciating sound of metal scraping metal, but once it's gone, there's an emptiness, like the air is missing something. No blaring taxi horns or curses from bike riders vying for space on congested streets. Instead, the hollow sound of a church bell in the distance marks fifteen minutes past the hour, although I don't know which hour, thanks to jet lag.

And *what* is that smell?

Shit. Literal shit. The dense, earthy scent of what I assume is animal manure from a nearby farm invades my senses, and I grimace. I'm definitely not in New York anymore.

The other passengers have already disappeared as the wind picks up, spitting icy rain droplets on my face. I dodge the miniature lakes forming between the uneven cobblestones, crossing the road as instructed by Cara's exclamation point-filled texts (*Hi Juniper! At the cafe until you arrive!! Can't wait to meet!!! Xx*). At the end of the block, past a row of colorful homes, I turn onto the main street. Sun-weathered wooden signs protrude from the rainbow of building facades, including a clothing store with knit items on display and a rustic pub with a red awning. Ballygrá looks exactly like the photograph I stared at online so often that I bookmarked the page. I'm there. I'm *here*, and this town lies before me in all of its charm and glory.

Then I see it: Cara's Cafe. Golden twinkle lights hug the door frame, and a thin layer of steam has accumulated on the windows. A standing figure comes into focus at a table near the front.

Is that her?

It's one thing to send messages back and forth, but something else entirely to meet this woman I'm connected to by blood. The blurry human form stills, and I want to bolt. I didn't even care about that damn DNA kit. I only used it because I arrived home pissy and spiteful after my editor passed me up for yet another promotion. There also may have been happy-hour cosmos and venting to my best friend Lissie involved. My buzzed brain imagined taking the test as a cosmic middle finger to my workplace.

Gutted with panic, I twirl, race across the street, and shoulder open a weighty ornate door. Inside, I find a different world—an Irish pub, but not like the ones in the city. To my left is a sophisticated oak bar top, and a hazy late-morning glow shines through the stained-glass windows. The room smells musty, like this very space was packed with patrons only hours ago. An elegant banister that looks hand carved leads upstairs to my right. The sign above the old-timey cash register says McCarthy's Pub: Cash Only.

A little liquid courage can't hurt, so I check the time. 11:19 a.m. I usually reserve morning booze for weekend brunch, but considering the circumstances, I'll make an exception.

A tinny guitar solo blasts from a speaker in the back. At the far end of the bar, a slim bartender faces the wall while bobbing his head to the song. He holds what looks like a professional camera, and the LCD screen has him so transfixed that my unceremonious, soggy plop onto the closest barstool doesn't catch his attention. Only once I plunk my bag and backpack on the ground does he shift his gaze my way, thrust the camera to his side, and scramble to lower the volume of the music.

He is not some rotund middle-aged man, which is sort of how I envisioned all Irish bartenders. This guy appears to be a couple years older than me at most, with a wispy mop of dirty blond hair and an angular face. As he moves toward me, his mossy-green eyes meet mine mid-stride.

"Anything," I blurt out before he has the chance to ask me what I want. "Well, maybe something strong. Please."

His mouth half opens as if he's about to speak. The man sizes me up, and I wriggle on the seat under his attention. An abrupt wave of self-consciousness hits me. What do I look like—or worse, smell like—after a transatlantic flight and getting drenched on the walk from the train station? I finger-comb my wet bangs and pray I'm not a complete walking disaster.

"Whiskey for breakfast?"

The man's thick brogue almost knocks me off my chair. I've heard all varieties of accents in the city, but nothing could have prepared me for this Irishman's smooth lilt.

"Not quite," I say, straightening up. The last thing I need is someone judging me for requesting hard liquor before noon. "I ate, so this is more like a digestif."

"Posh." He turns to grab a glass, and my gaze drags down his broad back. Yup, he's just as good-looking from behind. I could definitely have fun with this guy in the bedroom.

My phone vibrates as if it knows I've forgotten the reason I flew to Ireland. Work. And Cara. I don't have time to leave a trail of one-night stands in my wake, as much as I would like the release. I look at the screen, half expecting to see my editor demanding an update on the piece already.

LIS: Proud of you bb. You got this <3

I'd love to jump through the phone and tackle her with a hug. Whether she's bringing a bottle of wine back to the apartment to celebrate work wins, or we're binge-watching the latest reality TV shows to forget some terrible date, I can always count on Lis.

> **JUNE:** Why are you awake right now? Isn't it the middle of the night there?

> **LIS:** This was a test. I set an alarm for 5am to see if you'd message when you arrived and you did not, so you have officially failed the test

Lis needs to give me some credit. Just because I've never traveled overseas doesn't mean I'm a clueless tourist. Living on my own since I turned sixteen and spending nearly a decade in Manhattan count for something.

> **LIS:** Remember the travel advice I gave you, but most importantly, enjoy your time with Cara. Nervous?

> **JUNE:** Not really

> **LIS:** You know she's going to love you, just be yourself <3 She didn't have to invite you to her wedding, but she did because she wants you there

> **JUNE:** You are too good to me

> **LIS:** I know

"Here." The bartender slides a short broad glass filled with tawny liquid toward me. "Put it on the rocks for you. I think the cold'll remove some of the bite."

The way he says "you" seems almost like he's cut the word in half, shortening it to a brief soft tone, and his "think" comes out sharper, more like "tink." His manner of speaking is melodic, with valleys and mountains of sounds.

"Thanks," I say.

"Rough morning then?"

"You could say that," I answer with a rueful smile, grateful to have a hot guy to distract me. While meeting newly discovered half sisters in a foreign country is not my forte, flirting with cute guys in bars most definitely is. Not that I don't want to meet Cara, but her enthusiasm intimidates me. We'd talked on the phone for about three minutes tops before she invited me to her wedding. My editor overheard me talking about the call the next day, and if not for that mistake, I wouldn't be here.

Family has never done any good for me. While I wished for a real, normal household with all my heart growing up, at twenty-six years old, I've given up on that dream.

DNA tests don't lie, though.

The whiskey tumbler jitters in my hand, so I release it from my death grip. All I have to do is walk across the street, go into the restaurant, and meet the sibling I never knew existed. Easy enough.

The thought flicks on a job-related light bulb in my head, and I use my Notes app to jot down my ideas.

"Sorry," I tell the barman. "Quick work thing."

He nods, giving me some space but not turning his back to me. He rolls up one of his sleeves to wipe down his workspace, and the veins tracing up his arm make my mouth go dry.

I rip my eyes away from him to type out my note. *All I have to do is walk across the street, go into the restaurant, and meet the sibling I never knew existed.* Perfect. This is the slice-of-life journalism my editor has requested lately. I'm here to prove I can write more than fluffy roundups of celebrity photos and bogus astrology quizzes. And if this goes well, Ethan promised me a recurring column on any lifestyle topic I want.

My own column.

It's almost enough to make me forget that they gave us DNA tests as bonuses in lieu of something more useful. I would have preferred a Starbucks gift card, but Starbucks didn't move into the same building two floors above us. The Starbucks CEO also didn't start dating our editor in chief.

"So." I stash my phone away, and my eyes glide over the empty seats. "Busy morning for you then, huh?"

"You could say that." The corner of his mouth turns up in amusement, and he gives me another quick up-and-down. "Haven't seen you here before. Just get in?"

"Yeah. About ten minutes ago on the train."

"Welcome. I'm Aidan."

We shake hands, and I admire the sculpted curves of his forearms up close. I don't know what I like more—the strength of his hand or the rolling musicality of every word he speaks.

"Marissa," I reply. He seems harmless enough that I could give him my real name, but old habits die hard. Lis and I have a pact to not share personal information with anyone whenever we go out, for safety's sake, no matter how disarming their accent. Not like I'll run into this guy again. Ballygrá is a small town, but really, how small can it be?

"Marissa." A grin appears amid his five o'clock shadow. "Pleasure to meet you."

Chapter Two

Aidan

I don't have the heart to tell the woman who stormed in like a hurricane that we're not open for another fifteen minutes. On my way in, I must have forgotten to lock the front door, but who needs a pint at this hour? I know all the folks who pop into my da's pub—the loyal regulars. Most of them remember me from twenty-eight years back when I was toddling around here in nappies. They've their dedicated times that they saunter in for a drink, and they stick to those habits like the law.

"Nice to meet you too, Aidan." She flashes a mischievous grin that shakes something inside me.

She's clearly American, based on how she talks. I sift through past conversations with my best friend. She has a half sister coming into town for the wedding any day now, but did Cara say that was today? Tomorrow, I think, for breakfast. Besides, that woman's name is Juniper, not Marissa. Of that I'm certain.

We sometimes get tourists who have the sheer fortune of making a pit stop in Ballygrá on the way to the coast. Or, less frequently, ones who did dedicated research to unearth an old family pub like ours.

This woman looks and acts different, though. She's not gleefully ordering a pint of Guinness, and there's no guidebook glued to her palm. She's soaked, so I see no harm in giving her a drink.

"What's brought you here?" I ask.

"It's kind of a long story."

"Well, you're in luck, 'cause I've got nothing but time."

Marissa glances out the window and bites the corner of her lower lip.

"No pressure, of course," I say. "Normally, we get people who've had one too many and take any opportunity to overshare. Go on, be mysterious if you prefer."

She takes my invitation to not talk about whatever's troubling her and nods to the front wall instead. "Is that...sorry, is that a sheep on your dartboard?"

"Oh, aye." I chuckle as I recall the day my brother printed that photo and taped it there. "That sheep was a menace to society."

"So you throw darts at him?"

"No. I mean, yes we do." Christ, I sound like a lunatic. "I promise, no sheep were harmed in the making of that dartboard. Funny story, actually."

"Okay." She sits up straight and folds her arms on the counter. "You said you had nothing but time."

"And you?"

"I've got enough time for you to explain yourself."

"Well, when I was maybe twelve or thirteen, objects started going missing from people's gardens. Small things. Deck—" I stumble over the word and take a breath to slow down. "D-decorative gnomes, potted plants, clothes drying on the line. That sort of stuff. The incidents increased to where they brought the Gardaí into the schools to talk to the kids. The police. There was a clip in the newspaper about it too, all about people losing their garden decorations and bedsheets without a trace."

She listens intently as I find my stride in the story, and the amused curve of her lips draws me in. I regale her with how one Saturday afternoon, someone disturbed the summertime calm by yelling down the main street.

"Everyone hears, 'Thief, thief!' and they poke their heads out of the windows to witness a chubby ram tottering down the road with boxers in its mouth. Right behind it is old Mr. Langley, buck naked, arse out, waving his arms like a lunatic."

This prompts an eruption of laughter from her, and the sound gives me a heady feeling.

"Was that his only pair?" she asks with a giggle.

"An excellent question that we may never have the answer to."

"What was going on?"

I smile, pleased she's interested in hearing more. "Turns out, this clever ram had a tucked-away spot on the far side of a hill—a grove where he'd been collecting all the stolen treasure. Every family in town had something there."

"Did you?"

"My mam's favorite dress."

"Sounds like this sheep had style."

I exhale an easy laugh. "Absolutely. People stopped by and salvaged what they could from the heap, and most forgot about the spot altogether." My hands beg for something to do to not look awkward in front of her. I shove them both in my pockets. "My brother and I thought the place was special, though. Somewhere we could hide away and get up to mischief with friends, or girlfriends, when we got older. Escape the constant watch of folks in town." Good memories of him send a dull ache into my chest. "Growing up where everyone knows everyone means privacy's a valuable resource."

"And the sheep?"

"Exiled," I reply, and her jaw drops. "Humanely. We're not monsters. He lived off the rest of his days at a farm where the fencing's sturdier, I imagine."

"Good. I'd hate for him to walk in here and see his face up on that board." Her response comes out dry, but her smile tells me she's in on the joke.

I need more of this—joy, joking, anything to make the workday less monotonous. Serving drinks at the pub isn't how I imagined my life at this age, and I'm not suited for it the way Michael was. Still, it's the right choice—for Mam and Da, and for my brother. He always put family first.

But this woman's mere presence almost makes me forget I'm here. I toss a towel over my shoulder and wonder how long I can tempt her to stick around with drinks, but it looks like I don't have to bother. Her glass sits in the same spot, untouched and full to the brim.

"Everything all right there?"

"Yeah. No. I'm not sure." She angles in as if to tell me a sweet little secret. Like a reflex, I shuffle closer too. "What would you do if you had one of those moments coming up where you knew...you just knew your life was about to change? And your brain is telling you to run the other way, to do the thing you've always done. But you can't, and everything will be different, and you don't know if you're ready."

"Well, I'd...Christ." I comb a hand through my hair, not sure how to respond. If I'd known what would happen to my brother, how it would rip my family apart at the seams, what would I have done? "None of the big, life-changing moments I've had were ones I could plan for."

"Yeah, it's probably a weird question anyway."

"No, no, I understand what you're asking, I think." *Focus.* That wholesome all-American accent distracts me to the point that I have to reboot my brain to form a response. The way this woman's voice mesmerizes me means I'll have to watch out for Juniper when she's here—no need to be caught drooling over my best friend's long-lost half sibling.

"Well," I continue, "I suppose...I'd go into that moment ready for the shift. Embrace it. It's lucky to know beforehand that your life won't be the same, because sometimes change happens without you preparing. So enjoy it, go all in."

Marissa seems to give genuine consideration to my advice, but I know I'm a hypocrite. A man whose days look the same, doling out sage advice on epic life changes. If anything, I want to prevent change. There should be some way to pin an asterisk to what I say. No doubt my ex would laugh at hearing me talk about embracing transformation when I wouldn't even follow her to Dublin.

"You sound like my best friend." She tucks her dark brown hair behind her ears, though some strands promptly slip out. "Did she tell you to say that?"

"Take my input with a grain of salt. What am I but a lowly barkeep?" I say the last bit with a flourish of sarcasm, but the words taste bitter.

"You're a photographer, aren't you?" She nods to the back corner of the pub. She caught me flipping through pictures this morning, so I'm not as smooth as I'd like to think.

"That? That's just..." I trail off, picking up my Nikon from the counter. "It's a hobby."

"What kind of photography?"

"Oh...landscape, street photos. Depends on the location." The inkling of that intrepid photographer I want to be stirs, combined with a hint of dread. This week, I've an interview for the master's program where I'll have to talk about myself, my work, and what I've done since putting my studies on hold.

"Can I see?"

"Sure." My thumb rotates the camera dial in circles, and I show a few photographs to her while her big brown eyes widen with awe. More of her chin-length hair falls out from behind her ears, bringing a whiff of her floral shampoo with it.

"Not my best work," I say, ignoring the scent, "but it's what I could catch this morning."

"You're fantastic. For just a hobbyist, that is." She grins again, boosting my ego. "How long have you been doing photography?"

The faint sound of footsteps rises from the storeroom downstairs. No doubt that's Da. My shift has gotten derailed in the best way possible, but that means I've yet to dry all the glasses. The pub's not open.

"Uh, since I was a teen."

"Only a hobby, though?"

I shrug in response, using indifference to will our conversation in a different direction.

"Not many bartenders carry a camera to work, but plenty of photographers bring their cameras everywhere they go, like you."

He'll walk in any minute, and I hate him a little for squashing this moment for me—this tiny blip of time where someone sees me for what I'm good at, not simply as Aidan McCarthy, the son of a man who owns a local pub in County Kerry, or as the younger brother of the town's favorite bartender.

"You there?" Da's voice rumbles in the back office above some paper rustling.

"I'm here," I call out, shoving the camera below the sight line of the bar—a rapid motion that the woman's eyes track.

"Need you downstairs to help me move up a few more of the kegs 'fore we open."

"Down in a second."

The thud of his footsteps fade, and what luck that he didn't waltz in here. I'm in no mood for an argument, which our conversations almost always turn into these days.

"You're not actually open, are you? Oh my god, I'm so sorry."

"I don't mind, if—"

"*So* annoying of me. I barged in and—"

"Really, stay," I tell her. What's another ten minutes?

"Oh shit." Her tone shifts as she surveys the floor. She sets a duffel on the barstool and digs through it. "My purse. Where's my purse?" Her voice sounds strained, and her hands are frantic as she searches the area around the bar. She lifts her duffel bag and pats the seat, as if the correct motions will make the item appear out of thin air, like a magic trick. "My *passport.*"

"Is it on the ground?"

She looks at her feet, then shakes her head, eyes wild. A quick rummage in her coat pockets produces only a few crumpled euros and a folded-up paper. "Shit."

"We'll get it. We'll find it. You might've dropped it on the way here. Can't be far."

"Mhmm. Yeah."

"Have a seat." I set my hand on the bar top mere millimeters shy of hers, hoping to calm her. "I'll grab the phone from the back, and we can make a few calls. Okay?"

She nods, and I allow myself to fall into those dark brown eyes for a split second before fetching the land-line. When I return from the office, she's gone.

Chapter Three

Juniper

The front door to Cara's Cafe dings as I step inside, and a blast of warm air welcomes me. A grill sizzles in the back, and the whole place smells peppery and savory, like bacon. Two women by the wall chatter over tea and empty plates, and a man by the entrance keeps his eyes glued to his newspaper.

A young woman with a tall, sturdy build stands at the cash register, reviewing a receipt. Fiery red hair cascades down her back. *It's her.* I hug my duffel closer, letting it double as emotional armor. When Cara notices me, her face widens into the biggest smile.

"Juniper?" Her voice sounds like sunshine, all light and bright.

I gulp. With a nod, I brush my hood back, once again painfully aware of how travel-weary and wet I am, especially after scouring the streets for my purse. I'm sure I look how I feel: as grimy as a little subway rat.

"Hi! How was the trip? Are you well?" She swoops around the counter while firing off questions. "Can I get you a drink? Tea, maybe? We've coffee, too, whatever you like." She stops in front of me, radiating an innocent gap-toothed smile.

"I'm good."

I would have guessed a handshake to be the most appropriate choice to greet a relative I learned about less than a month ago, but Cara doesn't bother with pleasantries. She leaps forward to hug me like I'm her closest friend and confidante. I stiffen, and she pulls back.

"Shite, you're drenched. You walk from Dublin?"

"Not quite," I reply, tucking moist chunks of knotted hair behind my ears. There's no way to avoid reliving my humiliating mistake, so I explain how I must have left my purse on the train. "I looked everywhere for it."

I appreciated that bartender's honest concern, but I didn't need to sit around and wait to find out if I dropped my leather purse somewhere on the platform or the streets. Every second that passed would give someone an opportunity to swipe it, so I left some cash on the counter and dashed outside to retrace my steps. Lis had given me the genius advice to stash my credit cards and bills in various places, like my duffel and coat pockets, so I haven't lost everything. But my crisp new passport—the one I'd gone through the trouble of expediting for this trip—was gone.

"No problem, I'll make a few calls later this afternoon and see if we can't find it." Cara pulls out her phone and scrolls through her contact list. "I know some folks who work on the rail, and I'm sure something will turn up soon. But if not, then we'll sort out a replacement one at the embassy."

"You don't have to do that," I say, shaking my head. This woman's getting married in less than two weeks, and I don't want to be more of a burden than I already am. "I'll figure it out. Not keeping track of my passport was so, so reckless of me, and an employee at the station gave me a number to call."

"Please, I'm happy to. We're sisters."

Sisters.

I bite my bottom lip. Despite more protesting on my part, Cara won't accept no as an answer. She slips behind the counter, grabs a planner from her bag, and schedules her new to-do. I'd rather handle my own messes, but the time difference and lack of sleep must be getting to me, because I give up the fight.

Cara waves to the cook, telling her that she'll return soon. Handing me an umbrella, she leads me down the road to her apartment. As we walk out of the one-block radius of downtown, our feet patter on the wet sidewalk past modest street-facing homes.

My heart's beating a thousand times per minute, but Cara seems carefree. She begins with polite small talk—how was the flight, did I find her restaurant with no trouble, and is the jet lag terrible? I tell her about my journey and my realization about the passport.

"You're an early drinker then?" Her left eyebrow lifts with a hint of humor, and I wish I'd thought to omit that detail.

"Not usually. I needed..." I sort through lame excuses in my head to explain why I went into a bar directly across from her restaurant. "I was exhausted from the trip and I missed it. The sign was staring me in the face but it just, uh, didn't register."

"You met Danny at the pub then. Lovely, isn't he?"

"No, I think the guy there was named Aidan."

I *know* the guy's name was Aidan. I'm half tempted to sneak off to the bar during my stay and ask around for him.

"Aidan, that's him," Cara says. "He's Danny to me. My best mate and best man at the wedding too."

"Oh." I stop in my tracks. "Oh no." Knowing I'll see him again sends a flutter of anxiety through my stomach. I regret rushing out of there like I did and for introducing myself as Marissa. "I was sort of stupid and

I, uh...this sounds silly, but I introduced myself under a fake name."

When I explain why, Cara laughs like I deserve my own comedy special. "I knew someone in college who used to do that. She'd make up an entire identity and tell men she was a flight attendant or something like that. You were cautious, so no harm there. But where I live's incredibly safe, you've no need to worry."

"I actually had the exact thought, 'How small can one town be?'"

"Small." A laugh bubbles out of her again. "Small enough that your bartender is also your sister's best mate. Here, this flat's mine." She unlocks the entrance to a pastel-yellow building.

Her apartment contains mountains of cardboard boxes labeled *table decor* and *candle holders FRAG-ILE*. They crowd the cozy space, although the occasional trinket or picture frame appears between the cracks. Miniature potted succulents dot the windowsill by the kitchen sink, throw pillows right out of an Anthropologie catalog rest on the sofa, and a few strategically placed mirrors make the living room look more spacious.

"Apologies for the clutter. That's one thing nobody ever mentions about having a big wedding: where to put all the stuff."

"You sure you don't mind if I stay with you? I'd hate to add to your wedding stress."

"You're not! I'm thrilled to have you," she says with another massive smile as she rearranges a pile of boxes. "There's only like one B&B in town, and I wouldn't wish it on my worst enemy."

My work stipend from *The Edge* will barely cover meals, so having a place to crash helps with my budget. But as I navigate the maze and set my bags down on the precious last patch of visible carpet, concern pinches my heart. I'm in the way.

"Okay, living room's here obviously, there's the kitchen, and tap water is fine." She points to various spots in her home. "Loo's down the hall. Also, I've an air bed hiding here somewhere, but I won't have the chance to look for it 'til tonight. Feel free to use my bed, because the sofa leaves much comfort to be desired."

"Thanks." I hope I caught all of that. Cara speaks faster than lightning strikes. "Anything more horizontal than an airplane seat will do."

"I made a few sandwiches at the cafe, plus a green juice, if you want."

My stomach doesn't know what it needs, but I should try to eat. "Sure. I've got some extra money in my duffel. How much do I owe you?"

"Don't be daft," she says, waving her hand to dismiss me as she offers the brown takeout box. "I'm happy you're here, and I'm more than happy to feed you. It's one of my love languages, feeding people. That's why I opened a cafe."

We perch on the edge of her firm couch, and while the need for sleep tugs at my eyelids, I bite into the food. My sandwich has a crisp, satisfying crunch, and what Cara prepared tastes incredible—it's packed with verdant lettuce and cool tomatoes. This beats my corner bodega hoagies any day.

"I see why you opened your own place," I say before taking another bite.

"Thank you." She flashes a proud smile that brings forth her dimples, two profound pinpoints on either side of her face. "We make what we can in-house or source from nearby businesses. It's been a dream in the making for a long time, and we've been open for about three weeks now."

The shock almost causes me to choke on my food. "You're getting married in like a week and a half."

"Mad, isn't it? Not sure I could handle even one more stressful thing right now, to be honest. But the venue wasn't available for another two years. We might have considered different places, but..." She doesn't finish her thought and picks up some chips. "Planning a wedding is more than what I want or what my partner wants. Everybody has an opinion. Family drama. You know how that goes."

Not really, but I nod along anyway. I didn't understand until after my mom died and I was a little older why she popped in and out of my life. And my grandmother had no desire to do anything above the bare minimum as a guardian. We had no family drama because we weren't much of a family.

"Everyone's dying to meet you. When I told Mam about you, she nearly fainted. I mean, a *half sister*." Cara speaks like she's reciting the words to some kind of mystical spell and then adjusts the fillings in her sandwich. "And that article? You're brave, putting yourself out there. Fair play to you."

"I'm excited." On edge, too, which must explain this pit in my belly. "I've got the chance to write something meaningful and personal, and obviously it involves you too, so I want to do it justice."

"You will, I'm sure of it."

Hopefully she's right. I can't mess this opportunity up. I got lucky when Ethan hired me eight years ago since no one else would give a degreeless writer-wannabe like me a shot. The pay covered my monthly costs and little more, and the office had that we-have-a-foosball-table-in-the-common-room start-up attitude. But landing a salaried position was the first step to making a home of my own. Still, as much as I appreciate *The Edge*, I don't know how much longer I can write mindless roundups.

"And I understand—I'm sure you have lots of questions about our da. Not only for the article but also, well, your own curiosity. We can talk about him whenever you're ready. My mam knows more than I do, though."

"Sure. That would be great."

I suppress that deep-rooted part of me that hates my dad. He means nothing more to me than any other stranger on the street, but he's also my father, whether I like it or not. Plus, to round out this piece, learning more about him is a necessary evil to face.

Lucky for me, sitting on the couch half asleep in day-old clothes doesn't seem like the time to dive into a revealing discussion about my—*our*—biological dad. Cara talks about our plans for the next two weeks instead. Tomorrow morning, if I'm rested enough, she wants me to meet who she's marrying and re-meet Aidan. That thought in particular sends my stomach into a nosedive. She details all the relatives who will soon trickle into town for her wedding, including great-aunts and second cousins and great-grandparents, countless first cousins, and family friends who are essentially cousins. My heartbeat sprints from the oral history of who's who. Being family with Cara means becoming family with all of the O'Sheas, not just her. I type out a quick note on my phone to refer to later when I'm writing.

my family has grown from zero to one to a few trillion

"We're having sort of a massive Catholic wedding, with...with some exceptions."

"Like what?"

"Well." She clears her throat. "My fiancée is...her name is Yasmine. And we can't marry in the church, but the spot's lovely. Grand. Just not a *church*, you know? Which I maybe should've told you before you arrived, since some people only think it's a proper wedding if it's in a church. Trust me, I know."

Cara toys with the ring on her finger, her bouncy energy replaced with something more subdued. I don't care where she gets married, but then the realization of being somewhere else—somewhere that's not the tiny bubble I've created for myself in New York—sinks in. She's not worried about the church. I almost can't believe that she'd think I *wouldn't* be okay with her marrying whoever she wants, but that only highlights how little we know each other.

"It's fine. It's great," I say, giving her a small smile to put her at ease. "I'm glad you let me know, but it's your wedding, your partner."

The tension in Cara's shoulders releases, and that bounciness comes back to her body.

"Ireland's quite progressive, but I've...there's still challenges for me, which I won't bore you with. Yaz said

I should have said something before you got here, but I thought maybe telling you face-to-face was better. And if you'd known, you might not have come. Not like I could hide that fact for much longer."

"You told me at the perfect time."

Cara's smile shines again. "When I was growing up, I hoped my mum was secret royalty or something, and on my sixteenth birthday, she'd tell me I was a princess. But I think finding out about a sister is better."

"It's definitely a surprise," I say, half laughing. *Understatement of a lifetime.*

"The whole situation's pure mad, isn't it?" She has glistening tears pooling in her eyes. Sandwich in hand, Cara envelops me in another bear hug as a few stray pieces of lettuce go flying. "Really, Juniper, I can't tell you how happy I am."

I'm seeing that all! those! exclamation marks! in her texts were honest-to-goodness real. She is genuinely overjoyed to have a sister, but she's also overjoyed that sister is *me*. We met half an hour ago, so I don't understand her eagerness, but I can't sit here rigid as a streetlight with her arms around me.

"Me too," I whisper. It feels like the right thing to say, and I let myself melt into Cara's embrace.

Chapter Four

Aidan

On the way to Cara's Cafe for a late breakfast, I catch myself replaying scenes of the woman from yesterday. The rest of my shift went by as usual—same folks, same drinks. Perhaps in the delirium of boredom, I made Marissa up. A figment of my imagination. Anytime the pub door opened, a sliver of hope pierced me thinking it would be her.

Life *has* felt lonelier of late. Michael's gone—the one-year anniversary of his death in May hit that fact home. I've remained single since Mary and I broke up after he passed, and Cara's so consumed with wedding planning and the cafe that she's barely got time for Yaz, much less me. My focus has remained on the pub and keeping Mam and Da on good terms, and I've done little else. If I had made up some dream woman yesterday to pass the time, I wouldn't be surprised.

At least Da hired a couple new bartenders so I don't have to come in every bleedin' day. With the extra help, he could take time off for himself. Spend evenings with Mam, which they need. Then maybe we can try to get back to some kind of normal, the three of us, and maybe I can pick back up with my life.

For now, though, I have best man duties for Cara. Pre-wedding errands, hen party planning, all of it—including dining today with that half sister of hers.

Conversation hums as I walk into the cafe. "Hello, you. Right on time, too." Cara greets me with a warm smile and walks over for a hug. "Testing out an original recipe and the timer just beeped."

"Smells class." I get spoiled in the culinary department by having a best friend who can cook and bake like Cara. She enjoys testing new recipes on me and Yaz, and we never complain.

Cara bounces back toward the kitchen, and that pep in her step means she is giddy. Things must be going smoothly with this Juniper woman. Having female friends in her life is a sore spot for Cara, so getting to reignite that bond with other women—a half sister no less—means a lot to her.

"Here he is," Yaz calls out in her low, velvety voice. "I was singing praises to Juniper about how you're keeping me and Cara sane through this whole wedding planning process. This is Juniper. Juniper, Danny."

The person sitting at the table is not Juniper, though. She is the woman I've had playing on repeat in my mind since yesterday. She's Marissa, from the pub. Marissa, the American girl, is Juniper?

"You told me your name was M-Marissa," I sputter.

"They met already, remember?" Cara says to Yaz, setting a mug of coffee down for me. "Hey, you didn't find a passport lying around, did you?"

"Your name's Juniper?" I'm far too confused to smile at this lucky second encounter.

A rich red rushes onto Marissa's—Juniper's—cheeks.

"Fair play to you," Yaz says. "Never give your real name to a man in a bar. And this one? Can't blame you."

Cara cackles, and I send her a withering look.

"You two're hilarious," I say, deadpan.

A timer dings from the kitchen, and Cara recruits Yaz to bring the meal out. Juniper squirms in the booth, smooths out her skirt, and fiddles with her hair. I sit down beside her, marveling that she's real and here, right in front of me. I didn't think I'd get to see her again.

"You dashed out before I could call anyone," I say, baffled over her behavior yesterday.

"Yeah. I needed to find my passport, and it wasn't at the bar, so I went back to the station to look."

"I was trying to help." A beat passes as nothing but the instrumental background music flows between us. "I'm Aidan, by the way. Danny for short. Nice to officially meet you, emphasis on officially." I extend a hand, and hers fits into mine like a key in a lock. "What is it you said your name was?"

"Look, I've never traveled abroad before, and I wanted to stay safe. I wasn't sure—"

"No, makes sense. But if you're after a kidney, there's plenty of folks back in America you could've contacted."

"I'm not here harvesting *organs*." She blushes again—a striking pinkish tint like sunset. Judging by how the corner of her mouth angles up, she understands I'm teasing her, but she continues explaining herself anyway. "I got off the train literally five minutes before we met, and you were a total stranger. I had no idea you knew Cara. It's not suspicious that I wouldn't tell you my name."

"It's not *not* suspicious."

"Dan, stop giving her grief," Cara says, emerging from the kitchen while performing a balancing act of plates. "Make room. Your first meal out on the town."

"This is the finest food you'll find in all of Ireland," Yaz adds, and Cara feigns embarrassment with a

chuckle. "It is! Juniper, she's worked so hard on opening this place, and she pores over every detail of what
she serves here."

They settle in across from me and Juniper, and I
take in the spread. The cafe's got to serve some classic breakfast foods to appease the folks who only ever
want something traditional, but Cara works innovative
flavors into quiches, pastries, and salads. I don't know
how she decides which ingredients to pair together, but
whatever she whips up always impresses.

"So what did you get to do yesterday?" Yaz asks.

"Not a lot," Juniper says, her attention flitting to me.
"I was pretty jet-lagged and passed out on Cara's couch
the first chance I got."

"After eating here, there's not much more to explore
in town," I say as I scoop up food with my fork.

"Not true. The pub," Cara says. She turns to Juniper
to add, "Danny's da owns the place."

Juniper quirks her brow at me in what looks like
surprise.

"Ooh, maybe you and I can stop in tomorrow night,"
Cara suggests to her half sister, a glimmer of hope
hiding in her dimples.

"Sure. It'd be good for me to get to know the area
where you live, the places you like to go. That sort of
thing."

"That's right. You've an assignment." I pierce the egg on my plate and the yolk runs a vibrant yellow. "How's that work? You do interviews or something?"

"No, it's more casual than that. The piece is a narrative personal essay. My site's branching out and wants to publish more of those, kind of like *The Atlantic* or *The New Yorker*."

"*The New York Times* has those too, I think," Yaz says to Cara.

"That's the dream." Juniper's face relaxes into a smile, like a flower blooming in spring.

"What will you write about?" I ask.

"My experience," she says, using her utensil to usher the potatoes side to side on her plate. "Not every day you find a relative halfway across the world."

When Cara mentioned the assignment, I found it odd for someone to work on something so intimate. Perhaps it's not much different than people posting their lives on social media, but I don't understand that, either. Their story is extraordinary, though. Cara wanted to do a DNA kit for ages because she'd always wondered...what with her da not being around. When she got her test results with zero close matches and a handful of extremely distant cousins—which must've been years ago—she sulked for a solid week. But the message from Juniper changed everything. New family discovered an ocean away, two sisters who never realized the other one was out there. No wonder the site Juniper writes for wants to hear about them. And since she speaks about her writing with passion, like she genuinely cares, I have a hunch my best friend is in good hands.

The conversation shifts to the wedding—every decision, big and small, that's gone into the upcoming nuptials. What cake to eat, which flowers to hold, which song to dance to, what plates to use. How in the world they've planned all of this while Cara also opened a cafe and Yaz continued to work her way up to partner at the law firm is beyond me.

"We hired a day-of planner, thank goodness," Cara says, "because otherwise I've no idea how we'd manage. But until then, we're on our own."

"Keep your mind on the honeymoon." Yaz wraps an arm around her fiancée and plants a kiss on her temple.

"Where are you going?" Juniper asks.

"Sardinia, but—" Cara replies at the same time Yaz says, "Isle of Man—"

"Well yes, Isle of Man the few days after the wedding," Cara explains. "What all the bridal magazines call a minimoon. Then, April next year, we'll be off to Sardinia to sit on the beach and consume too much pasta and wine."

Juniper laughs again, a chime like church bells. "What a dream."

"Have you been?" Yaz asks.

"Um, no." Juniper's attitude goes from open to something more guarded. "Neither place. They both sound nice, though."

"Oh, speaking of the wedding." Cara digs in her back pocket and pulls out a folded-up piece of lined paper, offering it to me. "Before I forget. Sure you don't mind taking care of these things?"

"Positive. Consider me your errand boy."

"Wish my brother had that attitude," Yaz says, chuckling into her orange juice.

"Thank you," Cara says while I look over the list of tasks she needs help with. "I'll bake you all the apple cakes you could ever dream of. And the air bed?"

"Gave mine away. Remember?"

"It's fine," Juniper says to my friend. "I've slept in worse spots. Your couch is perfect."

Cara gnaws on the cuticles of her thumb for a moment before her eyes light up. "Can Juniper stay at yours?"

Juniper's head whips to me, and I let out a strangled "What?"

"Say no if you'd rather not," she says, "but Yasmine's mam is staying at her house, which means no room for me there. And rather than have you on the sofa, perhaps you could go to Danny's. If—" She looks back at me with pleading eyes. "If that suits you?"

"Oh, um—"

"I'm totally okay on your couch, really," Juniper says. "I don't want to be in anyone's way."

"Not possible. You're welcome to stay with me, but that thing is a rock. You must be sore in twenty-five new places this morning."

Juniper hesitates. "That's probably from the plane ride."

"I want you to be comfortable, and he's only down the road. I've no clue where that air bed has gone, and I'd like to host you, but his guest bedroom will be better." Cara flips her attention back to me. "Can't believe I didn't think of this before. Wedding brain. That good with you?"

The thought of Juniper under the same roof as me sends something like panic coursing through my veins, but I can't pinpoint why. I keep the spare room tidy, and no one's staying there. She's my best friend's sibling, so I should extend the same kindness to her as I would to Cara. And based on how Cara's awaiting my answer with her hands clasped in prayer position, I'd lighten some of her load.

"Sounds good to me." I give Juniper a no-big-deal kind of shrug.

"Yeah, I don't mind."

"Brilliant. Thank you, Danny." She kisses my cheek as she stands up to prep for the lunch rush.

Juniper and I head out with a long list of to-dos, which now includes moving her things over to my house. As we exit the cafe, I glance down at the list. The last item reads: *Take care of Juniper!!*

Juniper picks up a box of cereal and examines the back. With her staying at mine, we make a stop at the supermarket so she'll have some food around the house. She tosses some healthy-looking bran flakes into a shopping basket hooked on her arm and continues walking.

"Have I successfully convinced you I'm not on the hunt for a kidney?" she asks.

"For now. Never thought of myself as so intimidating that someone has to give me an alias."

"You're not intimidating," she says as the corner of her mouth lifts.

"Your question from the pub makes more sense, though. About change, and about not feeling ready for it."

She falters while reaching for something on the shelves, and her cheeks flush. Clearly, she's put on a brave face coming to Ballygrá, but the reality of the situation is a shock. It certainly was for Cara.

"I understand. Cara's been a wreck this whole week over meeting you. If I gave you a hard time about the name thing, it's only because I'm looking out for my friend." After how quickly some people in her life ghosted her, I have to, although Juniper's level of street smarts is what I'd expect of someone from New York.

"You didn't tell me your dad owned the pub."

"Unimportant."

"And you introduced yourself as Aidan, *not* Danny."

"That's a common nickname, I'll have you know. Not as much as Marissa is for Juniper, though."

"Okay, ha ha." Her response oozes sarcasm, and she gives a dry laugh. "Call me June. Juniper's fine, but to most people, I'm June."

"All right, June," I say, tasting her name on the tip of my tongue. So full and juicy for such a short and simple word. "Sorry about your passport not turning up."

"I was careless." She adjusts her grip on the basket, struggling under the weight of the food she's picked.

"Here."

"Oh. Thanks." Her arm brushes mine as I take the basket full of groceries, and the brief contact shocks me with awareness. "Anyway, I can get a replacement passport if needed, but Cara knows a few people who work for the train. Fingers crossed somebody turns it in soon."

"Cara's good like that. Always has a person to call. Plus she's a solid friend. Be warned, her natural talent for baked goods will ruin you for all other pastries. But if you had a choice of all the sisters in the world, you chose right."

The supermarket owner, Mrs. Abernathy, peers over the newspaper as we approach the counter and removes her dainty silver eyeglasses. She paws around the table-top for our items without looking at them, drilling her attention on me and June with an overenthusiastic smile. The wrinkles in her cheeks fold like velvet curtains.

"Danny! Lovely to see you, m'dear."

"You too, Mrs. Abernathy. How's things?"

"Oh, always the same for me. I like you poppin' in here. How're your mam and da?"

"Grand."

She leans over the counter. "I told them at the memorial, and I'll tell you again now. Anything you need, anything at all, you tell me and Edwin. Don't be shy about it."

"Will do."

"Miss that lad. And nights at McCarthy's? Not the same."

My body has tensed, so I give a terse nod. Everyone adored Michael, his easy smile, and how he made them feel like his best pal. But it's not just the pub that hasn't been the same since his crash—nothing has.

Mrs. Abernathy picks up each item one by one, entering the price on the keyboard with a clumsy clink of the plastic keys, but something seems to distract her. Or rather, someone. "An' who might you be, sweetheart?"

"I'm Juniper."

"Oh! An American girl," she says with a combination of intrigue and approval. "Well, Juniper, I'll tell you, this one here's a keeper. You'll never meet a more gentle gentleman in your life. And you two look the part together."

"Mrs. Abernathy, June is—" I explain while June says, "I'm actually—"

"I noticed you having a glance by the yogurts, and I'm glad you found someone, Danny. After that last lass of yours—oh, what was she called?"

Please make this stop. Mrs. Abernathy won't, though, and bulldozes me with the name.

"Mary! That was her."

Christ.

"After Mary, I saw how down you were. Sulked around town, and you were doing your best, but it was a sad sight altogether. Now to see you out and about with someone warms m'heart. How'd you meet?"

"We met yesterday, at the bar," June interjects amid the rambling. Mrs. Abernathy's mouth falls open, wordless—something I've never seen from her before.

Before the old woman shares any more of my humiliating romantic history at the till, I make introductions.

"Mrs. Abernathy, this is Juniper Martin. Remember Cara's half sister she was telling you about? This is her."

Cara mentioned June to a few of the more talkative residents of Ballygrá, expecting the natural flow of gossip from one nosy person to the next to spread the news. Somehow, that news failed to reach Mrs. Abernathy, or she outright forgot, and we stand in an uncomfortable silence as she mentally puts all the pieces together.

"Oh," she chirps. Something's clicked, and she comes back to life. "Why didn't you say so, love?"

This unfolds into a fifteen-minute Q&A. Lucky for me, Mrs. Abernathy only cares to talk to June—and lucky for June, the questions don't probe too deeply. Where did she grow up, how does she like Ireland, and is she seeing anyone?—Pennsylvania, lovely so far, and no. I pull June out of there before Mrs. Abernathy asks for her unabridged life story, or worse yet, tells mine on my behalf.

We step into the brisk early-afternoon air, both of us holding paper bags of groceries. I want to say something, anything, but what I've got is even more embarrassing than what Mrs. Abernathy has already divulged—like how Mary and I called our relationship off ages ago and I'd long gotten over her, or how I most definitely wasn't ogling June in the yogurt aisle.

"She's a chatty one, isn't she?" June asks.

"She can get carried away."

"No, she's sweet. She'd make a talented writer. The curious type."

"Don't give her any ideas. A gossip column is the last thing we need here."

"When Cara said Ballygrá was small, I didn't realize just how small she meant. Must be annoying living somewhere where everyone knows your dirty laundry."

"Sometimes." It was certainly a pain in the arse just now. "I've grown used to it, but you're right, you can't keep secrets for long in a place like this. Heaps different from New York then, isn't it?"

"Yeah." June walks on the ledge of the pavement like a gymnast on a balance beam. "More anonymous. I'm never weighed down by anyone's baggage or worried about what they think of me. Except for Mike."

She throws out his name like he's someone in our social circle, a lad we hang out with on weekends sometimes.

"Who's Mike?" I don't care, but June told Mrs. Abernathy she didn't have a boyfriend.

"My corner bodega guy. He's great. Teddy bear, born and raised in the city, and he knows pretty much everything about me. My comfort foods, my work drama...and he always stocks my favorite stuff. Chocolate, wine, tampons. Things like that."

"Ah, now that's what you should lead with. I've run the tampon errand for Cara before, and it's not a task for the faint of heart." The path ends, and we stroll side by side on the springy grass of the road shoulder. "You could say living in Ballygrá is the same as living in a town where everyone, including Mrs. Abernathy, is your bodega guy."

She laughs again, one of those energizing laughs that brightens me up from the inside out. June tucks a stray strand of hair past her ears, and I wish I had my camera on me. My brain works like that—I see images in the making as I go about my day. Fleeting moments of life I have to choose between experiencing for myself or capturing forever behind a lens. Without my camera, all I can do is enjoy this sliver of space and time.

That night though, as I wash and dry my face, I keep thinking about that little sliver. Christ, I really should stay on task. June's my best friend's sister. She's here to visit Cara for her wedding and then she'll head back to the States. I don't need to get some schoolboy crush on her.

"Did I leave my necklace in here?" June stands in the doorway, and somehow the whole house feels more full with her in it. More interesting.

"Mmm." I dismiss that thought and scan the counter. Behind the soap holder is a gold chain and pendant, and as I hand her the jewelry, the softness of her palms heats up my arm.

"Good night, Aidan." She gives me a quiet smile before turning to walk to her bedroom.

"Night," I finally call down the hall.

All I have to do is treat June like I would my best friend, and everything will be fine.

Chapter Five

Juniper

I wake up groggy and disoriented from the time difference, wiping drool from my cheek with arms as heavy
as lead pipes. All those travel articles advised me to get
out of bed at a normal time, no matter how impossible
that felt. Well, it *is* impossible. With a rejuvenating,
full-body stretch, I reach for my phone on the nightstand. Above a few missed call notifications from an
unknown number, the clock reads 5:19.

In the evening.

Sleep evaded me for hours last night. The second my
head hit the pillow, I couldn't stop thinking about, well,
everything. When I'd find my passport. What Cara
thinks of me. What Aidan must think of me.

At some point, I fell asleep and probably turned
off my alarm in a fog. Aside from stumbling into the

kitchen for some cereal while it was still dark, I've been
out cold.

I stretch again to wake up my limbs. When I check
my phone, my focus breezes past the missed calls and to
the bolded text messages from an unfamiliar number.

> Got your number from Cara. Out for the
> day, but ring if you need anything. Left
> a set of keys on the table by the door.
> Also let me know when you get these
> texts so I'm sure I'm messaging the right
> American girl. – Aidan

I grin and save his contact in my phone.

> JUNE: No Juniper here, just Marissa

Scrubbing a hand over my face and heaving an enormous sigh, I stand to shower and get ready to go. Last
night, Cara proposed a one-on-one hangout at the bar.
I call Ethan on my way over, since he hoped to check in
yesterday but got slammed with meetings.

"Juney! I was hoping we'd connect." I picture him
with his feet propped on his desk, twirling a pencil
between his fingers, like a cocky frat boy who somehow
landed on the masthead of a popular digital magazine. "How's the trip? I've been missing your little face
around the office."

I cringe. Ethan's sexist comments have been a regular part of the job. Confronting him about his behavior
wouldn't get me anywhere, and I'd much rather have a

salaried position at *The Edge* than none at all. With this assignment on my plate, I definitely won't say anything.

"You slept the entire day?" Ethan interrupts as I share what I've been up to since arriving. "Juney. I know you went for a family thing, but you're there to work too."

"Of course. I didn't intend to crash so hard, but my body was down for the count. I'm here for two weeks, so I'll just catch—"

"No 'just.' No excuses. Listen." Ethan lowers his voice. "There's been some tension in the office, with you on this assignment and all."

"What do you mean?"

"I've heard some rumblings from some of the senior staffers about preferential treatment, that sort of thing. It's all bullshit, in my opinion, and they're jealous, but I can see their side of things. A huge article. We've sent you to another country to report. We're covering expenses."

"You told me you'd cover a portion of expenses." They offered a paltry daily stipend that barely put a dent in my flight costs. *The New York Times* this is not. Working at *The Edge* for years should earn me some seniority, but I don't argue. This is the first piece I've gotten that's not a clickbait-y listicle, but something legitimate. It hurts that my coworkers can't show any support for me, though.

"There's a lot of promise in this story. I mean, what are the chances your test would turn out like this? It's why I supported you doing this from day one. I did, didn't I?"

When he heard me talking about my test results in the break room, he latched onto them like a leech. He may have had good intentions, but I can't pretend that potential page views didn't also influence his actions.

"Sure," I say, "but I—"

"And look, I want you to have your own column just as much as you do. Word got to Nancy, and you know, if the editor in chief is buzzing about a piece that hasn't even been published yet, then—well, let's say this could mean some very good things for your career here."

"Right." The din of McCarthy's Pub grows louder as the golden lamp out front comes into view. "*Very good things.*"

"How 'bout this? You want the story to perform well, don't you?"

"Of course," I say without hesitation.

"Me too. I know what the readers come to read, but we need this to be perfect. Show everyone that this decision to go out on a limb and send you there made sense. I'd like to work on this more closely with you, so can you write up a rough outline in the next few days?

Just something that organizes your thoughts a little. In the meantime, I'll set up a shared folder where you can drop your notes and your progress."

"We're working together on this?"

"More like I'll supervise," he says with typical Ethan nonchalance. "If you knock this out of the park, it'll reflect well on the both of us in Nance's eyes. Win-win, right?"

I bite my tongue. I don't need the hand-holding, but I'm in Ireland already, and I have no other realistic options. If a group project is what it takes to secure my column and finally take on bigger and better assignments, then I'll do it.

When I get off the phone and step into the pub, I may as well have a flashing neon sign above my head. A poster near the cash register advertises live music, but by walking in, I feel like I'm the one putting on a show. Even after the bar patrons resume their impassioned conversations, I have the eerie feeling of their eyes on me.

"June!" Cara's ever-exuberant voice sounds behind me. She's snagged a spacious booth by the window and waves me over. "You made it. Welcome back to McCarthy's Pub. Drinks on me."

"Thanks." When I sit down, the cracked leather bench squishes underneath me and releases a puff of air. "Did I do something wrong? Why is everyone watching me?"

"Everyone's curious 'bout the American girl. Never mind them, they'll sort themselves out soon enough. Fancy a pint?"

I nod and Cara gestures toward the bartender, who nods back at her. An older gentleman pours the drinks, so Aidan must not be working tonight.

"So what's the craic?"

"The crack?"

"Not crack, the *craic*." Cara chuckles. "Sorry. It's like asking how you are. Or you could say someone's good craic, like they're good fun."

"Oh." I stash that bit of Irish slang in my brain. "I woke up about an hour ago, so either great or terrible, depending on how you think about it. You?"

"You poor thing, you must still be exhausted." Cara pushes a plate of fries toward me to share and dips a fry into a blob of ketchup for herself. "Today went well. I found someone to step in for my shifts next week while I take time off to enjoy being a bride and all, which is a tremendous relief. I want to offload all responsibilities for the minimoon. With my sous-chef getting sick while all of this is ramping up, I've been scrambling."

Just then, the bartender approaches the booth with two pints of amber liquid. He has a lean, friendly face framed by salt-and-pepper hair, and he walks with an almost unnoticeable limp.

"Noah, I'd have come up and got the drinks."

"Well, I hoped to meet this fine lass m'self," the man says, his soothing accent laced with sweetness.

Cara introduces us while Noah sets down the foamy glasses and wipes his hand on his apron. "Noah's known me since I was a small one, so any embarrassing stories he tells you are entirely fabricated."

"I intend to save those for the wedding." He pats her shoulder with a grin. "So June, been to Ireland before?"

"No." Then, quieter, I add, "First time abroad, actually."

"First time!" he exclaims, and I brace myself. I shouldn't have said anything because I bet he's ready to chastise me for not traveling more in my life. If I could have traveled, I would have, but my grandmother was so inconvenienced by having to take me in that going on vacation was out of the question.

"Well, you chose a grand first country for your first-ever holiday," he goes on, and I relax a little more inside the booth. "You've also got the best sister, you're in the best town, and you've come to the best pub. M'family's owned this pub for almost a hundred years. Passed down from my granda, to my da, to me. And then someday—"

The crisp sound of glass shattering jerks his attention away. "Oi!" Noah calls to the back as a group of people part, dodging the blame.

"Gravity spike," a gentleman's voice whoops.

"I'd best take care of that, but you two let me know if you need anything."

Noah shuffles away and pulls a broom out of the closet.

"He's nice." I watch as he sweeps up the broken glass. "Aidan's dad?"

"Yup. Top man, he is. You'll meet Danny's mam soon, I'm sure. She's not here right now, I don't think..." Cara peers around the bar before shaking her head with what looks like a tinge of disappointment. "But Noah's lovely, like Danny. They're both men with generous hearts. Both have been through a lot. Both're stubborn as hell too, so they butt heads all the time. Sort of how my mam sends me up the wall sometimes, but I still adore her to bits."

I nod, pretending to understand. All my mom and grandma did was fight—over me, over my mom's addiction, over whatever—and it never looked like love. But neither did my interactions with my grandma, though we fought on rare occasions. Raising another kid in her sixties was not part of her plan, especially after struggling with her own daughter, so she resorted to apathy. By the time I landed in foster care in my unadoptable teen years, I discovered the silver lining to my situation—I didn't owe anything to anyone, and I only had to worry about one person: me.

"Okay, you've got to promise not to laugh at me." Cara's fizzy glee interrupts my spiraling thoughts. "I've a list."

"A list?"

She unfurls a food-order ticket covered in writing from her pocket. "Afternoon was slow at work so I brainstormed some questions. Favorites and things like that." Her megawatt smile dims, and she folds the paper back up. "Sounds daft now that I say it out loud, doesn't it? Forget it."

"No, no, it's not." I rest a hand on her forearm, surprising myself at the physical contact, but I don't like seeing her beat herself up over something when I can tell that she's just being nice. "We have to start somewhere. So...what's on it?"

She lights up again, flattening the paper full of questions on the table for us to discuss, one by one. Things like my most commonly eaten food (pizza), my favorite movie (*Spirited Away*), and my biggest fear (heights). I ask Cara the same—her answers are chips (what the Irish call french fries), *The Princess Bride*, and clowns, and we dissolve into giggles as she shares a story about her first and only visit to the circus.

"Fancy another pint?" she asks with a glimmer in her eyes.

"Sure." I smile and down my drink as Cara holds up her thumb and forefinger toward the bar.

Only one drink later, the alcohol makes my limbs loose and fills my mind with a pleasant haze. The sun has set here, but my body thinks I woke up in New York, which means I'm essentially having beer for lunch.

"So. First trip to Europe," Cara says. "That's exciting."

"Yeah." I chew the inside of my cheek, ashamed that I've never experienced another country outside of the United States. "Getting time off from work is tough."

"Did you go places as a kid?"

"Day trips around town, but not packing up for two weeks abroad."

"I get that," she says. "My holidays growing up were road trips and camping with my mam. Never went far. Couldn't afford much more with her raising me solo and all."

Understanding dawns on me like the lights brightening up a notch. I'd kind of assumed that Cara had what most normal kids had—memorable family vacations to faraway lands, masses of presents around a Christmas tree, and more than a duffel's worth of clothing. But with a single mom, that would have been tough.

"Wasn't 'til my mam started going with Roger that we did more holidays and such."

"When did they meet?"

"I was fifteen, and they married a year later. I was a little fecker to him too. Absolute brat."

"Really?" I can't help but laugh at her confession and her accompanying devilish grin. "You seem so...I don't know, *not* that."

"I'm easygoing, sure, but when someone crosses me, I can be a terror. Though, at the time, a lot of that was teenage hormones. Growing up, Mam and I were a team. There for each other no matter what. So when she and Roger got together, I turned into a complete nightmare."

"You get along with him now?"

"Best mates. Mam jokes I like him better than her, and sometimes she grates so far under my skin, I'd agree. Guess I needed time with Rodg. And to not be a teenager." She shrugs and wraps her fingers around the pint glass. "I treated me and my mam like a secret club he couldn't join. But he was a part of it all along. He made her happy and only wanted the best for me, and I was putting this arbitrary limit to how many people I could love."

She holds up her drink, waiting for my cheers. I tap my glass against hers, and she gives me a big grin in return.

The responsibility of writing about my time with Cara seeps deeper into my conscience. Perhaps a bit foolishly, I'd envisioned that I'd land here, and after a couple weeks, I'd have this monumental article. But I overlooked that this work has to come from somewhere. From opening up and forming some bond between us. Between sisters.

And Cara treats me like a *sister* sister.

"What do you remember..." The beer has made me brave enough to ask. "Do you remember much about your dad? Our dad?"

"Some, but not a lot. Mam's lookin' forward to telling you more. I recall thinking he was fun, good for a laugh. But I guess that's easy to be when the responsibility's not on you. My childhood was all my mam, and I never felt like it lacked. She sacrificed a lot, I'm sure of that, working double shifts and telling me to take the last bits of dinner because she was full. Looking back, I know she wasn't." Cara's memories are the kind that I fight hard to keep from people, but she seems so at ease sharing them. "As for our da, I saw him a couple times at birthdays when I was younger and that was all. The nature of his work had him moving around all the time."

In an email, Cara wrote about how our dad worked for an organization that responded to humanitarian crises worldwide. He spent his life helping others. It doesn't seem to bother Cara that he wasn't around for her as a father and ended up dying for the job. I can't detect a hint of resentment in her voice.

"What was it like for you growing up?" Cara asks me.

My stomach clenches. When people ask me these kinds of things, I never know how much is too much to tell. I don't need pity, and everyone has a different limit on the amount of trauma they can handle hearing. I learned to pack my upbringing away and stash it out of sight instead. Compartmentalization is a beautiful thing.

But something about the way that Cara rests her head in one hand, and how her eyes are gentle and unassuming, shows her question comes from curiosity rather than nosiness.

"Growing up was tough," I admit, tracing doodles into the condensation collecting on my glass. "When I was young, I didn't understand what was going on with my mom. Why she would be in charge of me sometimes and why, other times, she disappeared and I'd stay at my grandma's. By the time it was just me and my grandma, she was so furious at my mom that I don't think she could really—she wasn't a great caretaker."

"I'm so sorry."

"It's fine. Around fourteen, she wasn't fit to care for me anymore, so I went into foster care. No big deal."

"What happened to her? Your grandmam?"

"Dementia," I say matter-of-factly, modeling some of the same easiness Cara showed while discussing her past. "She's in a care home now. I don't really..." I take a big gulp of beer, questioning whether I should go on. "I don't see her."

"That makes sense." Cara offers a sad smile. "Sounds complicated."

"I was lucky. Didn't spend my entire life in the system, and there were people who helped me along the way." People like my ninth-grade teacher who always packed too much food for her lunch and would offer me some, or one of my first Couchsurfing hosts in New York who let me stay two weeks longer than we'd originally agreed. "There were people who pushed to make sure I had needs met. I'm white so I've had privileges other kids didn't have. And the second I could emancipate myself, I did."

"Still," Cara says, interrupting my rambling. She tilts her head with a sympathetic look, concern swimming in her eyes. "It's awful all the same. You were given difficult circumstances. Things no child should have to deal with."

As she reaches across the table to pat my arm, my face prickles with the urge to cry. I could shout, roll around on the floor, and beat my fists against the wall. I never had a family, not with my mom, my grandma, or at any temporary homes. Cara may have had her mom growing up, but she understands a little of what my life was like. We have something that tethers us together—our father. A man who left Cara just like he left me.

We found each other, and I should be happy about that. But why did I have to live twenty-six years before finding this kind of connection?

I chug some more of my beer, risking a bout of alcohol-induced hiccups to hide the frustration stinging my eyes.

"Thought I'd find you two here." Aidan appears at the end of the booth, his breezy accent disarming me. He ushers in a fresh bundle of cold air that clings to his bomber jacket like an aura. "I was out shooting the sunset. Mind if I sit?"

"Not at all!" Cara scoots closer to the window to make room for him.

He takes a seat across from me, and despite the chill he's brought in, I remain toasty warm. The wind has tousled his hair, and a five o'clock shadow darkens his jawline.

"What'd I miss?"

"Sisterly bonding," Cara says. "The usual."

"Part getting to know you, part therapy session."

At this half-joke, half-truth of mine, Aidan chuckles, and his lopsided smile knocks my thoughts off track.

"Get any good shots?" I manage.

He tucks his backpack further underneath the table, as if that would help him avoid my question. "Not really."

"He's lying," Cara says. "He always gets something worthwhile."

"He showed me a few of his photos."

"What?" She looks at her best friend like she's never seen him before in her life. "It took *years* before you shared a single photograph with me."

"Not years." He reaches for her beer and then says to me, "She exaggerates."

Feeling protective over creative work is something I'm familiar with as a writer. I probably just caught him in a sharing mood the other day while he scrolled through his photos.

"So what's this about lunch tomorrow?" he asks.

"Right." Cara sits more upright and leans into the table toward me. "Mam and Roger are dying to meet you, June. Want to head over to theirs tomorrow? You both, obviously."

"I don't want to intrude on sister time."

"You wouldn't be," Cara says. "We've so many folks coming in for the wedding, so I thought it'd be nice to have some time together before then. Besides, Rodg has a new point-and-shoot he's got to show off, and he has a million questions about it."

"I'll join, so long as you're okay with it?" Aidan locks eyes with me. His appear darker than before, like the trees in Central Park during the summertime dusk.

"Sure. Of course," I say, ignoring the flicker of want in my belly. "You should absolutely come."

I don't have any issues with Aidan being there. I sensed some kind of attraction between us when we first met, but knowing how close he is with Cara puts any thoughts of getting tangled in his bedsheets to rest. He's Cara's best friend, and I'm staying at his place, so I have to get used to him being around, that's all.

"Tomorrow then," Cara says with finality.

Meeting her parents. I swallow, nod, and wash my concerns down with the last of my drink. I can do this. Meeting Cara, meeting her parents. This is part of the deal, anyway—part of having a family.

"Yup. Can't wait."

Chapter Six

Aidan

"You about tomorrow mornin'?" Da sets down a fresh pint for me and a basket of chips in the middle of the table.

He'd best not be roping me into the starting shift. Aside from my plans with Cara's parents, I have my own activities going on.

"What for?"

"Breakfast with your mam and me. Thought it'd be something nice, and seeing as you've the day off, we could all be together."

"I-I want to, I do." Of all days, of all mornings, he organizes family time for tomorrow. "But I can't."

"Not even an hour?"

My focus wavers, and I match June's gaze from across the table. I wish she didn't have to see this messed-up side of me.

"I'll stop by the house when I'm done," I tell Da.

"Done with what?" He rests a fist on one hip. "S'only breakfast. Can't you do your business after?"

"I said I'll stop by later tomorrow morning." The firmness in my voice startles Cara and June and even me, so I ease up. "I won't be too late."

"He's swinging by mine just before lunchtime," Cara says, stepping on eggshells.

"I'm meeting Cara's parents," June adds, and my da softens. "Hangout time."

His mood changes almost instantly, and I doubt she realizes how much she drained the tension from the room.

"I'll visit by then," I assure my da before he heads back behind the bar.

"Is tomorrow the interview?" Cara whispers.

"We shouldn't talk about it here," I say, rubbing my temples.

"You'll have to tell him eventually."

"No, I don't."

"Tell him what?" June asks.

"Danny's got an interview for uni tomorrow."

"That's exciting," she says, examining my face. "Right?"

"It is. His master's." Cara turns her body to face me. "And you know they'll ask you back, so he'll find out about it sooner or later."

"I'll let him know when the time's right. And that's *if* I get in at all, and they don't laugh me off the campus."

"They wouldn't." Cara pats me on the shoulder. "You belong there. You did before, and you do now."

At least Cara believes in me. She has an effervescent personality that bubbles over, but she takes care to only ever say what she means—and I needed to hear something positive like that from her.

We leave the pub early so I can rest up for the hour's drive to Cork in the morning. I fill up a glass of water in the kitchen, and June lingers by the hallway. I haven't gotten used to her presence in my place yet.

"With your interview tomorrow, Cara made it sound like you've already been to this school," June says.

"I did. I came back here when...some personal things came up."

"So you want to go back and finish what you started," she says while twiddling the hem of her jacket. "Makes sense."

"I think so."

"You don't seem very excited."

"I am." I toy with the glass on the counter rather than drinking from it. "I'm worried about the interview part. The being-good-enough-to-get-in part."

"Someone once told me to embrace change and go all in." June takes a few steps forward and leans onto the gray island at the center of the kitchen like she owns it. "You should try it."

"He sounds incredibly wise," I say, tempering the flare of excitement at her standing so close. "Or maybe incredibly stupid."

"Wise. I've seen some of your work, and Cara's right, they're probably excited to see you. But if not, that doesn't mean you're any less great. Ultimately, the choice is up to you. You can say no."

"Now that..." I whistle in surprise. "That's wise."

"Good luck tomorrow." She laughs and exits to the guest room, and I realize I'm smiling as she goes. For the first time, I might be ready for what the next day brings.

That confidence fades once I arrive on campus in the morning. I navigate across the green and past the aging buildings covered in ivy. The school resembles a castle with its walls of gray stone, and in one of the massive sections of window, a professor lectures to a packed class of students measuring liquids in a lab. When I enter the arts building, its familiar faint scent of mildew greets me.

"Ah," a woman says. "You must be Mr. McCarthy."

"Er...yes, that's me."

"I'm Professor Murphy. I've been expecting you. Please." She leads me to a room halfway down the hall and motions to a wooden chair across from her desk. "Have a seat."

The prim professor opens a drawer to her left and retrieves a manila folder. One by one, she removes papers from inside and sets them next to each other like soldiers in a line. My application, admissions essay, and portfolio pieces.

"Is this your first time visiting our wonderful campus?"

"No. I-I was in the program before. I had some—"

"Ah! Yes, I recall. Mr. *McCarthy*. Here we are." She holds one piece of paper closer to her face, scouring the page. "That's right. You had your deferment, which expired at the end of summer semester. Professor Bennett told me all about you."

"I see. Good things I hope."

Professor Bennett left for an early and well-deserved retirement, but he wrote me a recommendation for my reapplication. Based on how Professor Murphy's thin lips stretch into a forced smile, I'll need any help available to me.

"This is a chance for us to chat, you and I. See if this is the right fit for what you aim to achieve in life and at our program."

I shift in the chair. "Sure, sure. Well, as my application mentions, I attended for almost two full semesters before I left. So I'm looking to pick my studies back up where I was."

She opens her mouth, but I trample over her like a blubbering eejit.

"I fully understand that all the classes I took before, I'll have to retake them. I'm prepared for that."

"What have you worked on since you were last enrolled?"

"Uh..." I inhale. "Family stuff. I went back to Ballygrá, where I'm from, for a while. Death in the family. So I've been there, working and helping at my da's pub. My brother was sort of set to take it over, and with him gone...I needed to be there."

"I'm sorry for your loss." Her mouth twists into another locked-up smile. "Have you done anything creatively in that time? Grief is obviously quite a hurdle, so it's understandable if not. Have you had any projects as a photographer or artist since you left?"

"Sure." She doesn't care about the bleedin' pub or all my family drama or the car accident that changed everything. "I've, well, I've been taking photos. Mostly 'round town. Sometimes I'll take day trips to the coast and such. Explore other spots. It's been enjoyable and I think I'm—I know I'm ready to return."

Professor Murphy nods, shuffling some of my prints around on the desk. She leans back in her seat while her eyes bore into me. For some strength, I think of June's encouraging words last night—how this is my decision in the end, not the school's.

"Mr. McCarthy, as you already know, the photography program here is intense. Full of some of the most talented students from across the country and the world. Enjoyment...well, naturally that's part of any creative process. But assignments are demanding, grueling. They'll push you. We don't cover merely the artistic side, but theory too. Considering this is such a rigorous program, what is it you hope to gain by attending?"

Reasonable question. I applied to *one* university after unending support from Cara—a university I'd already gotten accepted to a few years back. And now I look like a complete arse, waltzing in as if they'd see me and immediately write *Approved* in breezy cursive letters on my application.

"Mr. McCarthy?"

"Skills, I suppose. I hope to get some skills as a photographer. To get better, get some practice in, and have other people to work with and get better at...improve my—"

"Skills?"

I scratch the stubble on my chin where I missed a spot shaving.

"And you're able to dedicate yourself to the challenging hours of the program, correct? This will involve classes, coursework, as well as darkroom time, and you'll also be required to complete two separate internships or work programs."

My phone rings, and I jump to my pocket to silence it. None other than Da ringing. "Shite. I mean—sorry. Sorry. Uh, yes. Yes, I can commit."

Professor Murphy thumbs through more of the photos, holding a few up while I wait.

"I think that's all I'll need, then," she says, resuming eye contact with me. "Thank you for your time, Mr. McCarthy." She extends a hand and plasters on one last bitter smile. "We'll be deciding spring entrants in the next few weeks."

I don't need to wait to hear her decision, though. The weight of my failure makes my feet drag to the door like I'm wearing steel boots.

"Oh, Mr. McCarthy?" Professor Murphy's no-nonsense voice stops me at the doorway. "I have one last question. How does photography make you feel?"

"Feel?"

"Yes." She rests her elbows on the armrests, and her jewelry jangles on her forearms. "I love asking applicants this. When you go out to take photos and you look through the viewfinder, how do you feel?"

Sliding both hands into my jacket pockets, I look at the ceiling as if the answers will appear there. I recall June's supportive comments from last night. *That doesn't mean you're any less great.* I don't think *great* is how Professor Murphy would describe me, but I can at least walk out of here with some dignity.

"Free, I guess," I say, letting the words tumble out. "I feel free. In control. Like the universe around me could crumble, but I might not notice until after I click the shutter. Because that's all that matters."

Yet another stiff smile appears, which she breaks as she gathers my papers and stuffs them back into the beige folder. I've somehow said everything wrong during this interview, and I wish I could disappear.

"Thank you, Mr. McCarthy. You can go now."

"A waste of my morning, and hers."

"I'm sure that's not the case," Cara says over the phone.

"You weren't there. Christ, rather than taking the trip out to Cork, I wish she'd called me, asked her questions, and let me rattle on with my nonsense that way. Would've saved us both some time." I rub a palm down my face, wishing I could scrub away the last two and a half hours of my life. Getting accepted once was enough of a miracle—expecting to get in twice was pure fantasy.

"Where are you now?" she asks.

"Parked at my folks'."

"Need me to come over? I've got tons of muffins left over from the cafe yesterday, if that'll make you feel better."

"No, thanks." I turn off the ignition and take a heavy breath. "I'm grand."

"Okay. Say hi to them for me. See you soon. And Danny—" Cara's voice rings out before I hit the end call button. "No need to beat yourself up about this morning. The fact that you showed up is...it's a big deal. I'm proud of you."

I unbuckle my seatbelt and whisper thanks before we hang up.

When I open the front door to my childhood home, both Mam and Da are hunched over their plates at the dinner table. Guilt nags at me—it'd be one thing if my interview went brilliantly, but to throw away a morning when my parents are in the same room together? I wish I could've been here.

"Danny. Oh my sweet boy." Mam's eyes brighten, and she gets up to greet me. She's clad in a fuzzy blue bathrobe, and her hair is still damp from a shower. She opens the fridge. "Want some juice?"

"Sure. No, don't worry, I'll grab it."

"Get my message?" my da asks. "I called, too."

"I saw," I say through gritted teeth. "I was driving and couldn't answer."

"Long drive, eh?"

I ignore his comment. "Would've come by sooner. No one told me we'd be doing this 'til last night."

"Danny," Mam says in a warning tone. "Please. Y'just got here."

I give a concession of a smile. "Sorry."

Once I settle in at the dining table, all three of us fall into a clumsy conversation—updates and gossip from Aunt Brianna in Sligo, the new hires Da made for the pub, and how Cara's managing with the wedding.

We don't spend much time like this together anymore. Grief swallowed Mam whole once Michael died. It left her unwilling to leave bed some days, and she's spent weeks on and off with her sister for a mental refresh. Da dove into work, taking over her responsibilities. And I returned here to sand down the rough spots.

Today, I get the sense that we're all on the same team—something I haven't felt in a long time.

"Can't believe Cara's getting married in a few days," Mam says, cheerier than usual. "Seems like yesterday you two were running 'round the yard and making mischief. How's everything with that new sister of hers?"

"Far as I can tell, they're getting on."

"Seems like a brilliant girl," Da adds.

"She's..." How can I describe June? Brave. Funny. Refreshing. "She's lovely."

"Any thoughts on when we can talk inventory?" Da asks.

"Noah," my mam whispers, "do you really need to chat about that now?"

"It's related to the wedding," he says, turning his attention back to me. "Once you've finished your time off, I'd like to go over the process."

"I figure Mam'd come back and handle that again. When-whenever you're ready, 'course."

Da removes his silver frames and rubs both eyebrows with his thumb and forefinger. "You'd be doing us both a favor by taking that part of the pub over for now."

I fear what *for now* might mean—no deadline, no expiration date. And why would I take over work from my mam? She's been getting better, going out more, and readjusting to our new normal. I wouldn't have considered interviewing at all if she didn't seem well.

"What about Lucas? The lad you hired?" I ask, hopeful. "He said he'd take more hours."

"The kid's a fine bartender for now, but I'd like to know he's someone who'll stick around for a while before I pass off a task as important as inventory to 'im."

"Now's not the time," Mam interjects.

"It's a fine time. Danny, the pub may not be as big a thrill as jetting off and taking pictures, but it's also not a bad gig." He sweeps his hand around the room. "Keeps the roof over our heads."

McCarthy's Pub, by some miracle, is not a financial burden on our family. Every month, we have the funds to pay the staff a fair wage, buy what we need to keep operating, and earn enough profit to keep the lights on. We can thank the Irish and their love of drinking for that. Our lives have never been lavish, but I never got the sense that was my da's goal. If he aspired to life beyond the four walls of McCarthy's Pub, he never let on.

"I'm not looking for a thrill," I say, a little ashamed that my desire to do anything but the pub is so glaringly obvious to Da. "I'm fine stepping in, but Mam should know we'll welcome her back anytime. We can look forward to that."

"Love, if you—"

"Always a fuss with you." Da throws his arms up. "Your brother gave his all, whenever we needed—"

"I'm not Michael. Sorry for that." Michael would have done anything for the family and the pub, but I'm at my limit—and drowning in guilt every time I realize it. "Don't know why you always have to bring him into this."

"He's part of this family too. Forever. Michael's not here with us, God rest him, but that doesn't mean I don't think about him every day."

"Noah."

"Well me too. He may have been your son, but he was my brother."

"So our sadness is a competition now?" my da asks, his voice steeped in anger.

"You bring him up every chance you get. It's like living with a ghost."

"Would you two stop?" Mam stands with a sob, tears trickling down her cheeks. She opens her mouth to say something else but gives up. She leaves and slams the door to the bedroom. The guest bedroom. I'd hoped her and Da's relationship was improving, but that must've been wishful thinking.

"I think..." Da pauses as if he has to handpick each word. "I think if we can give your mam a longer break without that responsibility...not going into the pub where she saw him in there every day. With more time, we might make the situation easier for her here. Let her ease into things at her own pace."

As much as we disagree, my father and I have the same desire. He's begging me to say yes without getting on his knees, all to take care of Mam. No doubt, her taking the time and space to grieve with us in Ballygrá sounds better than her running off to Sligo again, or even further. I want her to stay, so I'll do anything.

The memory of my interview this morning slaps me in the face. Michael would never have done something so selfish. He never would have wanted *me* to do something so selfish. Maybe all I'm destined to be is a bartender who dabbles in photography, and I shouldn't expect anything more—not in my career or in my personal life—and I need to learn to live with that.

"How's Tuesday after the wedding?" I ask weakly as I pinch the bridge of my nose. "Should still be quiet at the front, and we can talk inventory."

He pauses, then solemnly bobs his head once. Da sorts through some papers that clutter the skinny worktop of the kitchen island and offers them to me without meeting my eyes. "For the post," he mutters.

Not until I step out to my car and peek at the letters do I notice my hands quivering with frustration.

Chapter Seven

Juniper

"June? Juniper, wake up, will you?"

A firm hand grips my shoulder and rocks me out of whatever restful wonderland I fell into last night.

"Stop," I grumble like a whiny five-year-old, swatting around blindly. "So tired."

"June, we need to go soon."

Aidan's resonant, husky voice eliminates all remaining hope of drifting off to sleep again. My vision blurs into focus to find him standing by the side of the bed, and he holds my gaze for a nanosecond before his eyes dart to the ground. Those green irises make for quite a wake-up call. I groan and roll onto my back like a lazy dog looking for a belly rub.

"Here." A soft blanket lands on top of me, and Aidan coughs. The buttery knit throw melts in my arms, and on instinct, I cuddle it closer. If he needs me to get out of bed, he chose the wrong plan of action. I hug the worn-in wool, which feels like cotton candy against my skin.

My senses become more grounded as I wonder where my pajamas are. I grip the flimsy blanket around me as my body flushes with embarrassment. Sometime between staying up until 3:00 a.m. because of the time difference and getting ready for bed, I passed out in nothing but my bra and underwear.

"Why didn't you knock?" I snap, wrapping the fabric around me and under my arms like a bath towel.

"I did. Quite a bit. Worried you were dead for a minute."

I wish I could die right now. I'm no prude, but he's caught me in that unattractive morning state—hair unbrushed, pillowcase creases on my cheeks, and nearly nude. At least I have my nice lacy black bra and panties on.

That doesn't matter, though. I clutch the blanket closer to me and fumble to make myself decent.

Aidan readjusts the hem of his shirt. "You coming to Cara's mam's this afternoon? You slept all morning, so it's about time to head over."

"Already?" The clock on the nightstand shows it's almost noon. "Uh, yeah."

"We'll grab Cara on the way. Think you can be ready in fifteen?"

"I'll try," I utter and race down the hallway with the throw still draped around me.

Aidan has a knack for finding me in uncomfortable states—hopeless tourist who lost her passport, suspicious young woman caught lying about her name, and lazy lady sprawled out half naked on a dainty floral comforter that his grandmother probably knitted for him.

After the world's shortest shower, I rifle through my bag. I only have a few outfits to rotate through, but I alternate between each bottom and top, holding them against my body in the full-length mirror. I land on a sweater, a corduroy dress that ends mid-thigh, and a pair of tights that are so warm they've made the snowstorms in the city feel like a tropical breeze. This seems like an appropriate meet-the-parents-of-your-surprise-half-sister kind of outfit. Looking in the mirror, I dot a lip stain over my cheeks and lips, and I smooth out some feathery pieces of hair.

As ready as I'll ever be.

Aidan drives a car that must be from the '80s, based on how the maroon paint has long faded and lost its glossy sheen. When I pull on the handle, I do a double take at the dry leather of the steering wheel.

"We drive on the correct side of the road over here."
Aidan opens the opposite door and smirks as I switch to
the passenger side. Rather than trade with me, though,
he waits there and closes the door once I'm settled in.
His chivalry chips away most of the remaining anger I
have about my unfortunate wake-up.

I settle into the light musky scent of the car—or
maybe that's Aidan? We're nestled so close together
that I can't tell. He twirls a knob on the center console.
Once he's satisfied with the melancholy Morrissey song
on the radio, he places his camera in the minuscule
backseat.

"How'd the interview go?"

"Don't remind me," he says, backing out of the driveway.

"That bad?"

He grunts in response, which stops me from prod-
ding further. I can't imagine a school disliking him and
his work that much, but I understand if he doesn't want
to talk about it. I'm content to drive around and listen
to the radio instead.

I type notes on my phone in the shared document
that Ethan set up. *Abrupt awakening by Aidan,
Cara's BFF and my temporary roommate. En route
to meet Cara's mom and stepdad, and while I
shouldn't be nervous (after all, they're not my parents), I can't help but worry—*

"Sorry," he says.

"For what?"

"Being short with you," Aidan says. "Shite morning."

"I get it. Happens sometimes."

"You...you ready to meet Cara's parents?"

"I think so." My voice quivers, unmistakably, and I sit up straighter to fake self-assurance. "Cara doesn't seem to remember much of our dad, but she said her mom will. That's kind of weird for me."

"Evelyn's lovely, you'll like her. She's really...motherly, I guess is the word. She can expect what people need in the moment, same as Cara."

"I hope she likes me." Is that why butterflies are swarming in my stomach? "She sounds cool, is all."

"She is. And she'll like you, both her and Roger will. They're good folks." He drums his fingers on the steering wheel. "I understand why you'd be anxious, meeting the parents and all."

"Yeah. Never got used to the process."

A familiar apartment complex sneaks into view, and Aidan parks by the curb and clicks his hazards on. "*The process*?"

"Meeting new families in foster care. They were all nice enough, but that didn't make the experience less bizarre."

"Ah, I thought you meant meeting the parents. Like when you're seeing someone."

"Oh no, no," I shake my head in distaste. "Although I'm sure that's nerve-wracking in its own way. Wouldn't actually know."

"Really?"

"I mean, I date." My face heats up like an oven. "I'm just not a serious-relationship kind of gal, you know?"

"Right."

"No one questions men when they choose not to couple up long term," I ramble on. "I prefer to occupy my time with what matters to me—work, my best friend, life in the city. I just..." My attention drifts to the driver's seat where Aidan is listening, not a hint of judgment in his eyes. "I'd rather not attach myself to another human being, that's all. It usually ends in disappointment."

"That's true." Aidan's tone leads me to believe he knows this firsthand. "But you'd have nothing to worry about meeting any parents, because you're...you seem great. You met my da, and he thought you were sound. So anyone would be lucky to take you home to meet their folks."

"That's...yeah. Thanks."

Aidan has probably comforted Cara the same way hundreds of times before, but I still smile to myself in the passenger seat. In less than twenty seconds, he gave me the pep talk I didn't know I needed. The added confidence is a mental boost.

Cara steps outside and waves so hard her arm might fly right off. She squeezes into the backseat, which is a miracle considering the space is more of a glorified storage area for Aidan's camera gear. Even though she's hugging her shins and her knees block her vision, she bursts with energy.

"Mam has been texting me all morning. She and Roger are *buzzing*."

"I'm excited too," I say, then resume chewing on my bottom lip.

Cara leans forward, resting an elbow on the back of each seat, and stares Aidan down. He takes in a deep breath before asking, "What?"

"How you feeling?"

"Grand."

"Be honest."

"I'd love to not talk about it."

Cara nods once. "Understood."

"I'm ready to crash your brunch if that's fine with you."

"You know my mam and Rodg wouldn't have it any other way."

Only one minute outside of town, we cruise down perilously skinny roads, passing fields of sheep and quaint family homes. I can't remember the last time I escaped the city for more than a long weekend, and the scenery fills me with the longing to rent a car and drive around the countryside all day. Without a driver's license or a private chauffeur, that won't happen, but a girl can dream.

We arrive at Cara's parents' home within minutes, and I swallow the anxious jitters crawling up my throat. Cara's mother and stepdad await us on the front porch, with a large weary-looking dog lying dutifully at their side. They wave as we pull in and then walk up to greet us at the car—the epitome of loving parents.

"You must be Juniper." Cara's mom extends her arms out wide, the sleeves of her dress flowing behind her like feathers on a peacock. Her voice has a milky quality to it, and she wears an enormous quartz crystal neck-lace that digs into my cheek while we embrace. "I'm Evelyn, but call me Evvie. I'm delighted to meet you, love."

"Nice to meet you," I say in a daze.

When Cara sent some photographs during our initial emails, I struggled to spot any resemblance between the two of us. She has a heftier bone structure, a long oval face with a rounded chin and nose, and flaming red curls, while I'm more compact, with straight dark hair and sharper features. Seeing her mother, though, I understand why we share almost no physical similar-ities—Cara is a carbon copy of Evelyn, twenty-some-thing years younger.

Her stepfather, a wiry man who stands a foot shorter than his wife, looks like he could explode from joy.

"Such a delight to have you here," he says, suffocating me in a hug. "Ab. So. Lute. Delight."

"Careful, love, she needs her ribs," Evelyn says, pulling me toward her and hooking an arm in mine. She does the same to Cara on the other side, leading us down the pathway and past a well-tended garden of violets, pansies, and chrysanthemums. Evelyn pats me on the elbow. "I'll stick the kettle on. We've some catching up to do."

"Stop," Cara groans, drawing out the word into three separate syllables. "Rodg, really."

He's had a palm-sized camera tied to his wrist from the moment we walked in the door. "One more." Cara's stepdad presses a button, and we're all blinded by the aggressive flash. Roger waves Aidan over and holds the device up, displaying the screen on the back. He waggles his eyebrows like he's impressed with his own work, and Aidan leans in to give him some pointers. The camera is clearly far less advanced than what Aidan uses, but he doesn't roll his eyes or look bemused while giving his advice.

"I'm so sorry," Cara says to me. "I'd no idea he'd go mad over meeting you."

"I don't mind," I say, smiling to hide my bewilderment about the intense fanfare.

"*Mo stoirín*," he begs his stepdaughter. "One day you'll thank me for these. So much is happening this week. First your sister's in town, then the wedding, then, then..."

With that, his face crinkles like tissue paper as plump tears flow freely down his cheeks. Aidan pats him on the back as Cara, unable to ignore the pitiful sight that is her stepdad weeping like a wounded child, gets up to hug him. Winnie, their senior German Shepherd, casts a concerned look but doesn't budge from his spot in the middle of the floor.

Evelyn remains mellow and laid-back, dancing over to my seat with a cup of tea. "Don't mind Rodg. He's worried he's losing his girl this week, and it's got him all worked up."

He wails again, the sound muffled by Cara's hair, as a fresh onslaught of tears forms. I've never seen a man fall apart the way he does at the mere mention of a wedding.

"So, love," Evelyn says, getting cozy in the dining chair next to me. I prepare for all kinds of questions—and to be judged with hypercritical eyes. "I can only imagine what a whirlwind this whole trip has been."

"Kinda crazy." I adjust in my seat, aware that everyone here is watching me. "In a good way. But aside from losing my passport, I'm enjoying it."

"A real shame someone didn't do the right thing and turn your bag in." She shakes her head and makes a *tut-tut* sound with her tongue. "Although you might end up a small bit thankful to have the excuse to get a replacement in Dublin. We've so much to do for the wedding, and Cara's probably ready to put you to serious work."

"Mam," Cara says in a low warning voice.

"Aidan and I have a list already." I don't think I've said his name out loud before, and the novelty of it sends a shiver up my spine. "More his list than mine, but I'm helping."

"Well, Roger and I are thrilled you came. Really. And to get the time off...I honestly didn't think you would with such short notice. What was it you read, Rodg? That most Americans only have two weeks of vacation, but—"

"But..." He dabs his eyes with a hanky and rejoins us at the table. "Over half don't take a holiday. Can you believe that?"

"Technically, I've got work while I'm here," I admit, ashamed to be the living proof of that hard-working, never-vacationing statistic. "But that meant my employer would approve the time away."

"That's right, you've that story Cara told me about." Evelyn claps her hands as if my assignment is the world's finest piece of literature. "Can't wait to read it. You'll let us know when the article prints? We'll want a copy."

"She writes for a digital magazine. It'll be online," Cara says with a hint of annoyance, like she and her mom have had this conversation ten times already. "If you want a copy, we'll have to print it ourselves."

"Well, we'll do just that. And we'll need you to sign it."

As we sit around the table, sipping on tea and munching on cookies, I can't help but compare this to all of my foster families. I remember first visits full of stop-and-go discussions and long pauses, punctuated with even longer lists of rules. They were tame and orderly, if a little uncomfortable.

Here, I'm included. With Roger's jovial chuckles and unexpected outbursts of happy tears, Evelyn's kind eyes and habit of waltzing rather than walking around, and Cara's eye rolls and giggles, this feels so...normal. Not like I'm an outsider, but I'm in on the joke too. There's polite arguing over the right number of sugar cubes to put into tea, and discussion on when Roger definitively knew he loved Evelyn ("At first sight, I say," to which Evelyn swats his arm and turns a bright shade of crimson). All of them—including Aidan, who leans against the counter across from me—chat over each other, recalling birthday parties and graduations. I make intermittent notes on my phone, but mostly I sit and witness everything unfolding.

I guess this is what a family can be.

"We've some old photos in here somewhere." Evelyn floats off to a bookshelf and pulls some notebooks from the shelves.

"She doesn't need to see those," Cara says, her agitation palpable.

"Oh, I think I do," I say, giving Cara a teasing look. "Baby pictures are a must."

"Journalistic research," Aidan adds, a smile playing on his lips.

"Exactly."

She glares at us both, but mirth causes the corner of her mouth to twitch. "I'm not sure which side you two are on."

"They're adorable photos," her mom says, "and I bet you could use some for your newspaper assignment."

My phone vibrates—it's the same unknown number that called yesterday. I silence it while Evelyn sashays her way back to the table with three hefty notebooks.

"Now, when Cara was a child, she had a terrible habit of lifting her dress up and showing her knickers for everyone to see, so—"

"Oh my *god*."

As I look at Cara, Aidan catches my eye. "It's true," he mouths, which causes me to burst into laughter.

"Let me try to find at least a few decent ones where she's actually looking at the camera and not flashing it."

"If I'd known you'd pull out the albums, I would have made other plans for us this morning." Cara sinks into the chair. "I'm so sorry for this," she grumbles.

Evelyn reaches out to pat her arm, which Cara deftly evades. That dynamic that Cara had mentioned—where she loves her mom, but her mom also drives her crazy—fills me with a kind of yearning. A recognition of what I never had.

Evelyn shares cute photos of Cara dressed as a witch for a costume party sometime when she was four or five, pictures from her sixteenth birthday, which are less cute and more angsty, and many, many images of Cara in her childhood with her dress flipped up over her head. Evelyn didn't lie, that happened a lot.

Another book has memories from before Cara was born. "Oh, look at these." Evelyn points to the people in the photographs, some in black and white, introducing me to them and giving me the chance to take photos on my phone so I have them for future reference. "These are my aunts and uncles, all of whom'll attend the wedding. Oh, and this is Cara's godfather, Conor. And here are my own mammy and da."

"Will they be at the ceremony as well?" I ask. Evelyn's shoulders tighten, and everyone looks over me or around me. Less than an hour in, and I've stuck my foot in my mouth. I assumed Cara's grandparents were still alive, and now I've brought up painful memories.

"Sorry." I panic, worried I can't climb out of this hole. "I shouldn't have said that. I didn't realize—"

"Nothing to be sorry 'bout." Evelyn rubs my back and sweeps that mistake under the rug as quickly as she turns a new page in the photo album. Her sheer graciousness undoes some of the tightness in my body.

Cara's mom lets out a delighted *Oh!* when she sees what's next: pregnancy photos. In one, she stands in a kitchen with the glowiest of grins, cradling her baby bump. In another, Evelyn holds up a onesie to the camera.

"I loved being pregnant." She strokes each photograph like they're precious jewelry, and I'm hit with that yearning again.

"I've only a few photographs of your father," she goes on. "By this time, we both knew our relationship wouldn't work."

A buzz from my phone interrupts us once more, and the only way to end the spam calls once and for all is to answer and demand they take me off the list. Agitated, I excuse myself, step around a sleeping Winnie, and go out to the back porch, hugging one arm to my chest for warmth.

"Hello?"

"Is this Ms. Martin?"

"It is. I don't know where you got my number, but—"

"I'm a representative at Double Helix Labs. My name is Andy."

"Oh, um. Hi." I turn and face the yard.

"How are you doing today?"

"I'm good." Aside from this call, I'm doing great. Talking to Cara and her parents went better than I could have imagined.

"I'm, uh, calling to discuss your DNA test with us." In the background, I hear papers shuffling. "Specifically, an error may have taken place with your results."

A chill forces my body to shudder. "What do you mean?"

"We're not 100 percent certain whether an issue occurred. There's a chance your sample was compromised at our facility." His voice switches into something more formal. "We at Double Helix recognize the immense amount of trust placed in us by our customers, but mistakes can sometimes happen." The bland surety of his delivery sounds like he's reciting a scripted explanation. "We want to make this right, so I'd like to send you a replacement test kit at no charge to you."

The world around me screeches to a halt. So this means Cara and I might not be half sisters at all? "My results are wrong? That means I..." I traveled here for no reason. I got a taste of what I'd been missing out on my whole life, only to have that ripped away.

No. This has to be a mistake.

"Your results may still be valid," he says, and I nod, as if my agreeing with him makes any difference. "The retest will tell us for certain."

"What happened to the first one?"

"Uh." More paper shuffling. He clears his throat and puts on his Official Customer Care voice. "One of our technicians discovered a potential problem after your report went out, so we've been reaching out to clients—I wanted to resolve the issue with you personally."

"But what happened?"

"There's a possibility of an...a potential algorithmic error."

"What does that mean?"

"I, uh...the lab only shared the basic details." He takes his tone into something more personal, like he's taking off a mask and can speak more candidly. "It usually means a software problem at the time we analyzed your results. The simple retest will clear everything up."

I rest a hand on the wooden handrail to steady myself. "Well, I'm...I'm out of the country right now, I can't do anything."

"That's no problem. Double Helix is the most widely used DNA testing service, with labs in over thirty-two countries and shipping to over ninety."

In the same staged tone, Andy explains my options. Something about mailing one to me at home. Lab locations in Ireland, if I'd prefer. Expedited results as a courtesy.

"There's, of course, the chance that everything did process accurately. And I want to emphasize that this second test is just a precaution. We won't know for sure until you submit a new sample."

"Really?" I squeak.

"Yes. Our goal at Double Helix Labs is for this additional test to ensure 100 percent accuracy."

I want to believe him. I do. How comforting to think I'll give them another vial of spit, and we'll confirm what we thought all along: that Cara is my long-lost half sister. Then, I can continue the trip like this call never happened, I can write the article I intended to write from the beginning, and I can have the sister I never knew existed.

Except I can't fight the thought that maybe my gut feeling was right—that this was just a fairy tale. Did I really think I was so special that I had some father from another country and an entire group of relatives to meet here?

"Do I have to retest? I mean, if it's just a precaution, and you're pretty sure that everything's fine, then maybe I don't need to."

"This is the standard protocol. In these highly unlikely scenarios, we work one-on-one with the client whose kit was compromised. From there, if a mistake indeed occurred, we'll reach out to anyone who matched with your account as a courtesy."

"Right." I suck in a breath. "Okay. I need to figure out what the best option is for me since I'm not home. Could I get back to you later?"

Andy obliges. He says he'll email, and I can let him know when and how I'd like to retest, giving me more time to sort out my options.

Until then, I'm a living, breathing question mark.

"You keeping well out here?"

I twirl around to find Aidan stepping onto the patio with my jacket in hand. He must have seen me trembling. With a swiftly muttered goodbye to Andy, I hang up and exhale a massive puff of warm air.

"Mhmm. Thanks," I reply through chattering teeth, draping the coat over my shoulders. My whole body shakes, but I can't blame that on the temperature. My reason for coming to Ireland might have just imploded.

"You're a hit, by the way. A natural O'Shea." Aidan tucks his hands into his pockets and nods toward the window with a crooked grin. "I told you—nothing to worry about."

If only you knew. I attempt a smile at his generosity, although my face contorts into something more like a wince. "Thanks."

"You fit right in."

Another collective laugh roars from inside the house, and we peer in the direction of a joyous Cara, Roger, and Evelyn.

My heart plummets, wondering if they're destined to be the family I almost had, so close yet so far. Maybe my results are fine. But I can't ignore the nagging worry that this is all too good to be true.

Chapter Eight

Aidan

June sits in the passenger seat, hunched over the papers on her lap as she writes in her information. "Sorry you got roped into this," she says without looking up from her work. "I doubt driving to Dublin and back was at the top of your list today."

"Don't mind."

Cara truly does know the best people, and a friend from the embassy called right after June stepped out for a chat on her mobile. A last-minute cancellation for this afternoon meant she could squeeze in and get a temporary passport. She couldn't just email paperwork to the embassy in Dublin, though—June had to show up in person with all the documents. She already missed the train that would have gotten her to the city in time, so that left her with only the option to drive—or rather, to be driven.

I could tell Cara hated asking me to give June a lift, but I dismissed her worries because I couldn't avoid Dublin forever. The odds I'll run into my ex are slim. She's one person in a place of hundreds of thousands, and I'm a grown man who doesn't need to hide from a former girlfriend.

"You shouldn't go out of your way for me on Cara's behalf," June says as I drive. "You're her best friend, I get that." The way her fingers flip elegantly through the papers distracts me for a split second. "But I'm already crashing at your place, so no more special treatment."

"You're special to Cara, so you're special to me." That's a simple truth—anything or anyone that matters to her matters to me too—but saying so out loud feels too intimate. "I only mean, so, you're her half sister, and we've known each other for ages. Cara and me, I mean—you and I just met. And even though you only got here—"

Christ, my roundabout talking won't stop. I never get this tongue-tied around Cara or Yaz.

"I understand," June chuckles, putting me out of my misery. "Thank you for the ride. Better option than the bus."

"That would've taken you twice as long."

"I'm used to the subway. I can get from my apartment to pretty much anywhere in New York in less than an hour."

"That's different, though. The Big Apple versus all of Ireland," I say.

"Nobody calls it *The Big Apple*. No one who lives in New York, anyway."

"Not the point. The whole world is all of it, the big cities and small towns and the in between. Folks in cities think they're the center of the universe, but life's bigger than Dublin, or New York, or any place on a map."

"True. Guess I'd feel kind of trapped if I didn't have as many options to get around, that's all."

I swallow. Trapped is precisely how living in my hometown feels some days—like I can't leave, no matter how hard I try. Life would look different if Michael hadn't gone out that night.

"Okay, I have a question." June takes a sip from her water bottle, leaving a few miniature droplets on her rosy lips. "And if you don't want to talk about it, I understand."

"Whatever you're imagining happened at my interview, make it two hundred times worse."

"I wasn't going to ask that. But why did you leave in the first place? Stop school?"

"Oh. Family stuff." I wait, unsure if sharing all the not-so-pretty details with her will make June regret asking. But she spent the whole day being vulnerable around me, what with meeting Cara's parents. And this morning in the guest bedroom, when she had almost no clothing on.

I blink that beautiful thought away.

"My, uh, my older brother passed," I continue, "and I had to come home for a time. School got put on hold."

"I'm so sorry. That's awful."

"It was. It is."

"On top of losing him, you made the sacrifice of coming home and leaving school. Your parents are lucky to have a son like you."

"It's nothing," I say, almost laughing her observations away.

"I don't think it's nothing."

"Well, I...I'm pleased to do it. I might not always be pleased *about* it, but I couldn't imagine carrying on while my parents are...and Michael. He would've done the same if the situation called for him to."

"Were you two close?"

"Quite the journalist, you are."

She shrugs. "Just curious."

Curious about *me*. I don't want her to dig too deep and not like what she finds, though.

"We were close how brothers are, which means I idolized him and wished I could've been that cool. I was the shy kid who kept to himself and spoke as little as possible, but he made friends with everyone. Chatted up anyone who walked in the pub's door."

"You're surrounded by reminders of him there too. That's hard."

I swallow the lump forming in my throat. Few people understand what a challenge it is to push my parents to move forward with their lives when the pub is so closely tied to Michael.

"But you'd rather not stay there? Continue working with your dad?"

I can't bring myself to say no, but I let my shoulder hike up a little as I nod.

"They could hire someone to take your place. Then you could follow your own dreams."

"It's more than the pub." I swallow. "I'm kind of holding the family together, so to speak. That's the priority, not a degree."

"Sure. Not that you need one, though."

"How do you mean?"

"You could spend all your life sitting in classrooms and not learn a thing," she says with a shrug. "People do it all the time. I get the appeal of school. I wish I'd done more myself sometimes. But there are people attending class all around the world studying how to become half as talented as you are. Real experience has as much weight as a degree, in some cases."

"I think you're talking rubbish with what you say to me, all because you and Cara are siblings."

Her demeanor changes from warm to cold in a moment—like the sun dipping below the horizon at the end of the day. I don't think I said anything wrong, but June seems more interested in quietly watching the world go by as we make our way into Dublin.

We arrive ten minutes before closing time. June races inside while I wait in the car. I chew over her suggestion that I don't need school. I can't effortlessly pick back up where I was, and maybe I shouldn't, because I'm not who I was a year ago. But once Mam and Da return to a happy equilibrium, what should I do if I don't do school?

June takes a while, so I'm certain she's had some luck. I people-watch from behind the wheel. A group of business folks in grayscale peacoats and fancy leather shoes wait at the traffic lights. A middle-aged woman pushing a buggy is power-walking on the other side of the street. A bicyclist rings his bell and signals with an outstretched arm before racing past rows of two-story brick buildings.

The last time I was here, Mary and I were hunting for apartments. That was when I realized I could never be what she wanted. She outgrew me, and we both agreed we weren't going to work, no matter how much we tried.

"I can't wait around forever, Danny."

The crack of the car door snaps me back to reality. June slips into the passenger seat with a frustrated frown on her face. "Well, I've got good news and bad news."

Although we arrived late to the embassy, June met with Cara's friend and dropped off all of her documentation. June says that's the good news. The bad news is the passport won't be ready until tomorrow.

"You've already helped me a ton driving me here. You can go back to Ballygrá, and I'll catch a train in the morning."

I shake my head. What is it with June and feeling like she's an obligation?

"I won't abandon you here tonight. We'll...we could get a hotel?" My offer comes out more like a question, since a hotel would mean uncertain sleeping arrangements. Would we share a room? Book separate rooms? We'd have dinner together at least, wouldn't we?

"Yeah, a hotel could work." In the setting sunlight, June's cheeks turn rosier. "Or if you or Cara have friends here, that's fine. I'm cool with couch surfing."

"I might have someone. As long as he's available, I'm certain he'll have us."

"Okay. Is that what you prefer?"

Her boundless eyes catch mine, and for a split second, I get the sense she's daring me. My gulp echoes in the car as I envision us checking into a hotel room together—one hotel room. But no, that's out of the question, and certainly not what Cara meant by taking care of June.

I call up my friend, Max, and he invites us right over. So much for the hotel fantasy.

"Been too long, man," Max says in his loose American accent. He waves June and me into his Dublin flat with a grin. "How've you been?"

I met Max the spring semester of my postgrad. The company he works for in Dublin did a series of nationwide pop-up museums, one of them in Cork, and his time there coincided with my flatmate needing a subtenant. We roomed together for months, and he even liked my photos enough to feature two of them in the pop-up. Because I hurried home in the spring for the funeral, I missed the exhibit, though. We've kept in touch with texts here and there around holidays, but I didn't know how he'd react to a surprise visit.

Turns out, he's thrilled.

He sweeps the brunet chaos of his ear-length hair away from his face—in vain, since the waves fall right back into place. "Hey there," he says, holding out his hand. "Max."

"June. Nice to meet you."

"You're American too?"

"You remember my friend Cara?" I ask. "This is her half sister."

"Cool, Cara's great. Glad to have you," Max says with his signature warmth. "Make yourselves comfortable."

He fetches drinks from the kitchen, and we relax into the living room. His flat looks similar to a few of the places I scoped out in the spring. It has some grit to it but still looks hip—with exposed brick and high ceilings, sleek furniture, and a bookcase packed with literature. The whole setup is what I'd expect from Smithfield, the trendy area we're in. The closer June and I got to Max's address, the more quirky coffee shops and tiny restaurants we saw.

Max gives us some water and then sprawls out in a plush chair, swinging his legs over the arms. "It's great to see you."

"Sure we're not putting you out tonight?" I ask. "We can sort out a few rooms somewhere if that's easier."

"I'd be offended if you did. You should've told me you'd be in town."

"That's my fault," June says. "I'm the one who needed to get to Dublin. Aidan offered to take me last minute."

"It's kismet. You're both welcome here as long as you'd like." Max looks at me. "Last time we saw each other must've been when you were here looking at places with Mary."

"Sounds about right."

I offer nothing more about my ex and steer the discussion toward how Max has done up the place, asking him where he got the art on his walls. I'm not in the mood to talk about what happened with Mary, certainly not in front of June. Not that she'd care, but there's no need to go into the gory details of my last relationship. Since she arrived, I've finally had someone around who hasn't been weighed down by every piece of my baggage.

Max inflates an air bed for me and tells June to take his bedroom. "I'll sleep on the couch," he says to her. "It'll give me some precious pillow-talk time with Danny over here."

"Down, boy," I say with a chuckle, although something like disappointment nestles into my chest. Part of me wants to watch June during those soft moments before bed. A laughable thought, though. If Cara were here and not her half sister, would the sleeping arrangements bother me? I need to usher those thoughts far, far away.

Since we hadn't planned on the overnight stay, June goes out to purchase a few toiletries. Max points to a shop across the street through his living room window. I offer to go with her, but she insists she'll be fine.

As the patter of her steps disappears into the stairwell, Max sits his lanky body on a stool. "So how're you doing?" He rests his feet on the footrests, knees like arrows pointing in opposite directions. "Last you told me, we were gonna be neighbors out here. Then you text me that you and Mary are through, and that's about all I've heard since."

Max has a way of asking the right questions and listening, really listening, for the answers. I'd joked with him more than once that if he ever pursued a career as a therapist, he'd manage fine.

"Been better, I s'pose. You won't believe where I was this morning."

"Where?"

"Cork. Interview to go back."

"Nice."

"It was shite," I say. "Total, utter shite."

"You really are your harshest critic. I've seen your stuff. I've *advocated* for your stuff."

"Don't think spring's gonna be the ideal time to pack up and leave anyway."

"How's the fam?"

"Also shite," I snort. "Da's on at me about the pub, Mam's...she's partly here. It's like a piece of her died when Michael did. Which I understand, you know.

She's his mam. But..." I look up to Max, who is nodding his head with understanding—a concerned frown on his face, and his eyebrows wrinkled together as if he can hear what I don't speak aloud.

But she's my mam too.

"They need more time," I go on.

"I couldn't imagine doing what you're doing for your mom and dad. You're loyal, I'll give you that much."

"I wish I could let them handle the situation themselves."

"Why can't you?"

I scratch the stubble on my chin, imagining a world where I ran off to pursue my own dreams rather than putting my family first—one where I faced the guilt instead of sacrificing myself out of duty to my parents. "I don't know."

"That's fine. You don't need to know. When you're ready, and if you ever change your mind about Dublin, I'll be here."

I kick off my shoes and lean into the couch, my legs tingling from the first stretch after a long afternoon of driving. "Even if things were going better between my mam and da, Dublin's not me."

"Yeah, it seemed like an odd fit when you'd mentioned it, to be honest. But I can contact some friends. Ask around, find out who's looking for a photog. Or I could see who's hiring. You've got a great eye, and that translates to all sorts of jobs."

"Sure."

"I'm serious. I get it, man, this past year sucked for you. Your brother, the breakup. But anyone would be lucky to work with you, and I know this because I have. You're the most talented photographer I've ever met." He pauses, making sure that I see the earnestness in his eyes. "You're also the most talented photographer I've ever had the pleasure to live with."

"Christ, you're full of it," I bark, tossing a pillow at him, which he diverts with an expert kick.

Pulling the focus away from the shambles of my life, I ask Max to fill me in on his past few months. The latest of who-knows-how-many pop-up museums he's curated has been a massive success, landing him features in papers and magazines worldwide. His mam and da are still at the law firm, and his sister's an honor student at school.

"I broke up with that bookstore owner I started seeing in May."

"Sorry to hear that."

"Eh, I'm not," he says, nonplussed. "Just wasn't feeling it."

"Still friends?"

"You know it."

Max is a good guy all around, especially when it comes to dating. While I've never seen him head-over-heels ecstatic about someone, his relationships always seem fun and easygoing. He also doesn't seem too bothered when the flames cool down, and Max somehow manages to remain friends with almost all his ex-girlfriends. I wish I could channel some of that casual energy in my own life.

"I might've had to travel for some new pop-ups, so we wouldn't have lasted. What about you and..." Max's eyebrows hint toward the door.

"June?"

"Yeah. She's cute, seems fun."

"No. No, no, no," I say, as if the more I repeat the word, the better I'll get my point across. "She's Cara's half sister. And she lives in New York."

"And?"

"The woman's *related* to my best friend. That makes anything between us beyond friendship automatically...I don't know. Awkward? I wouldn't put June, or Cara for that matter, in that position. Some kind of rule about friends and their siblings."

"Rules are made to be broken. Besides, if you both like each other, who cares?"

"I've no reason to believe June feels any particular way about me."

"My mention of Mary piqued her interest."

I'm more pleased with myself than I should be. "Well, that—that doesn't matter. I don't want to get in the way of her and Cara getting close. Besides, even if I *were* attracted to her, she lives in another country. Long distance is a beast of its own. I c-could do it for the right person, but that's a lot to ask." I clear my throat. "We could mess around, but I don't...I'm more a relationship man. Huge surprise, I'm sure, considering my previous relationship lasted almost a decade."

Max processes my word vomit in stillness. "Hm."

"*Hm* what?"

"Nothing," Max leans back and cradles his head in both hands like a hammock. "Seems like you've put some serious thought into your hypothetical attraction to her."

I roll my eyes again and chuck the other pillow at him. "You really are full of shite."

Chapter Nine

Juniper

Dear Ms. Martin,

I'd like to apologize again for any inconvenience regarding your test results. As I mentioned on the phone, we would be more than happy to extend a complimentary retest to you, either through the mail-in method or in person at one of our hundreds of labs worldwide. Please let me know how you want to proceed.

Best,

Andy Johannsen, he/him/his
Manager, Customer Relations, Double
Helix Labs

I'd hoped that Andy would take his sweet time sending that email, but unfortunately, he's a diligent, albeit inexperienced, employee of his word. I can't ignore him for long. And maybe the results *will* work out with no change, like he said they probably would.

But if they don't...

I star the message and give my inbox another scan. Something from Ethan with the subject line *DNA journey article status update??* makes my stomach drop. If my career-altering piece is all potentially based on a mistake, I don't know what to tell him. Ignoring Ethan's email for now, I walk down the street and dial up Lissie.

"Not even kidding," she answers, "I was just about to call you."

"Yeah?" The thin metallic sound of a streetcar hums down the block, and I strain to hear her response. "Everything okay?"

"Do you still own that pair of knee-high leather boots? They have around a four-inch heel and a zip up the side."

"The black ones?"

"Yes! They make your butt look great."

"Thanks." They do make my butt look great. They also make my feet feel like I've been tiptoeing on a cheese grater all night, so I only ever wear them when I'm on the prowl to hook up. "I still have them. I didn't pull them out for fall yet, so they're in the storage tote under my bed. Got a hot date?"

While I walk, Lis tells me about an audition she has later today for one of the witches in a steampunk retelling of Macbeth. The neighborhood Max lives in seems trendy. The buildings vary—some are all silver and glass and sharp angles, others have fresh murals in bright hues that hide the age of the structures. I pass a coffee shop the size of a closet and a vegan restaurant. Groups of friends walk by, laughing and trickling into various bars and restaurants.

"Borrow away," I say. "Another audition is good news."

"It's not a big one, but I'll take whatever I can to get in front of those casting directors."

"And show off that memorable butt."

"That too." She laughs, and a throb of homesickness hits me. "So what's up there? You texted that things were getting interesting. And you're in Dublin now? Do tell."

I can almost see her big blinking blue eyes craving all the details. My best friend's voice makes me wish I could curl up on our cushy couch, open a bottle of rosé, and spill. I lean my back against the chilly brick facade of a store and watch another silver and yellow train go by.

I explain the first part of the day at the O'Shea's, which feels like it happened weeks ago. My head is a jumble, sandwiched between the bureaucracy of getting an emergency passport and the reality that I might have booked a trip to visit a half sister who isn't really my half sister.

"How did the lab not catch this sooner?" Lis asks, and the outrage in her voice gives me reassurance.

"No clue. I can put you in touch with the guy who called if you'd like, but he'll just rattle off some prewritten response to explain it. Something about an issue with the algorithm." I kick my heel against the wall behind me. "I feel so stupid."

"You're not stupid. Their stupid lab is stupid. You didn't do a single thing wrong."

"I should have known." I tip my head back a little too hard, as if doing so will knock some sense into me. "Did I actually think, with my family history, I'd have a half sibling in another country? And now I'm writing this article, and—"

"Hey, stop that. As far as you know, Cara *is* your half sister. Lots of Americans have Irish heritage, so let's not doom spiral just yet. The lab said the second test is a precaution, so that means they're pretty sure it's fine, and they just have to double-check."

She's right. If the lab knew with 100 percent certainty that my test was wrong, Andy wouldn't lie about it.

"This is stressful," she goes on, "but you couldn't have prevented this. What did Cara say?"

"I didn't tell her yet."

"You should talk to her, see what she thinks."

"Not tonight. And I won't be back to Ballygrá until tomorrow."

"Oh June." Her voice has a gravity to it, a seriousness that I've only heard a handful of times before. "Just call her right now and explain. Rip off the Band-Aid."

"I...I can't."

"Why?"

Would she be disappointed? Would she tell me to forget the wedding until the truth comes out, or would she ask me to stay anyway?

"I'd hate to drop a bombshell like this over the phone when she has tons of other stuff on her mind. She opened her restaurant a few weeks ago, and she's planning a wedding. Why stress her out for nothing if the results come back fine?"

When we met, Cara told me she couldn't handle any more stress. Plus, she looked happy this afternoon, and I don't want to break the spell on what we had. It was my first time sitting around a table with a family like the O'Sheas. No reason to take that away prematurely.

"That's fair, I guess," Lis says. "Not adding to her worries if you can help it. And she seems chill, so she'll understand. So what're you gonna do? Next steps?"

I groan. Lis isn't letting me get out of this easy. "I guess redo my test."

"Great. Get that done and out of the way, sooner rather than later."

"This whole situation sucks."

"It does, but no matter what, you are brave for going out there and opening yourself up."

"Thanks." I blink my eyes a few times, realizing I've started to tear up. With an angry swipe of my thumbs, I hide the evidence.

"I hear you sniffling, you big softie."

"I'm not," I say, embarrassed that I'm so worked up. "I'm pissed."

"Okay. Remember what I told you?"

"My butt looks good in those boots."

"No," Lis says, unamused. "Be yourself. You're amazing. Even if the lab results end up different, and I'm sure they won't, you'll be fine."

My body shivers in the brisk cold of the evening. I slink inside the store to warm up and go to the second aisle to peruse the skincare.

"So it's you and that cute bartender in Dublin for the night, huh?"

"He has a name, you know."

"That's right. Aidan." She releases a dramatic swoon at his name, and I roll my eyes. "Is his accent sexy? I bet it's sexy."

"Sure." I refuse to gush about how attractive I find the rhythm of his voice and the hard r's on his tongue. "I'm not here to sleep with hot Irishmen, unfortunately. And definitely not ones who are best friends with a woman I may or may not be related to."

"So he is sexy?"

"I'm hanging up now."

She squeals with hysterical laughter.

"I have other things to deal with, like this DNA test."

"But you said yourself you're not gonna call Cara right now. There's nothing you can do that will make the situation any better, so enjoy tonight." Her energy lifts my spirits, giving me hope for the evening. "You deserve to have fun. You're in Europe for the first time ever, so go out and get some juicy Dublin memories to share with me when you get back."

Aidan and I walk into the bar, snaking our way through a lively crowd of people drinking and smoking outside, and I snag us a table near the back corner. Max has an early meeting for a new exhibit, so he couldn't join—a fact that sent my heart racing. Just me and Aidan. Lis got all in my head about him being cute, which I vowed to ignore, but she was right that I'm on vacation, and I deserve some fun.

And his accent *is* kind of sexy.

"Here." Aidan sets down a couple of beers. In order for me to hear him over the other patrons and the man singing a John Denver song, he has to lean close. Close enough that his breath moves my hair and warms my skin. "To lost passports."

"May I never lose one again." I tap my glass against his. "I'm glad we got out. I think I'm finally adjusting to the time zone."

"Max said this was his favorite pub."

"It's nice, but..." I scrunch my nose up. "My heart belongs to McCarthy's Pub."

He slaps a hand to his chest as he gives me a bashful smile that sends my stomach fluttering. "You're too kind."

Foot traffic forces Aidan to scoot his chair closer to mine, bumping our knees together in the process. Lis's question rings in my head again.

So he's sexy?

I really can't think of him like this. My trip has already become complicated enough without flirting with Cara's best friend, so I resist the tempting impulse to lean my leg back into his. I can have fun, but not that kind of fun, and especially not with Aidan.

After a couple rounds, my body tingles with a carefree glow, thanks to the alcohol. I tell Aidan about New York and how, in my first few years there, I scraped by working any odd job I could get—florist, dog walker, babysitter. The more I talk, the more we both stop moving our knees out of the way when they bump into each other, but that's only because we're crammed in a corner. It's a purely space-saving move.

"So am I right in assuming that Mary is a girlfriend?" *Oh my god, my stupid buzzed mouth.* I want to dig a hole and bury myself in it. "Sorry, that's none of my business."

"Ex-girlfriend. Why do you ask?"

"She keeps coming up," I say, wholly disinterested. "At the grocery store, and then Max mentioned her."

"We, uh, stopped dating shortly after we visited here together to look for a flat. Turns out she wasn't exactly the most faithful partner."

"Oh, jeez. I'm sorry. Losing trust in someone like that, it's..." I meet his eyes, regretful to have made him relive those memories. "That's shitty."

"Some guy from work at one of their other offices. She insisted nothing sexual happened between them—that it was just an emotional connection, and I believe her."

"That's almost worse."

"It was, I guess." He trains his eyes on his beer, and I wish I could reach for his hand without making it weird. "We grew apart over the years, and with my brother's passing...we weren't the best fit anymore. So she went to Dublin, and I didn't." He takes a few gulps of his drink. "And you?"

"What about me?"

"You're not seeing anyone?"

"I never said that."

"In the supermarket. Mrs. Abernathy asked if you were."

"Someone's paying close attention," I say, resisting the smirk that pulls at my mouth.

This is Aidan. This is Cara's best friend. This is a Very Bad Idea.

"No," I go on. "I'm not dating anyone. I'm more of a casual dater."

"That's right. Not into serious relationships."

"I'm comfortable on my own, and I've never met someone who made me want otherwise."

"Mm."

"*Mm?* What's that mean?" I lean toward him, close enough to smell that delicious scent of his. It's too subtle to be a cologne, but it might be his body wash or shampoo. It's nice. A little spicy.

"Nothing." He lifts one shoulder in a carefree semi-shrug. "Trying to figure you out."

"And what have you figured out?"

Before he can reply, a bright orange purse flies into view and knocks his glass over. A woman wearing a thick pile of makeup gasps. She wobbles and apologizes profusely, grabbing a few napkins to dab the table. When she offers us a new round, Aidan declines, since we have an early morning and a multi-hour drive ahead of us. Although I'd love to see where a few more rounds could take us, at least he's keeping a clear head.

The bar has filled up by the time we leave, and two and a half seconds pass before another couple dashes over to claim our table. We've surfaced in a sea of drunk people, and I can't tell which direction to go.

"Here." Aidan's so close, I could reach up and rub the whiskers on his cheek, and that thought distracts me from his hand linking with mine. Confidently, like he owns the place, he carves a way for the both of us, holding onto me with a kind of gentle strength that makes me crave some fresh air.

No reckless decisions. I'm in a supremely buzzy state—happy from one too many beers, but also from the thrill of being somewhere new. And maybe a little from the company of someone more handsome than he has any right to be.

We step outside, and when Aidan lets go, I grab my phone and swipe through a few apps to keep my hands busy. He's about to call us a cab when my throat tightens, and I squeak out a high-pitched hiccup.

"Oh, no," I sigh, resting a hand on my stomach.

"Gonna be sick?" Aidan asks, guiding me to a bench. "Need some water?"

"No, I drank too much beer, and when that happens I—*hic!* I get the hiccups." I hold in a breath, hoping to control the spasms. "It's not too far, is it? A little walking could help."

Hic!

"Of course."

"Sorry," I say with another *hic!* and hope Aidan doesn't pick up on my mortification.

"A nighttime stroll by the river'd be grand."

To get to Max's place, we walk beside a winding body of water that runs right through the middle of Dublin. Aidan says it's called the River Liffey. Shimmery golden lights reflect on the rippling water, illuminating our path.

"Should I scare you to get rid of those hiccups? Make you drink a pint of sugar water?"

"Please, no. I need to walk around a bit, and then I'll be—*hic!*—fine."

We share a laugh at the fact that I can't speak one full sentence without chirping like a squeaky toy.

"So how's that article of yours so far?"

"Rough," I say before I can stop myself. The alcohol has weakened my filter. "I mean, not bad. It's fine. I have to check in with my editor and give him some updates."

"How'd you get into writing?"

"I was working a few different jobs, one of them was as a nanny for this crazy-rich Upper East Side family. We're talking—*hic!*—totally loaded. Multiple Mercedes, vacation-homes-in-Tuscany kind of extravagance. And I'd hang out with all the other nannies at the playground and stuff. We'd all talk." A chill travels down my spine, and I tug my coat tighter around my torso. *Hic!*

"Here," Aidan says as he sweeps his jacket over mine. "Don't want you to freeze."

"Thanks." I'm wrapped in a cocoon of warmth and take a measured inhale. "Anyway, I saw a call for pitches from this new site. I'd had some stuff published before, nothing major, but enough to give me the confidence to send something in. It was a list, kind of like, 'here's the things you'd never guess about the job.' I asked all my nanny friends if I could include their experiences, anonymously of course, and threw in my perspective as someone who did the job too. Nothing particularly deep, but compelling. People love reading about the lives of others, especially rich others. The editor liked it, and they signed me on."

"That's where you work now?"

"Yeah." Another hiccup. "Eventually, I'd like to write more interesting articles, but it's mostly whatever my skeezy editor tells me to do. Not a bad gig, though."

"Skeezy?" Aidan surveys me with a quizzical look.

"He's a nice guy, but he's what you might call verbally affectionate. And he likes to call dibs on female writers when new people come on. It's kind of weird."

"June, that's..." He appears genuinely concerned, and I realize I shouldn't have said anything. "That's not right, he does that."

"He's harmless. And I'm sure I'm not the only person—*hic!*—who has to deal with him acting that way."

"That's harassment. You deserve better than some jerk of a boss."

"Sure," I say, flicking my hair back, as if that alone could deflect his too-kind comments.

"Hey." He nudges my arm with his elbow, and I meet his serious expression. "I mean it. No one should treat you like that, and certainly not a supervisor."

I offer up a shy smile and a hushed "Okay, thanks," because I don't want to talk about work any more than I have to. Loving my job is less important than having something that lets me pay the bills.

Aidan points to the corner store I went in before, and I look to my left before stepping out into the street. I'm met by a myriad of sounds—a wailing honk of a vehicle, the shuffling of feet, and a muffled shout. Aidan's arms, warm and secure, wrap around me as a car speeds by, the driver shooting an angry middle finger in my direction as he passes.

"Are you okay?" Aidan exhales into my hair.

"I think so."

"Other side. We drive on the other side."

I release my grip on his biceps, which are more taut than I would have guessed. We teeter on the edge of the curb, Aidan's arms still holding me flush against his body. He peels back slowly but keeps his face close enough to mine that I could lean in and kiss him.

"My...my hiccups are gone, I think."

He shakes his head and grins, a wonderful expression that could light up the night sky all on its own. My heartbeat pounds in my ears, although that's probably the adrenaline.

"Let me at least get you back to Ballygrá in one piece." He juts out an elbow, and I thread my arm through so we can cross the street together. "As soon as Cara found a half sister, you'd be gone. Can't have that happen."

I gulp. "Nope. Definitely not."

Chapter Ten

Juniper

"Something bothering you?"

Aidan's loaded question forces me to make conversation.

"Just tired."

That's a lie. I followed Lissie's advice to have fun in Dublin last night, and now it's time for me to listen to her other words of wisdom: to retake my DNA test. Not only do I have to figure out how to do that without Cara, her family, *or* Aidan noticing—I don't want to say anything until I have the results for sure—but my thoughts keep spiraling.

My half sister, my dream assignment that could further my career—there's a chance that none of this is real.

So no, I'm not in the mood for small talk, but Aidan doesn't seem bothered. As he drives us back, I perch my feet on the seat, hug my knees, and let my mind wander to better things.

Like this morning, when I padded out of Max's room and into the bathroom. I caught Aidan stretching, his muscular arms reaching for the ceiling. My attention worked its way south to where his shirt crept up, revealing a smattering of hair the color of sun-kissed caramel directly above his waistband. The sweatpants Max lent him couldn't hide his generous morning wood, and *of course* I stared long enough for Aidan to turn and wave hello to me. Hopefully, I wasn't drooling.

With my emergency passport safely tucked away, we arrive back in Ballygrá. Cara's already at work, so I email Ethan saying we should reconnect about my article. I want to move forward, but I'm faced with all this uncertainty. I hate to admit it, but having him so hands-on with this piece might be helpful in the end.

Cara's mom sends a sweet text inviting me on a hike. A chance to talk one-on-one. *The retest is a precaution*, I remind myself, and if that's the case, then why not spend some time with Evelyn?

She lends me some hiking boots that are one size too big and offers me a metal trekking pole identical to the one in her other hand. Winnie is accompanying us, so Evelyn promises the walk won't be too strenuous for the dog's sake, but she likes to be prepared. We set out on a path that begins in her backyard, weaving underneath low branches. The leaf-covered trail opens up after a minute to a wide, shallow river.

"Do much hiking in New York?"

"Does walking when the subway's delayed count?"

She laughs, and the sound ignites a comfortable warmth in my chest.

"We're blessed with an incredible landscape around here and friendly neighbors. A perfect combination," Evelyn says with dimples that match her daughter's. "When Cara was younger, we spent a lot of time in the fresh air walking together. It's nice to get out with you too. Cara's so focused on work, she doesn't have much time."

"Owning a restaurant must keep her busy."

"That girl throws her heart and soul into what she does. How she's been since childhood." Evelyn stops for a breather and taps the end of her hiking pole against the ground. "She was born with an entrepreneurial spirit, you could say. Trace that back to roadside lemonade stands, moving on up to bake sales in school, and then getting through college with her own made-to-order cake business. After that, she had a mix of restaurant jobs and culinary endeavors—some of which have done well, and some not so much. And now, it's the cafe. She's resourceful, that one. We miss her, though."

"Miss her?" That seems strange to say, considering they live ten minutes from each other.

"Roger and I...well, we don't like to push. But with the wedding and the restaurant, we've seen her less than when she was getting her degree."

The walkway opens up to a muddy trail and a verdant hill that kisses the sky. As we ascend, the slickness underfoot makes me grateful for the gear she gave me.

"We catch 'er here and there," Evelyn goes on, a tinge of sadness in her voice. "On opening day, we stopped by the cafe while she was running around behind the scenes, so all we got was a quick hug. And we've helped with the wedding too. She's busy, and I'm probably making a fuss about it. The restaurant requires more of her energy than I can imagine. We miss the quality time, though." Her smile seems forced, like she's willing herself into a happier mental state.

"You're a good mom," I say to lift her mood. The pat on the back that she gives me is like a gold star.

"Yesterday was nice, having you and her and Danny over." She sighs as we near the top of the hill. "First time in a while she'd suggested doing something as a family like that, without us pulling teeth to get her to do it. Just us." Evelyn squeezes my arm and stops in her tracks, turning my body to face her. "Thank you."

"Evelyn, you don't—"

"Call me Evvie."

"Evvie." I indulge her, and she practically glows. "You don't need to thank me. I haven't done anything."

"Oh, you have. Here, let's sit."

She gestures to a wooden bench decorated by a few fallen rust-colored leaves. We've got a front-row seat to the Irish countryside. Buildings dot the hills of green, and herds of sheep graze so far off in the distance that they look like miniature white puffballs. The only sound is Winnie's light panting and a cool gust of wind.

Evelyn reaches into a jacket pocket, shakes her head, and then checks the other one. "Here," she says, pulling out a wallet-sized photograph. "This is the best photo I have of your da, taken right before he went off on assignment. He was charming, so generous, but so tough. I see some of him in you."

"Really?" I lean over to inspect it. The man in the picture has a salt-and-pepper beard, and his ears pop out on the sides of his head. The curve of his mouth gives him a reserved expression, like he has a secret, and his eyes are a light brown.

Just like mine.

I examine the image more closely to make sure I'm not imagining the similarity.

"Our eyes..."

"Mhmm, the same shape and everything."

My face stretches into a smile. Maybe the DNA test will turn out fine after all.

"He was a catch."

"How'd you two meet?"

She chuckles, and the hint of a blush travels up her cheeks. "Leaving the baker's one day, I flung the door open and clocked him right in the face. Felt awful 'bout it and insisted on taking him to the doctor to make sure his nose hadn't broke. Spent a couple months inseparable before work called him away." She admires the photo again.

"He knew you were pregnant?"

"He did, and I was so angry at him for leaving. A man with such a big heart, but not enough to give any to me or his own daughter. Or, well, *daughters*," she corrects herself. "He lived to help others, and he died for others too. I should've known what to expect of him from the moment we met, especially with how he had no intention to stay in Ireland long term. He supported us every month with a little money when he could, so I'm glad that Cara and I had that. He was many things, but a decent father wasn't one of them. Did your mam keep in touch with him?"

"No." I trace my finger along the edge of the photograph. "She was secretive about his identity." When I would ask, hoping to glean any information she could offer, my questions usually put her in a bad mood. I learned not to bring him up.

That curiosity pushes me to pull out my phone and write down some of what Evvie says. "What was he like?"

"Stubborn. Smoked too much. Flighty, as you might guess. At his best, though, thoughtful in such a purposeful way, with little gifts and flowers and such. He wasn't the most talkative person in the room, but he sure knew how to make you feel like the center of his attention. Funny, too. After witnessing so many disasters around the world, he still had a sense of humor. And determined. He did nothing halfway. He went in completely with whatever he took on. Cara inherited that from him."

"How—" I swallow the ball of nerves climbing up my throat. "If you don't mind me asking, how did he die?"

"I don't mind," she says, looking down at the photo. "He'd gone with his organization to Indonesia after a terrible earthquake. He entered a building to check for survivors, and..." She sighs, her eyes lost in memories I'm not privy to. "His coworkers said it happened quick. The entire structure fell in on itself." She looks at me with a bittersweet expression on her face. "I wish you'd had the chance to know him."

"Sounds like he traveled a lot."

"All the time. And he flew just about everywhere, so no wonder he made it to America and met your mam."

I give a hesitant nod. Since the phone call with Double Helix, I've been doubting myself, but Evelyn—Evvie—refills my hope. My mother's reluctance to share anything about the identity of my father makes more sense after talking with Cara's mom. She may have felt ashamed or foolish, getting pregnant by a man who left with little hesitation. Maybe she was angry too, just like Cara's mom. She could have been protecting me in her own way, while also protecting herself. Appreciation flickers in my chest as I consider my mom's silence as less of a barrier and more of a shield.

Evvie gives me a few loving pats on the thigh. "You should keep the photo."

"Oh no, I couldn't."

"I want you to. I've a copy. Besides, you'll need it for your article."

"Yeah." I scratch the back of my neck, uneasy that Evvie has trusted me with one of the few photos there are of this man. "I might."

"There'll be loads of people out there who'll benefit from hearing your story. It needs to be told."

I soften when she side-hugs me again. Evvie's a nurturer, treating me like I'm a part of the family. I can only hope she's right.

We stand up and readjust our scarves before we begin the descent.

"Let's head back then, shall we?" She loops her arm through mine, and we fall in step with each other, Winnie ambling beside us. "I've all the ingredients for scones that are begging to go into the oven."

"You're here! I'd hug you, but, well..." Cara motions to her apron, which features a smattering of colorful sauces and stains.

"No worries. I brought a bottle for tonight. Aidan said you like red."

"She doesn't discriminate with her wine," Yasmine bellows from the kitchen.

"She's right, I adore all wine." Cara ushers me into her home, which has become more cluttered with boxes of wedding supplies. "Get cozy. Dinner's almost ready."

"Can I help?"

Cara examines the kitchen, but as the owner of a cafe, she has everything under control. "Could you pour that bottle?"

"Glasses are top left." Yasmine points to the cabinet with her chin while she mixes a bowl of leafy greens.

Cara stirs one pot, lowers the temperature on a pan, and then glides skillfully to the oven to remove a dish. She makes cooking look as effortless as breathing, and

I fetch three wine glasses while she works wonders at the stove.

"How was your afternoon with Mam?" Cara thanks me for the merlot, and we cheers. "She didn't pry too much, did she? She can be aggravating."

"Your mom's sweet," I say. Our few hours together ticked by in an instant because I had such an enjoyable time with her. Hanging out with Evvie combined all the fun of time with Lissie, all the warmth of Cara, and all the wisdom and care of a mother hen. "She told me a lot about your"—I catch myself—"our dad."

The resemblance in the photo Evvie gave me has buoyed my mood.

"She let you get a word in? Woman knows how to *talk*."

"I didn't mind." Cara's mom was chatty, but I liked that. That took the pressure off me to reveal everything about myself, or to display my past in front of her. With Evvie, the message was clear: *Take your time, but I'm here for you.*

"So what's Dan's excuse?" Yasmine asks.

"The guy who was on the calendar got food poisoning, so he's filling in." I shudder, recalling the voicemail that poor employee left for Aidan, which I played on speaker as he drove. "Aidan begged me for leftovers. If I don't have any for him, he might kick me out."

"He's serious about Cara's cooking." Yasmine plants a chaste kiss on her fiancée's cheek.

We ferry plates and bowls and food to the table. When was the last time that I sat down for a home-cooked dinner like this? Years. My grandma was a TV dinner connoisseur, and the mealtimes in foster care were better, but I didn't have family meals quite like this. The closest I've come is pasta nights at home with Lis—Al Dente and Dish, as we like to call it—though what we make isn't quite as gourmet.

With a swig of wine, I silence the nagging voice of practicality. The one that reminds me that this might not be a family meal after all. *Nope, not now. Remember the photo. How our eyes look the same.*

They've prepared a mouthwatering feast—a forest green salad with decadent hunks of goat cheese and maroon beets, drizzled with murky balsamic, topped with a perfectly charred piece of chicken, and roasted vegetables on the side.

"This looks incredible."

"This was all Cara, trust me." Yasmine throws her arms up to the sky, unwilling to take credit for the meal. "I preheat the oven and throw some leaves together, but she's the master."

"Aw, thanks babe." Cara leans in for another kiss.

If the two of them lived in New York, I'd want to be friends with Cara and Yasmine. They watch each other talk with pride and love etched on their faces. Since I have a three-date-max rule—if I even reach that many with someone—I don't relate to this kind of adoration.

"Everything in Dublin worked out then, yeah?" Cara asks. "No troubles?"

"Nope," I reply. "We even went out for some drinks."

Yasmine's eyes go wide. "What?"

"Some place his friend recommended. It was cool."

What a sensible description of the evening. We got beer, I tried my hardest not to flirt with him, and he saved my life. *It was cool.*

"Ever since his ex moved there, he's not been back." Yasmine leans into her chair. "He dwelled on that woman for longer than she deserved."

"You're not giving him enough credit." Cara comes to his defense. "He got over her a long time ago."

I perk up, absorbing as much intel on this ex-girl-friend of Aidan's as I can without looking desperate to find out more.

"True," Yasmine says, "but he dated her months more than he should have." She shifts her focus to me. "We hated Mary."

"No," Cara says, pointing her wine glass at Yasmine. "I liked her until she cheated on him."

"You *hated* her," Yasmine insists.

"I didn't hate her, I just didn't like her very much."

"Coming from someone as friendly as you, that's an insult," I say.

Yasmine nods her head. "Exactly."

"Aidan's a brother to me, and he belongs with someone who sees how incredible he is. Yaz knows it, and you must know it by now too."

I readjust in my seat and try not to think too hard about him wrapping his arms around me last night when I stepped into the street.

"She didn't want to deal with the hard stuff with him," Cara goes on. "She wasn't an actual partner. The second life got hard, she turned to someone else. So good riddance to her."

While we each eat a slice of lemon meringue pie, Yasmine and Cara show me their wedding attire from their respective phones. I sneak a peek at mine to see if Ethan emailed me, but he hasn't replied. I have a text from someone else, though.

> AIDAN: I'm here the rest of the night, stop by after dinner if you'd like

> AIDAN: With the leftovers

A fire creeps up my neck, and I tuck my device away.

"I'm going classic." Yasmine flips through the images of her slender body outfitted in an elegant midnight-blue suit. The long line of the pants leads up to her shoulders in a V-shape. Yasmine appears to always wear suits of some variation, but this takes her whole look up a notch—it's simultaneously sharp and smooth.

"Okay, this is mine," Cara exclaims, positioning the phone so Yasmine won't see.

I gasp, pulling the smartphone closer to my face. "Cara, it's stunning."

"The veil will be shorter, and this bit at the back will come in here." She brushes her finger over the photos to demonstrate where the crisp white dress would change. In the last picture, her mother stands on one side, and both of them are beaming. On the other side is a scowling elderly woman who reminds me of someone I've seen before.

"Who's that?"

"Oh, that's Granny," Cara replies, tossing the phone back on the couch. Her grandma had been in the photos that Cara's mom showed me yesterday.

"She was ill that day and—"

"Her gran doesn't approve of our marriage," Yasmine interrupts. They share a look—the kind that couples do—like they can communicate with ESP.

"It's hard for her, that's all, and she *is* trying." Cara pats Yasmine on the hand to appease her. "She handled a daughter having a child out of wedlock. But she didn't foresee having a lesbian for a granddaughter in her future."

"When your mom showed me those photo albums yesterday, I thought she'd passed away because of how quiet everyone got."

"Oh, Christ. No, she's alive and well. Causing plenty of drama for the wedding."

"We have to act different around her gran."

"Why, though?"

"Some people will never accept us." Yasmine crosses an ankle over her knee. "Most folks in Ballygrá have known Cara for ages, so we don't run into too much trouble, thankfully."

"But she's your *grandmother*," I say. Flares of un-expected anger swell from a familiar kind of pain. "My grandma was...well, she wasn't all that great. But she didn't deny my entire existence."

Cara's eyes pool with sympathetic tears.

"Sorry," I mutter. "Didn't mean to make that about me."

"No, it's okay. I like feeling like I'm not alone in this," she replies. "It hurts, though, when the people who should love you unconditionally don't accept who you are."

"Do you think she'll come around?"

"When hell freezes over," Yasmine snorts.

"She's working on it. The Easter card she sent, she addressed to us both. As for the wedding, we have a seat for her, but we don't know if she'll sit in it." Cara raises her brows toward Yasmine, who acknowledges defeat with a sigh and a shrug. "Point is, Gran's making an effort. She's still choosing me, and that means something. Not like—" Cara purses her lips and looks at me. "So I had some close girlfriends that I fell out with a few years back. They'd introduced me to my ex, so when things with her ended..." Cara reaches down to busy herself with the hem of the tablecloth. "I didn't think the breakup would turn so ugly. But we'd been working together on this catering business, so going separate ways became messy. In the end, my three girlfriends chose to cut me out of their lives. They chose staying friends with her."

"What?"

"They didn't even sit down with me to talk about my side of things. They just decided." Cara sighs and does a full-body shake. "Sorry for all the sad talk tonight. But you're my sister, and if I can't share these things with you, then who can I share them with?"

My sister.

I swallow the knot that's formed in my throat. After such vulnerability from her, coming out with a confession now would shred the joy she's clinging to into bits.

"I realize we've known about each other for less than two weeks, but you are a sister to me, June. You will be forever." Cara looks to Yasmine, who prompts her with a swift nod, before straightening in her chair. "And since you're my sister, I have to ask—and I know this is last minute, *but*—will you be my maid of honor?"

I almost choke on my wine. "What?"

"Yaz and I talked, and it would mean the world to us. To me."

"That's an enormous responsibility." Backtrack, *backtrack*. "I'd have to help with the bachelorette, I have nothing to wear, I'm not sure—"

"We've got hundreds of guests, but all you've got to do is put on a nice dress and walk down the aisle before we do."

"Super relaxed," Yasmine chimes in, pushing for a hard sell.

"But—Cara, I'm honored you want to include me this way, but I can't."

With so much uncertainty surrounding our biological connection, I shouldn't. We're in a good groove, the two of us, and I hate to overload her with a bunch of unverified doubts. She and I have a week and a half left to get to know each other, and news like this could put miles of distance between us. But I don't know how to change the subject—taking her from the highest high of asking me to join her wedding party to confronting her with what's going on.

With what's *maybe* going on.

"It's an enormous ask," she continues, "and I've only seen people do this sort of thing in movies, but I've

missed having close friends—girlfriends. I lost my closest ones in an instant. And having a sister is like having
the ultimate best girlfriend, all the time. So why ignore
that on one of the most important days of my life?"

Cara clasps her hands together in her lap, and tears
have already started forming in her eyes. She looks so
hopeful, and I can't excuse myself from this without
shattering that hope into a billion tiny pieces.

I think of the eyes in that photo. How they look the
same as mine.

"You standing up there would make me the happiest
and most supported and loved bride," Cara says, beaming. "So will you?"

Chapter Eleven

Aidan

"So, maid of honor, what'll it be?"

"You knew?" June sets the leftovers on the counter, her head cocked to one side in surprise.

"'Course. Cara texted me earlier today asking if I'd mind sharing the responsibilities with you. I've dreamed of standing up as best man for her my whole life, so I'll admit I was a bit disappointed."

"You should've said no."

"I'm teasing you," I say, wishing my joke landed better. "The more the merrier."

"Oi, Danny! Two pints of the good stuff, would you?" one of our regulars shouts from the other end of the bar.

"On it," I mumble back, wondering if inviting June to the pub had been an error in judgment. But if I hadn't filled in for the poor fella who got food poisoning, Da would have—and what if he'd had a night planned with Mam? At least drink orders will slow down once the event upstairs begins.

After handing the drinks off, I mosey back to the spot across from June. "That's classic Cara, by the way."

"Asking people she just met to take part in one of the biggest days of her life? I'm impulsive, but this is next level."

"Charmingly spontaneous is how I'd describe her," I say, chuckling to myself. "She's the type of person who loves making others feel loved. She can come off as overeager sometimes, but she knows what she wants and has the best intentions."

With an exasperated sigh, June leans on her elbows and rubs both temples.

"Why shouldn't you stand with her at the altar?" I don't understand why she seems so upset. Maybe she's shy in front of crowds too. "You're her half sister, for Christ's sake."

"You're her closest friend who's known her for her entire life. I should have said no. This would all be way easier."

"I'll be up there too, so there's less pressure. We walk down the aisle, we both give a speech, that tops it."

"Don't remind me about the speech."

"No need for any of this to be complicated."

June's expression tells me she remains unconvinced—her eyebrows are stitched together, and her mouth is puckered like she's bitten right into a lemon. This reminds me of the first time we met. She looked nervous as anything then, and she's the same now. Like a wild animal preparing to flee.

"Can I get you a drink?"

"I'll take your strongest pinot noir."

I wink. A wink? Christ, hopefully she doesn't notice. June's presence makes me bold, makes me do dumb things.

She goes into detail about dinner, speaking with an electric passion that vibrates in the air around her. Every emotion shows on her face as she relives the meal, the laughs, and the big question at the end of the night.

June's lovely, I admit, but fancying her is just inconvenient. New York's her home, and even if she lived here, I don't know if I'm her type. Sure, I saw her looking at me that morning at Max's—the way her eyes flitted up from the bulge in my sweatpants sent a jolt of satisfaction through me—but she seemed preoccupied on the ride back. Lost in her own world.

So I invited her here tonight to let her unwind. A chance for me to get distracted by the elegant curve of her neck, the faint brown beauty mark on her left cheek, and the way she tilts her body forward to close some of the space between us...well, that's a nice bonus.

"Yasmine and Cara are really compatible," she muses. "Like, they complement each other. Yaz supports her and she has this solid presence, and Cara is a sparkly ray of sunshine."

"They're a smart match. I'm happy to see her with someone who loves her so much, because Cara is one of the best people I know."

"How'd you two become friends?"

"Our mams were pregnant at the same time, so we grew up together. My mam'd watch us in the mornings and afternoons, then we'd go over to Cara's when the pub shifts got busy at night." From the corner of my eye, another regular, Rory, approaches the bar and points toward his empty glass. I turn to fill up a fresh pint for him but keep my focus on June. "Cara's boisterous and loves life, and I was a bit more of a shy kid. Didn't make friends too easy, and Cara made me feel like I fit in. Opposites attract sort of thing."

"She cares about you a lot."

Rory can evidently no longer wait for a drink because he sways over and clangs his empty pint glass down on the bar next to June. "Yertha'mericangirl?" The sounds slur into a long one-word question.

She looks to me for confirmation, and I nod. "I guess I am," she says.

"Hm." Rory puts one hand on his heart. "I loved an American girl once. Esme. Esme Williams from New

Jersey. Loveamylife, you could say. Gorgeous soul, that woman had. Gorgeous...everythin'."

June's mouth turns up oh-so-slightly at the corners. "Special lady."

"She was. Her hair went past her shoulders in these long, flowin' waves, and 'er blue eyes were as mesmerizin' as the sea itself. An' she had absolutely enormous—"

"Here's your drink. Thank you." I shove the ale along with a glass of water toward him, and his face lights up. He slaps some money onto the bar top and teeters back to his seat.

"Sorry about him."

June shakes her head. "It's fine. You must get interesting stories like that all the time, working here. I enjoyed hearing about the love of his life and her enormous...personality?"

"Feet."

"Yeah, that was it."

We laugh. Our eyes meet over the bar as she swirls her wine glass, and Christ, is she pretty. I can't get over the fact that someone like her is sitting here, all with the purpose of talking to me.

June sighs and takes a generous gulp of pinot. "I'm worried."

"'Bout what?"

"Screwing up the wedding. Saying or doing something that would upset Cara."

"No world in which that could happen."

"You two have had to disagree sometimes, right?"

"Sometimes, sure."

We never agreed on Mary. I didn't understand why, but even before the emotional infidelity came out, my best friend never totally warmed to her.

"Why're you asking?" I lean back and rest my hands on the edge of the counter. June's attention flickers to my arms for half of a second.

"To understand her better. I've gone from stranger to half sister to maid of honor in her wedding, but we're still getting to know each other. What if including me ends up being one big mistake?" The words come out frantic. She pauses to chug the rest of her wine and wipe her berry-stained lips with her fingertips.

"I don't see that happening."

"Yeah, well..."

June looks at her empty glass, and I hold up the bottle of wine with my brow raised. She accepts without hesitation.

"You have a habit of asking for life advice from bartenders."

"You're easy to talk to, I guess."

It's a simple compliment, but I latch onto it with a content pride. I drink in the toasty brown of her irises, which send a jolt through me, like caffeine to my veins. I've really no business getting involved with someone Cara's so fond of. I can't believe I'm even letting a thought like that cross my mind.

But I can still enjoy her being here.

"Danny, m'dear," a familiar voice calls me from the entryway. "We set for upstairs?"

Maureen and Adam have arrived. I give them the go-ahead, and they walk up the staircase to get ready. Some of the bar patrons grab their glasses and head up as well.

"What's going on?" June asks.

"You're in for a treat. If you thought Rory's story from before was good, wait 'til you hear this."

I bet I could hear a butterfly's wings flap in the room upstairs. Everyone migrated up here, so I asked the barback to keep an eye downstairs and say something if he needed me. Maureen and Adam are sitting on stools in front of the fireplace as Adam finishes his tale to a rapt audience.

"The king was horrified. Reluctantly, he stood before the court, lifted the crown off his head, and let everyone see his horse's ears." Adam gestures to remove an imaginary headpiece, which he then reverently sets down on his knee. "And the people, well, the people didn't respond the way the king had feared they would. Rather than yell or run away, they clapped. They admired his honesty and his ability to show his truthful self. From that day on, the king never hid his ears ever again."

Satisfied applause and whistles fill the room as Adam bows his head in gratitude. They've music next, an upbeat tune with him on guitar and Maureen on the accordion, and from the first note, people's toes tap and heads bob side to side. The upstairs of McCarthy's Pub may lack in size, but the energy here shoots through the roof.

"This is so interesting," June says, her face shining with delight that I'd like to bottle up and drink. She stands close enough to me that our arms touch, and both of our backs rest against the wall by the stairwell. "This happens every night?"

"No, just time to time. Maureen and Adam are local but travel all around, so whenever they swing by we have 'em. They're friends of my da's, and I remember listening to them when I was a lad. Music nights happen downstairs, but with storytelling, we host up here for a more intimate space."

"I didn't know storytelling like this was a thing in Ireland."

"Not so common anymore." I lean in close so we can talk beneath the guitar strums—close enough that I can smell that flowery shampoo. "Ireland's got a long oral history, with stories being passed down for generations. There're some well-known folks who do this, absolute legends. But formal storytelling nights like this are rare. Makes them memorable, though."

"Guess I'm pretty lucky then," she replies as a smirk skates across her lips.

Maureen wraps up the song on a high note, stands, and touches her chest in thanks. "Now, we've got someone here who I know will need some coaxing, but I won't take no for an answer." Her eyes land on me and my pulse breaks out in a sprint.

She wouldn't.

"Danny, why don't you come up and share with us?"

Oh, she would.

"I'd—I would rather not."

"Ah, go on up there!" Rory shouts from the corner. I make a mental note not to give him a generous pour anytime soon.

But when June's face lights up with the anticipation that I'll be next onstage, I decide to tell a quick one.

Storytelling was a useful tool for me to become a better speaker and more sure of myself. I don't stutter anymore, although now and then, I trip over words when I'm nervous. As a kid, though, I struggled with talking out loud and was painfully shy, so my granda used to tell me stories and patiently sit while I recited them back to him. At family gatherings, he urged me to share in front of everyone. Nothing changed about how I disliked standing up and talking to a crowd, but I stopped getting bullied.

The audience offers some encouragement and a few jovial taunts. Not a soul in this bleedin' room's going to let the night pass without hearing me. I take a swig from my water, wishing it were whiskey, and then drag my feet to Maureen's seat. A whoop comes from somewhere in the crowd and heat crawls up the back of my neck.

"Didn't expect to be up here tonight." When no one laughs at my nervous chuckle, I indulge in another hearty sip.

"We've known Aidan since he was a lad about this high." Adam holds his hand at his side, about mid-thigh. "A lot of you probably do too. He's shared some incredible stories with us before, when he was young. What'll it be tonight, then?"

I scratch my chin, going through the rusty Rolodex of my mind. The panic of choosing a story to tell replaces the dread of standing up here—in front of June.

"How 'bout Finn and the oak tree?" Maureen offers, and a weight lifts from my body. If there's one tale I'll never forget, it's Granda's all-time favorite.

"Right. Well, like most of you, I grew up listening to tales from my family," I say. "This one's from my da's da, Niall McCarthy. He told it to me so many times that after not thinking about it for well over two decades, I can still remember every detail.

"The 1840s weren't exactly kind days for Ireland. And Finn O'Brien was a lad wise beyond his years—he sensed the worry in his parents' voices, and with no crops on the family farm, he knew they had no chance of surviving the long, cold winter."

The room appears more packed from this vantage point—every stool has an occupant, and people stand in the rear. No one speaks, though many nod along knowingly as I begin my tale. Every single person has their eyes locked on me, including June. She's given me her complete attention, and she looks angelic, almost out of place against the aged wooden walls.

"Um," I say and clear my throat. "And so, right—Finn. One day, Finn sat underneath an enormous oak tree, resting his back up against the scratchy trunk, and he closed his eyes. He didn't know what to do, or how to help his parents or his siblings. He had to think of something.

"'What are you doin' out here on such a chilly afternoon?' a dainty voice asked him. Finn was shocked to see the prettiest young woman standing in front of him. Her hair shimmered in the rays of the setting sun, and freckles dotted the bridge of her nose.

"'Are you a fairy?' he demanded, fearful. It seemed like the logical question to ask, since Finn had never seen one before but had heard plenty of tales of their treacherous deeds. 'No, I'm no fairy,' she responded. 'I'm a girl!'"

A steady laugh spreads through the crowd, and I savor the grin on June's face too.

"Well, this young lass, Rose O'Sullivan, didn't live far from Finn, but her life was as far from his as two lives could be. She lived in one of the nicest estates in town and wanted for nothing. Finn couldn't believe she'd sit under that oak tree and talk to him, but she did. He listened as she told him about her day, and he explained the troubles at his family's farm.

"Rose looked him up and down. 'Will you wait for me here tomorrow?' she asked, and to that he said, 'I'll wait for you.'

"They met every day under that tree and shared stories. Rose brought him food—oats and such that could get him and his loved ones through the harsh winter." The audience hangs on every word, and I gulp, hoping no one can catch the thud of my heartbeat or the drips of sweat on my brow. "Finn appreciated what Rose had done for him, but more than that, he enjoyed seeing her, hearing her voice. It was the brightest part of his day.

"Throughout the year, he fell in love with Rose, completely. But he knew if he were to walk into her home and ask her da for her hand in marriage, he'd be laughed right out. So instead, he didn't say a word and settled for their daily meetings, all while knowing one day he'd have to let her go.

"Two years passed like this, every day with the same question and answer. 'Will you wait for me here tomorrow?' 'I'll wait for you.' Finally, Finn didn't want to wait any longer. He'd never be good enough to ask for Rose to marry him, but he needed to tell her how he felt. So the next day, he picked some wildflowers and walked to the oak tree and he waited. And he waited. But Rose never arrived. And she never would again. She got sick that autumn and passed away before Finn could tell her of the love he had for her."

Faint *tsks* of disappointment float through the audience, and Mrs. Abernathy dabs a balled-up tissue at the corner of her eye.

I can't remember the last time I told this tale, and the despair of its ending resonates with me in a new way. How Finn was content with every day looking like the one before. How he never chased what he wanted. That's a kind of regret I hope to never experience.

"Finn married years later and had two children. But he didn't stop loving Rose. And if you look at the tree on the top of the hill, right off the entrance to the trekking route, you might see a shadow, a figure sitting at the base. That's Finn, waiting for his love. Forever waiting."

The room fills with claps and some hoots and hollers, and a few folks dry their cheeks. "Thank you," I say as I stand. "Now Christ, can we get Maureen and Adam up here for something more upbeat?"

When the entertainment ends, everyone funnels back down to the bar. I pour next rounds and move to stand across from June like she'd called me there herself.

"You were amazing! The many talents of Aidan McCarthy."

My full name on her mouth feels like an itch being scratched. "That's kind of you," I say.

"You were. And getting up in front of a room of people all so close they could touch you. I could never do that."

I hold back a broad grin as I refill her water glass.

"And that story...my god, so sweet. So *sad*. I can't believe your grandpa told you that as a kid. So depressing."

"Suppose it is. I grew up with it, so there's nostalgia there."

"Well, you were fantastic."

With her watching me over the bar, I'm unsure how to respond. I hold up a bottle like an eejit. "Another glass?"

She considers the offer, and after a beat, shakes her head. "No, I shouldn't. I have to answer some work emails."

"Of course." I should have guessed she wouldn't spend the entire night here, but already, the pub seems dimmer. I grab at the cup of water where she was sitting and spill some. "Get some rest. It's been a long day."

"Thanks for tonight. See you tomorrow?"

"See you tomorrow."

She walks out the door—and while I have a thousand reasons to feel otherwise, I can't wait for tomorrow to come.

Chapter Twelve

Juniper

Aidan drives me to a bridal store near Limerick, where the seductive voice of Michael Bublé croons through the speakers. A cluster of young women sit on an ornate ivory couch in the back, waiting while their friend slips into a gown in the dressing room. That will be Cara soon—she has work, but then she and her mom plan to join us here for her final fitting.

In the meantime, I'm on a mission.

Most of the store's real estate is taken up by crisp white dresses, but a sizable corner houses a plethora of bridesmaid options in every color of the rainbow, with enough pinkish, reddish ones to make me dizzy. Woodland berry, to be precise. Cara and Yasmine didn't pull out swatches, but they requested a dress, any dress, within that scheme of rich purplish red. With the wedding happening only six days from now, they crossed their fingers and sent me on my way to find something to wear.

I could have said no. I *should* have said no to the title of maid of honor. But she looked at me with such anticipation that a *yes* slipped from my lips without me realizing I'd opened my mouth.

This could be a whole lot of worry for nothing, but I won't know for sure until I take another DNA test. Lis was right—I just need to get this done. But I can't drive myself, and I also can't ask Aidan for a ride. Somehow, I have to handle this discreetly.

I really hope this dress is returnable.

Aidan pulls a strapless gown off of a rack stuffed with fashionable chiffon creations. "How's this?"

"Will there be dancing?"

"Absolutely."

"No, then. That's a disaster waiting to happen."

I resume my search, but Aidan doesn't appear to understand my distaste. He examines the dress closer, looking for what he missed.

"Boobs, Aidan."

"Ah. Fair enough. Not strapless then."

Seeing Aidan on that stage last night, commanding a crowd, allowed me to witness a different side to him. He was quietly self-assured, yet still the same person as the blushing man holding back a smile across from me. The more time I spend with Aidan, the more he surprises me.

We flick through the racks, our backs to each other. My fingers brush against intricate lace, meticulous beadwork, and silky satins as I rifle through the rows of outfits. I pick up every single woodland-berry-colored bridesmaid dress in my size, and a dutiful attendant named Diane places them one by one in a dressing room.

Aidan makes himself comfortable in the plush armchair at the center of the floor while I step into the fitting room. I go through the tedious process of unlacing my boots and stripping down to my underwear. With a zillion dresses to try in my little woodland-berry haven, I reach toward the metal dowel on the wall, eyes closed, and allow fate to pick the first one.

"How's it going in there?"

"Umm..." This dress fits me, and I can zip myself up since the back of the dress makes a low U-shape. Shoulder pads tower like mountains on either side of me, though. "I doubt this one will work."

"Does it fit?"

"Sure."

"Let me see then. We're not in the position to be choosy."

I open the door and step out in a flourish, arms spread wide to show off the outfit. No one needs to tell me I look ridiculous, so I might as well own it. Still, Aidan doesn't hold back—he roars with laughter, doubling over in his seat.

"Christ, those are some shoulder pads."

"Molly Ringwald can eat her heart out." I give him a playful twirl. "This is a definite no."

"You'd need a plus-two for the wedding."

I giggle as I poof up the sleeves so they stand higher. "Here, take a pic. Cara will get a kick out of this."

Since picking one without thinking didn't work out well, I peruse my outfit options and select something that has a minimalist style and zero sleeve action. The simple slip dress slinks right over my shoulders like warm butter and hits mid-shin.

"How's this?" I ask, modeling the outfit as I exit the dressing room.

Aidan looks me up and down and then exhales.

"That bad?" I ask.

"No."

"Then what?"

"It's..." He tilts his head side to side. "It's a little boring, is all."

"Anything compared to the last one will be boring. Plain isn't bad. The day is all about Cara anyway."

"Do you like this one? That's what matters. If you do, then grand, but I pictured you in something with more personality."

He pictured me in something? I almost ask him what exactly he pictured, but no. Flirty banter is not the goal here.

I march back into the dressing room since his admission threatens to put a cheeky smirk across my face. How does Aidan do this to me? When we showed up at the bridal store, I dreaded choosing a dress, seeing as I might be a fraud of a maid of honor. Now I'm tempted to put each of these dresses on, one by one, if that means I'll get his eyes on me.

In the next gown, I fumble around my back for the zipper with no luck. When I peek my head out the door, Diane has vanished. Without prompting, Aidan seems to know what I need. He rises and, with a turn, I clutch the front of the fabric in tight fists.

"Thanks," I say, all breathy and weird.

"'Course."

His warm exhalations on my neck send goosebumps down my arms, and I shiver.

"Hold on. I can't get the zipper to close all the way." He fiddles with the closure, his knuckles pressing into my skin.

"Maybe zip down a bit and then yank it up?"

"I don't think this is the kind of dress one yanks." Aidan gently works the slider up, and I become intoxicated by his touch, wishing his hands would explore other places. "There," he says and pats my waist, which sends a tingling up into my chest and down between my legs.

Relax, girl.

I scurry over to the mirror to check myself out. With an approving pout, I nod and twirl around to examine myself from all angles. This spaghetti strap dress hugs me in all the right places. The satin material sways with every move. The sweetheart top accentuates my chest without coming off too risqué, and a surprise thigh-high slit adds some sultriness.

"I like it," I say to my reflection.

Aidan stands behind me, not speaking, with his hands in his pockets.

"What? Too much?" Self-conscious, I survey the mirror once more. The dress channels old Hollywood glam, but maybe that's the problem. "Does this not fit with the vision or theme? Would one of the shorter dresses work better?"

Aidan works his searing gaze down my body and back up again. He examines me for one, two, three seconds, and I get another chill. "It's...no, it's a fine dress," he says.

"You don't like it."

"No, I do. I mean, you look perfect. The dress is perfect."

"Perfect? Well. Thank you." I rotate one last time in front of the mirror and agree. This one fits like someone sewed it specifically for me. "Great. That's one item we can cross off the list."

"What about the others?"

"I've got a good thing here. No need to try on a hundred more red dresses to figure out that this is the one for me."

"Woodland berry," Aidan corrects, and I exhale with a slight laugh.

Before I return to the fitting room, I hesitate. "Um, would you unzip me?"

Biting my lips, I remind myself that I'm not enjoying this, not at all. Not even as the hairs on my arms stand on end.

As he undoes the hook and eye at the top, the front door dings and snaps me out of my daydreams. A familiar voice fills the shop. "June, you look *gorgeous.*" Cara walks in while ogling me in the dress, slack-jawed. "Wow, Babetown, population: you."

"Is it too fancy?" I ask her, second-guessing my choice now that she's seeing the outfit herself. "Because I have every one of the store's woodland berry dresses in that changing room."

Cara loves what I chose, though, and she helps unzip me, which I am not disappointed about in the least. With the dress selected, I get to the much easier part of the afternoon: relaxing while Cara tries on her wedding gown.

"Is Evvie coming?" I ask Cara as I step out of the fitting room.

"She's on her way," Cara replies. She clenches her fists, giving off a frazzled energy that I've never seen from her before. "And guess who's with her?" She looks at Aidan, whose eyes go wide.

"Really?"

"Mam has been saying all week that she wouldn't show, but she's here."

"That's good. Right?"

"Mm. I want her at the wedding, I do." Cara nods her head, but her focus floats somewhere far away. "This'll give her more time to warm up to this weekend."

I'm about to ask who they're talking about when the front door chimes again. Cara's expression switches in a snap from worried to *happy, happy, happy*.

"Hi Mam! Hi Granny. I'm thrilled you're here."

"Ma'am. Ma'am." Granny waves at Diane. "Can you bring out some nibbles or refreshments?"

"I'm sorry, we don't allow food. There is a small supermarket next door, if you'd like something to drink. They've a nice selection of champagne."

Cara's petite grandmother can't hide her disappointment and dismisses Diane with an annoyed "Oh, never mind." Aidan volunteers to run into the store to grab some sparkling wine. Although Granny doesn't seem to notice, Cara mouths a *thank you* to him on his way out.

"Not even biscuits?"

"Gran, we're in a bridal shop, not a restaurant."

"Still, you'd think they'd have those small personal touches that make this less of a wedding factory. After all, this is my youngest granddaughter getting married. I want everything to feel special."

"Aw, Gran." Cara's eyes shimmer. "Thank you."

"Mammy, I'm pleased you came." Evvie drapes herself over her mother in a heartfelt hug.

"Stop fussing," Granny says. She notices me as if for the first time and does a poorly disguised up-and-down assessment. "Who're you?"

"I'm June."

"Who?"

"Granny, this is my half sister, Juniper."

"Oh." Granny lowers her voice, although not low enough we all can't hear, and mumbles to Evvie, "Unusual name."

I uncross and recross my legs, unsure what to do under her watchful eye. Considering what Cara and Yasmine have already told me about Granny, I struggle not to judge her in silence. Her treating me like I'm a reptile in a tank at the zoo doesn't help.

"Mammy." Evvie gives her a warning look and changes the subject to the dress, the alterations, and how Cara's sure to look incredible.

As the tailor gets Cara set up in one of the dressing rooms, Aidan returns with a chilled bottle of prosecco, napkins, and disposable cups. Cara's granny sips, smacks her lips, and announces that she would have gone with something drier, like a cava.

"You didn't have too much trouble finding something for you, love?" Evvie asks me.

I scroll through the photos Aidan took of me in the gorgeous slinky dress and show the best one to Evvie. For kicks, I also share the glorious '80s pouf that was a solid backup choice.

"Even in this dress, you're a star," Evvie laughs.

"The photographer had a lot to do with that," I say, turning to Aidan.

"It's all the sleeves."

I take my phone back from Evvie and smile at the image of myself. The lighting's awful and the gown is questionable, but I could still be mistaken for a retro-glam prom queen. "Have you ever thought of selling your photos?" I ask him.

"That's a brilliant idea," Evvie says. "You're out with your camera all the time."

"Pretty sure I need people to want to buy them first." He sighs and sinks into his seat.

"No, you need to sell them," I reply.

"To who?"

I turn to him and rest my head in my palm. "The site I write for works with a few freelance photographers, but those people don't sit around and wait for work. They're constantly pitching, sending in ideas, or updating their portfolios. You could put prints on your website."

"I don't have a site."

"Then do Instagram."

Crickets.

Rather than interrogate him, I offer some encouragement in the form of a real-life example. "I did this write-up once, a profile piece on the city's first pet-maternity photographer. Nobody *needs* twenty photos of their pregnant golden retriever, but if she has a business out of doing that, then you would have no trouble finding people interested in your stuff."

The scenery around here is breathtaking. Our drive to the bridal shop took us past a picturesque countryside full of petite farmhouses and rolling fields. The landscape is every photographer's dream.

"I'm not up with the trends, I guess," he says. "Besides, I've other things right now."

Other things, like the bar? I want to encourage him to reconsider, because I remember the photos he showed me the day we met. They were good. *Really* good. He should be working for magazines like *National Geographic*, and anyone can see that's where his heart is. But Aidan's crossed arms tell me he doesn't want to talk about it much further.

"Unless there's an enormous demand for maid of honor photos at bridal shops," he goes on, "I doubt there's any business in it."

"Maid of honor!" Granny whisper-yells to Evvie. "Ev, dear, is that the best idea?"

"Of course. It's what Cara asked for. June is Cara's half sister, so she should stand at the wedding."

I shift uncomfortably in my seat, not yet able to let that title stick to me.

"Everyone will *know*, though."

"Mammy." Evvie's ordinary amiable disposition cracks, and she sighs. "They already know I raised Cara alone and that Roger came along later. All the folks in town saw. That Cara's da had another child won't shock a soul." The brusqueness in her tone makes this sound like a conversation they've had before, many times over.

"I know," Granny huffs. "I only wish you'd be more—"

Before she can finish her sentence, Cara emerges from the fitting room. I gasp while her mother presses her hands to her own chest with a squeal, and I almost don't notice the sly way that Aidan—with the biggest smile on his face—pulls out his phone for a shot.

I saw photos of Cara in her dress, but with all the tailoring complete, she looks ethereal. The bodice features exquisite handiwork, and the flared sleeves are an unexpected addition I love. A column of dainty buttons runs up the back, and the skirt flares out and glides on the floor behind her. She is a goddess in ivory.

"You look amazing," I say, and everyone agrees. Even Granny grabs a tissue before kissing her granddaughter on both cheeks.

After a couple of spins, Diane shows us how to bustle the train in three swift moves. She makes the process seem as easy as tying shoes. "You'd be wise to have someone here unfasten the buttons now so they can get familiar with them," the tailor tells Cara.

The bride-to-be waves me into the fitting room, and after a few solid run-throughs with the bustle, I help her undress. I'm glad to have some practice with the back of her outfit in advance, because these buttons are slippery suckers that take some getting used to.

"How's everything going out there?" Cara whispers over her shoulder. "Granny can be difficult."

"I hadn't noticed."

"You're a miserable liar," she says with a low giggle.

My face burns at the accusation, even though she said it in jest. Maybe I *should* just tell her about the call from the lab. But I wouldn't be here helping her bustle this gorgeous gown if I did that, would I? And I'd only stress her out.

"But I appreciate you." Cara grips the bodice of her dress close to her chest, turns, and leans closer to me. "She can be a pain, I know. But she's here, so she is trying. Gran's on her own journey of acceptance, and I have to accept that."

"She'd be crazy not to share this day with her grand-daughter."

"Just embrace constant positivity with her. That's what my mam says. She's old and set in her ways, so when she's negative, ignore it and be positive, and everything will be fine. Absolutely fine."

I can't tell if Cara is pep-talking me or herself.

"Sure, I can do that. Don't worry. By the time cock-tails are flowing at the wedding, your biggest concern will be fighting for space on the dance floor."

Cara laughs some more and pulls me in for a firm hug. "Thank you. I'm so glad you're my maid of honor. I wouldn't want to get married without you."

Wouldn't want to get married without you. I soften at the words and squeeze her back.

While Cara changes into her regular clothes, we wait in the lobby. Granny totters around while examining the enlarged wedding photos on the wall. She shakes her head at one, moves along to the next, and then shakes her head side to side again.

"But what will she wear?" Granny says to no one in particular, but still loud enough that everyone can hear.

"The dress, Mammy," Cara's mom replies.

"Not *Cara*," she says, almost cutting Evvie off. "Yasmine."

"I'm not sure, Mammy, I haven't seen, but I've no doubt she has her own wonderful outfit."

"But..." Granny pauses. "Two white dresses? She can't wear a tuxedo, can she?"

Positivity.

"She's wearing a gorgeous jumpsuit." I hop into the conversation while making sure Cara isn't in earshot—I don't want to ruin the wedding day surprise for her. "She looks like royalty. They're going to make the most memorable couple."

"They will," Aidan agrees, and I let out a breath of relief knowing he has my back. "Two breathtaking brides."

Granny chews on this. She mutters an "Oh," and continues staring at the other framed photographs.

A different attendant slides behind the checkout counter and rings up the total for the tailoring, my dress, and the strappy heeled sandals that Diane strong-armed me into getting. They looked amazing, so I had to.

Evvie refuses to let me pay, nudging my credit card away. "Don't even think about it."

"I'm fine paying for my own clothes."

"I don't want you to."

"Oh..." I hesitate before putting my card back in my wallet, touched by her generosity. "That's nice of you. Thanks."

"Of course, love." She grabs my chin between her thumb and forefinger and looks me right in the eye. "I'm glad you're here with us and part of this day," she whispers, and my heart nearly bursts.

Chapter Thirteen

Aidan

"Is Cara's grandma always that way?"

"Sometimes." I hold the door to the floral shop open for June. "She has her moments."

Stepping inside from the dreary, drizzly car park, I see what Dorothy must have experienced when she landed in Oz. Brilliant blooming petals in every shade of the rainbow adorn the room from top to bottom. The scene is a carnival of flowers, and I've never seen so many in so many hues before. June gravitates toward a waterfall of blossoms, which she touches with the tips of her fingers before bringing her nose close for a sniff.

"Her gran can be kind when she wants to be. She's struggled to wrap her head around the marriage, though."

"I can't believe she treats Cara like that. Her own grandkid. And Evvie doesn't care what she says?"

"Don't blame Evvie for any of this," I say, coming to her defense. "That Cara's gran came today is a win."

June cocks an eyebrow to tell me she isn't entirely convinced, but I shouldn't be the one to explain the intricacies of the O'Shea family dynamics. She'll have to trust that Cara and her mam know how to best handle Granny.

"Afternoon," a delicate voice jingles from somewhere behind a heap of bouquets. "How may I assist you?"

A thin middle-aged man with slicked-back silver hair appears. He wears crisply pressed trousers, a white-as-snow shirt, and a smart-looking waistcoat. A shiny silver pocket watch rests in his breast pocket.

"I'm here to buy a bouquet," I say.

"Certainly. For what occasion?"

"Just for my mam. She likes 'em."

The gentleman's mouth drops open like that's the most touching thing he's heard all day. Truthfully, I regret missing brunch with her, so the flowers are for when I stop by later. Sometimes, I've no idea what to talk to my mam about, and I never know what her mood will be like when I show up. I have to monitor everything I say or do because she'll break down into sobs at the simplest things. She insists it's not my fault, just that she's sad, but I wish I had a way to make her not sad. At least less sad. So showing up to the house with a bouquet might cheer her up. The gesture is, at the same time, the least I can do and the only thing I can do.

The phone at the shop rings and the florist excuses himself, encouraging us to stroll down the aisles and see what stands out.

"What flowers does she like?" June asks, wrapping her palms around something that looks similar to a tulip.

"Peonies. Her gran had a peony bush in her garden, and my mam told me that the scent takes her back to balmy summer days as a four-year-old. No clue if they're in season."

"Not this time of year. Dahlias have a similar petal structure, though, so maybe these would work?" She holds up a few pinkish flowers from a bucket, water dripping off the ends of the green stems. "We'll pair them with something that drapes a little, like sweet peas," June goes on, her eyes darting around the room to find precisely what she has in mind. In this wonderland of florals, she knows just what to look for. "My grandmother had a small garden in her backyard," June says, answering the question that must be clear on my face.

"Ah. That's why you seem so at home."

I've witnessed June adapt to every new situation that she's encountered since arriving, but I like seeing her more comfortable. Like her defense has come down a bit.

"That was her peaceful place. Her one peaceful place. My grandma put love into her garden and could almost guarantee she'd get something good out of it." She pauses, her fingers trailing down some more flower stems. I'd listen to more about her past if she wanted to share. More about everything. "Sometimes I'd spend time with her there. Help out. She seemed lighter after an afternoon of gardening. Made life at home easier."

"Goodness, Dan? Is that you?"

A familiar voice brings my attention away from the tenderness in June's face to the store entrance. Mary stands there with her mouth open in surprise.

"Hi." I'd love to rewind the last five minutes and pick any other flower shop to walk into—maybe one that doesn't have my ex in it. "You're...you're here."

"I am." She laughs a little. "Oh, don't be so shocked. I was bound to run into you sometime when visiting home. Here for the weekend."

"Right."

I don't want to look at June and see the pity in her eyes as she watches this unfold.

"How's the form?" Mary hops to adjust the teal hand-bag on her shoulder, her blond locks cascading down longer than I remember. "You doing all right?"

"Can't complain. I'm, uh, buying some flowers for Mam."

"Oh, how's she?"

"Grand. Grand. Everything's—she's at home and well."

"Lovely. That's good."

A Colin Farrell look-alike swoops in and throws an arm around her waist.

"Heath," she says to him, "This is Aidan. Dan, this is Heath, my boyfriend."

"Good to meet you." Heath holds out his hand for a hearty shake. "Mare's told me a lot about you."

"Hi!" June interrupts my morose thoughts with an exceptionally bright tone of voice and a subtle glance my way that inquires, *This is* the *Mary?*

I nod in return.

"Mary, Heath, this is Juniper. June. She's come into town...well, she's visiting, but—with Cara's wedding, she—" June stands next to me through my excruciating rambling, and as I'm about to excuse myself to go scream, she steps in.

"I'm Aidan's girlfriend."

The proclamation pours out of her mouth, stunning me. Another subtle glance from her says *Play along*, and I'm too floored to do otherwise. The whole charade feels unnecessary considering I'm happy to have Mary out of my life and don't need a new partner to prove that point.

Although seeing Mary's pure and poorly hidden shock does give me a dose of satisfaction.

"Girlfriend," I say, as if testing the word out. "Right. June is my girlfriend."

We look nothing like a couple, though, with such a wide gap between us. June and I scuttle toward one another—she steps closer and I loop my arm around her. The sensation of our bodies pressed side by side jolts my senses. She fits me like we're two statues carved from the same stone. And does the shop smell like honeysuckle, or does June?

As the four of us talk with an abundance of politeness about the wedding, their weekend plans, and general catch-up, June melds into me more and more. Her presence gives me a kind of courage, helping me realize that after all Mary and I went through—after all Mary put me through—the bitterness about our relationship has dried up.

And more than that, I notice that standing by June is the most natural thing. When she tilts her head onto my chest—the act alone knocks the breath out of me. Our eyes meet, and I'm compelled to lean down and kiss her cupid's bow lips. I wouldn't—shouldn't—so I calm that impulse by tucking a strand of hair behind her ear. Her skin against my fingertips sends every synapse off in my brain, and for a second, nothing around us exists. Not Mary and Heath, not the store, and not the classical music playing on the radio.

Her eyes track my fingers, and for a flash, I fear that I've taken the ruse too far. But the moment passes, and the corner of her mouth tilts up in a fragile smile.

"Sorry for the wait." The florist reappears and breaks the spell between us. June pulls away. "Have you decided what you'd like to get? I can assist you with assembly."

"Yes," June says. "We picked out a few."

"I can help."

"No, don't worry." She places a swift kiss on my cheek before bounding away without a backward glance. "Stay here and talk some more, babe."

Mary and Heath continue chatting, but I only partially listen as I replay what just happened over and over in my head.

The knowledge of what June's body feels like, up close and personal, makes me crave more of what I can't have. As we climb into the car, I dream of reaching across the center console and pulling her face to mine—to find out just what those lips taste like. Those lips that should remain off-limits.

Those lips that were on my cheek only moments prior.

"You didn't need to do that." I turn the key in the ignition. "When word gets to Mrs. Abernathy, she'll be all over with the news."

"I'm sorry. I wasn't thinking. You just looked kind of panicky, so I said the first thing that popped into my head."

Panicky. She means I looked like a total eejit.

"No worries," I say. "Haven't seen her since the breakup, so in a way, I'm glad I got that done. We were going to run into each other at some point, since our families are from the same area."

"Small town."

"Everyone's your bodega guy." My callback to one of our first conversations causes her to chuckle, and the sound eases some of the tension in the car. "Sometimes...sometimes I get tongue-tied," I confess quietly. "I'm a bit embarrassed you saw me like that."

"What? No. From what you said, Mary was super shitty to you. And you don't plan to get back together with her, so...I mean, do you?"

"No." I can't emphasize that any quicker. "We're done. We've been done, and I've moved on."

"So you showed her that."

June looks at me long enough that I can admire the streaks of golden honey in her brown eyes. She shivers, so I turn the dial to get some heat going.

"You're a, uh, you're a very skilled actor," I say.

"*Moi*? Please, you were the one who was all...you know."

"What?"

"Like getting close to me and stuff," she says as her hand gestures back and forth between us. "If anyone gets an Academy Award here, it's you."

The creases at the corners of her mouth are flirtatious little hooks that reel me in. I stumble over my words again, and through the mishmash of thoughts, I insist that she leaned into me and not the other way around—a fact she vehemently denies.

"No, you scooted over and put your arm on me, and you pushed my hair back," June says as she recreates the scene on her own. "And you did the thing."

"What thing?"

"The *thing*. The *look*."

"You're mad."

"Come on."

"I've no idea what you're on about."

Except I do. I know what she means because I'm pretty sure the same one was on her face too. One of longing, desire. Christ, what I wouldn't give to see that look on her face again.

"You kissed me."

"On the cheek. That doesn't count."

"Sure, but still." A chaste peck on the cheek—of course it doesn't count. What am I, twelve? "We can stop the act, though."

"She almost fell over when you introduced me."

I smirk in satisfaction. To have the awareness in my heart that I don't regret the breakup with Mary is savory knowledge—for Mary to know that too, well, that tasted sweet. "We were together a long time." I fiddle with the radio dial to find a station not playing commercials. "Most of my twenties."

"I've run into guys before. Like in public, sometime after..." She breaks eye contact, but the masochist in me wants her to keep going. What type of men does June find attractive? Does she have a type? I shake the thought out of my head.

"Sometimes it's weird," she continues. "Not years-and-years-of-history-together kind of weird, though."

"Bet you handled it better than I did," I joke, using self-deprecating humor as a crutch.

"You were great. Very suave."

"*Suave*?"

"You were."

"Some people may disagree with that. Most people, actually."

"Well then, most people are wrong."

June says this like it's a fact she can prove from a textbook, and I'm too chuffed to argue with her.

We head back to Ballygrá with faint rock tunes from the '70s on the radio. Even though we've driven all over the place, even to Dublin and back, June keeps her eyes glued out the window. She seems fascinated by the small farms with herds of sheep trotting around and the lazy towns that we pass through. Cara mentioned that this is June's first time out of the country, and I enjoyed showing her some of Ireland. She'll go home a few days after the wedding—it's a shame I can't show her more than Ballygrá and a bit of the capital.

Best that she'll be gone soon, though. June's already got my mind all mixed up, and she's only been here a week.

"We've checked off a lot of Cara's to-dos on here." June holds the list in her lap and crosses off the tasks we completed. "This all seems very doable by Saturday."

"Most of what's left are miscellaneous jobs about town." I still have to pick up my tux, Thursday we have the hen party, and Friday marks the first of the wedding festivities. "I should sort out my speech by tomorrow too."

"Sure you don't want to give one for the both of us?"

I glance at her. While her voice is light and humorous, her expression gives away some worry.

"You'll do great. Standing up in front of a few hundred strangers isn't my idea of a Saturday night. But you're outgoing, and..." *Charming.* "You make easy conversation with everyone you've met here."

"I feel like..." She trails off and worries her bottom lip.

"What?"

"A fraud." We pull into my driveway, and concern has worked its way into her brows as she unfastens her seatbelt. "I would hate for Cara to regret this choice. To realize I shouldn't have given a speech in front of all of her family and friends."

"There'll be plenty to drink, so even if you make a fool of yourself, half the people there will be too pissed to remember a thing."

Her laugh fills up the car, and that dire concern seems to lessen. "Thanks." June sighs, resigned, and opens the door, but she halts before exiting. "Maybe you could help me?"

"How?"

"Well," she says, "since you refuse to do my speech for me—which, okay, fair—could we at least talk about them? Together?"

The cool air from outside the car sends a chill down my spine. "Not a bad idea. If we're both speaking, we should make sure they match up."

"Yeah, they should complement each other."

"Exactly. In that case, think about what you might say, and gather your thoughts. Then you can run ideas by me and give it a practice go. How's that sound?"

"Amazing. Thank you. Seriously."

I tell myself that my motives are entirely selfless and that I can't have June going into the wedding reception unprepared. But the way June's gratitude sets sparks off in my chest tells me otherwise.

Chapter Fourteen

Juniper

"I don't see what the problem is, Juney."

Obviously Ethan doesn't see the problem—he's not the one getting closer and closer to Cara and her family, and he's not the one assigned to write an article about the experience.

And he's *definitely* not the one cozying up to Aidan.

The thought brings warmth to my lower belly, so much that I chuck my jacket onto the bed. I'm glad Aidan drove to his parents' place so I can have some space alone.

Introducing myself as his girlfriend came out of instinct. If it had been Lis floundering at a bar, I'd step in and boost her self-esteem no matter what. I'd be the wingwoman. But Aidan played along with the act in a way that turned my legs to goo. How he held me electrified me, body and soul. I've had my fair share of lust-filled, sloppy make-out sessions with guys who were fun for a night or two, but nothing could top just *standing* next to Aidan McCarthy.

And that little kiss—I shouldn't have done it, but I couldn't help pushing the flirtation to the brink.

The more people I become friends with here—Cara, her parents, and Aidan—the more I'll inevitably have to sit down with later if this is all one big mistake. As I hang the maid of honor dress in the closet, I convince myself to consider the flipside. Perhaps that future scenario won't transpire at all.

But no matter the outcome, my assignment is also at risk.

"Sometimes," Ethan drones on through my phone, "stories go in a different direction than we plan. That's okay."

"But this isn't a new direction. This would mean no story, and that I'm not her half sister at all. The end." An uncertainty seizes me. Maybe we're related, maybe not. Maybe I can write the original story I pitched for *The Edge*, maybe not.

And if not, is this catastrophe how I want to propel my journalism career forward?

"This encompasses more than a story," I say. "It's my life, and it involves real people—people I care about. I've gone hiking with them, gotten beers with them, gone on road trips with them." I'll treasure those moments, even if there's a chance I didn't belong in them in the first place.

"Juney." My neck stiffens at his pet name for me, and the faint sounds of him tapping away at his keyboard hit me one by one, like a hammer to the head. "I've been looking through the notes you put in the folder. You have some workable stuff, and I really think this is salvageable. Plus, I want you to get this recurring column."

A column. My *own* column. Of course Ethan would dangle that in front of me.

I sit cross-legged against the bedroom wall, rubbing one hand through the shag carpet while contemplating what that would mean for my career. I love the idea of finally getting to do some real journalism—no more articles with "You Won't Believe What Happened Next" in the title and no more photo roundups of celebrities walking around SoHo.

Writing provided an escape for me as a kid—it was a place I found comfort when the rest of my life went to shit. When I got to New York, I didn't care if *The New York Times* hired me or some underground website did—I enjoyed sharing stories.

But after years of working under Ethan, this assignment marks the closest I've come to genuine career advancement. I can't let it vanish before my eyes.

"Aside from what you get out of this, Nancy doesn't want to fill our editorial calendar with a different article. Not after the investment and hype of this one. What message would it send for one of my writers to abandon a high-profile story like this when the going gets tough, and not at least try to work out some other related angle? I'm over here figuring out how I can justify to upper management that we keep on a writer who turns around and kills a piece with no guidance from their editor." Ethan releases a heavy sigh on the other end of the line. "I really need to count on you for this, but—"

"You *can* count on me," I shoot back, scrambling to salvage this situation and my own job, if I'm understanding him correctly. As one of the go-to sites for news, lifestyle, and New York culture, we receive hundreds of resumes every week. Ethan or anyone at *The Edge* could have me replaced by lunch break.

"Without me, you've got nothing," I say, grasping for the confidence to stand up for myself as I play the one card I've got. "What other writer in the world has gone through what I'm going through right now? I'm the only person who can write this."

"Yes, but it needs to be what we assigned to you."

"Aren't there ethics standards for sites like ours? Like, I should at least wait until I know more or—"

"What?" Ethan's tone turns deadly serious. I knew throwing out the E-word—ethics—would catch his attention. *The Edge* doesn't have the best reputation online. Every year or two a writer will depart for a better-paid, better-respected position elsewhere, and it's only a matter of time before they post some scathing account of their time at *The Edge*. Readers either don't care or can't get enough of the drama, because we continue to dominate with shareable content on news and entertainment. And Ethan will stand by our publication until the bitter end.

"This is real-life investigative journalism," he goes on, "and you can't always guess where the work will take you. That's all."

"Please, Ethan. Don't deny me an opportunity over something that might not be true. Could I move forward with an anonymous byline? There's still a story, but all the names get changed and I'm not attached to it publicly."

"Nance hates anonymous bylines and articles written by the generic 'Staff.'"

In my years there, no one ever published anonymously on *The Edge* ("This isn't Tumblr," Nancy once announced at a staff meeting in her usual unenthusiastic delivery). The publication claims to hold writers accountable, a roundabout way of shirking responsibility for the site as a whole. They ensure every article has well-labeled bylines. With my situation, I can claim the desire to preserve some of my privacy, but I doubt anyone will care what my reasoning is—they'll want my name at the top.

"I could turn it into a service piece on how genealogy works," I suggest, "and how professionals do it."

"That's a yawn for me."

"Then give me an extension. I'll have an article for you and for Nancy, but not as soon as I intended." Deadlines move around often, and if he'll oblige, then I can figure something out. "This whole thing would actually make for some good storytelling, right? A road bump I can write in, or...well, if things turn out differently, I'll still have a story to share. Just a different one, maybe on the efficacy of DNA tests. More research, less narrative, but with a slight personal element."

That's the last thing I'd want to write, considering how close I am to this—but I'm not asking Ethan to agree to anything. Just showing him that other options exist and encouraging him to push my deadline. He makes a familiar *hm* sound, and I can tell he's open to a grace period.

"Let me finish up here," I beg, "I'll get back to New York, and then you and I will make an amazing piece out of this. One that Nancy will love."

His exhale comes out long and irritated. "We're launching a lot of narrative pieces that week. It would be real nice to have this one among them. But..." Ethan clicks his tongue a few times, considering my offer from afar. "Fine. I'll see what I can do with the calendar."

"Thank you. I promise—"

"I want to see your progress on this, though. Keep uploading your notes to the cloud so it doesn't look like I signed off on you taking a two-week vacation."

"Yes, of course."

He's giving me time. I would kiss the ground Ethan walks on if I could. With an extension, I'll have to brainstorm an alternative yet equally eye-catching story to wow the pants off of Nancy. And although I'd rather not think about it, I need to sneak away for a new DNA test. But I've got this under control.

Right before I hang up, Ethan stops me. "Hey Juney—I need to trust you can do this."

"I can. No matter what that DNA test says, I will have something for you." I say this to reassure myself as much as my boss.

With that bullet dodged, I head into the kitchen to grab a glass of water. A woman with red hair peppered with silver sits with her hands clasped on the table, and I about jump out of my skin.

"Evelyn! Evvie, you scared me. What are you doing here?"

"Hi, love," she says with a wan smile. "I was dropping off some wedding decorations that Aidan said he had room to store. Who were you on the phone with?"

My insides clench and my heart drops. "How much of that did you hear?"

"Enough to think we need to have a chat. Come on, grab your coat."

"That's Jamie," Evvie says to me while we watch the ball dart around between players. "One of the sweet students I taught years back, that's his lad. Tea?"

She's acting chillingly normal. When I spat out the truth, Evvie hugged me and drove me straight to the DNA lab outside of Cork herself. Since that pit stop, she hasn't spoken a word about it. This must be the calm before the hurricane. I keep waiting for her to yell at me, take me to the airport, or call up Cara, but she remains interested in the scrimmage.

We secure a spot on the side of the field at her godson's Gaelic football practice, and we stand all bundled up in warm coats and scarves. Gangly kids who can't be a day over fourteen race around the grass like commuters at rush hour, creating a chaotic jumble of young people. One of the boys spies Evvie in the crowd and instantly brightens when she waves at him.

Cara's mom pulls out a thermos from the depths of her coat and gingerly pours me a cup, like this is what we do every afternoon. I burn my tongue and spend the next few minutes watching the kids follow a ball around and pretending my mouth isn't numb. In between measured sips of her drink, Evvie cheers on her godson with sharp whistles that startle me back an inch or two.

"Okay, love. Tell me. What're we to do?"

"No." I cover my face with both hands. "Don't do that. I don't deserve that."

"What?"

"*Love*. Don't be nice about this. I should have told Cara the second I found out. And I shouldn't go to the wedding, and I shouldn't be staying with Aidan who's her best friend, and this is just...this is a disaster."

"You've one thing right." She chuckles, but her lighthearted response makes no sense because nothing about this seems funny. "This is a disaster. Maybe."

If Evvie's saying that, then I might have eked out a small slice of sympathy for my situation. I shouldn't be surprised—the O'Sheas have only shown me generosity from the moment I arrived.

But the thinnest of threads connects me to them. It's fragile and fresh. I could leave their lives as quickly as I entered, and they would hardly notice my absence. For me, things are different. I've just gotten a brief taste of what it's like to be part of a family, and a tiny vial of my spit might take that all away.

"Life unfolds in ways we don't always predict or plan for," she goes on. "You did believe you and Cara were half sisters when you showed up here?"

"Yes. God, yes, 100 percent."

"And you still might be?"

"Right. I can't confirm until they call or email." The gentleman at the lab said that they marked my test a priority, and they've expedited the results, cutting down the usual time to a week or less. The thought makes my stomach tense. "Telling Cara during all the wedding planning and work, and when I couldn't give her a confident answer anyway...it felt premature, I guess. The not-knowing is killing me, but also..."

Evvie nods without a word, and I sense she understands what I mean. She offered me a ride to the lab, which relieves as much pressure as it creates for me.

"It's harder to bring it up to her than before," I continue. "Especially because, from the instant I got here, Cara has treated me like one of her favorite people."

"Because you are. Would you guess, she begged me for a sister when she was younger? You're a bit of a dream come true for her." Evvie loops an arm through mine and pulls me closer. "Cara has a lot of energy, but her enthusiasm is genuine. It's how she is. She doesn't withhold her love. Never has."

"Sounds like my best friend from back home." Maybe that's why, as much as I didn't want to get close to Cara,

I have. She reminds me of Lis. "Are you going to tell Cara what's going on?" I hold my breath. If Evvie says yes, at least I won't have to face my maybe-half sister's disappointment myself.

"Oh, I don't know. I think you're right to wait."

"Really?" I must not have heard her, but she gives a curt nod. "But you're her mom."

"And 'cause I'm her mam, and 'cause I love her, we shouldn't bring this up yet. Cara thinks the world of you, so much that you're her maid of honor. She's had too many friends abandon her, and if she felt you might back out now, well, I'd hate to see her like that again." Evvie reaches into her bag and pulls out a plastic-wrapped cinnamon bun that she probably grabbed at a gas station. After breaking the sugary delicacy in half, she offers one part to me. "By the way, if she caught me eating these, Cara'd let me have it. I adore her baking, but these buns are my guilty pleasure, and she can't take that away from me."

I don't know what to say. Rather than giving me an ultimatum, Evvie wants me to carry on like normal.

"Cara's ecstatic that you're here and part of the family. She's been consumed with the restaurant for a while, and I'm proud of her. But she's been all work, work, work." Evvie's eyes shimmer as she pops the last bite of pastry into her mouth. "Since she found out about you, Cara's making more of an effort to spend time with us.

Inviting me and her granny along to the dress fitting? If you weren't here, I doubt she'd have done that. She would've raced to the bridal store, tried on the dress, and left."

Cara's compassionate and thoughtful, but she's also ambitious, and opening a restaurant is more than a full-time job. She has put in active effort over the last week to hang out with me, but what if I'd never shown up? It's easy to picture her spending every waking minute at the cafe, and the rest planning her wedding in the most efficient manner possible.

"Oh, hey, fair play! Go on, Jamie!" Evvie claps along with a few other onlookers. As the scrimmage resumes, she turns to me with warmth. "You're a shining influence in her life, whether or not you realize it. Roger and I adore you. Aidan adores you too."

The mention of Aidan sets my ears aflame.

"Besides," she goes on, "none of this is your fault, is it, dear?"

"But what if, when the results come back, they're wrong and we're not related?" *Would they adore me still?* "And how do I tell Cara?"

"As my granda would say, we'll cross that bridge when we get to it." She nudges me, pulling me out of my stormy thoughts. "Even if you're not her half sister, she'll still like you, love."

"I guess." Since arriving, Cara's only shown me kindness. I can't discern how much of that is because of our shared DNA and how much is because she actually likes *me*. "She probably wouldn't care to have me stand in her wedding if I went to her now with what's going on."

"Sometimes life isn't as simple as what's right and what's wrong, love. You realize that too, otherwise you would've told her already. If you're not up there, it'll be a cruel reminder of all the friends who've walked out on her. My daughter has her heart dead set on sharing this day with you. She wants that, and we can give her that. She'll be crushed by the news, and worried and sad, and I don't want that for what's supposed to be the most special day for her."

"Cara's going to be at least a little mad at me for lying to her, though. If, well...you know." I consume my cinnamon bun support pastry. "And she'd be upset with you too. Oh god," I say through a half-chewed baked good. "I've made you complicit."

"We're making the best decision we can right now, given what information we have. That's all we can ever ask of ourselves." Evvie massages one of her hands with the other in some form of self-comfort. "With all of this wedding planning, she'll likely be grateful. If it comes to that in the end, which is a big if, you'll find a time to say so. Sit her down and explain what happened. But no use fretting over what may not be."

She has a point. I'm not purposefully hiding facts, but I'm sharing updates when I can be certain of them. This dilemma has caused me enough grief, so I can only guess how Cara would handle hearing about it, on top of all the things she has going on. By the time I get the results, Cara and I will know each other even better too. No matter what the outcome, the conversation will be easier.

And maybe, *maybe* by doing everything else right—being a stellar maid of honor slash half sister—Cara will understand. Just as Evvie said, Cara would still like me.

"You won't tell anyone, will you? What about Aidan?" I don't know why I care what he thinks, but I do.

"Our little secret." Evvie gives me a peaceful smile. "Family's not just blood. It's who you choose. Cara knows that, what with Roger and all. They aren't related, but he's her da. You've got folks like that in your life, don't you?"

"Mm. Yeah, I do." Never in my life would I have guessed that the random Craigslist stranger I moved in with would become my best friend, but Lis is as close to family as I've ever had. She knows me better than anyone and has shown up for me in more ways than I can count. "You're not upset that I've looped you into this craziness?" I ask, turning to her. "That I'm making you lie to your daughter?"

"You're not forcing me to do anything. Sometimes you do things for the people you love that are for the best, even when they don't have the entire story. It's not cruel, though. You do it 'cause you care. Like this?" She gestures to the field of uncoordinated kids dashing to one side of the grass and leans into me, lowering her voice. "I come here to support someone I love and watch his son run around like a lost lamb. I clap whenever Jamie or anyone else scores a goal. And I don't care to understand a thing about the bleedin' game."

My laugh makes some of the other people sitting on the bleachers shoot an annoyed look in our direction. "Have you told Jamie or his parents that?"

"'Course not! Taking that one to my grave, along with the cinnamon bun obsession." She elbows me and giggles.

Someone knows my secret—what a relief. Evvie cares, not only about her daughter but me too. She has both of our best interests at heart.

"Thank you," I say, my chest feeling lighter than an hour ago. She wraps an arm around me, and I smile to myself.

The test results will come eventually, but for now, all I have to do is be the best half sister Cara could ever imagine.

Chapter Fifteen

Aidan

"How many straws does he think we need?" Mam huffs, sounding utterly defeated. She sits in the middle of the stockroom, and only the top of her ponytail is visible as I enter. "We've at least a year's supply, and then some."

"I may be partly to blame for that."

"You ordered all these?" She peers over the battalion of boxes surrounding her, all of them stuffed with red straws.

"No, but Da's been asking me to help with inventory and I, uh, I hadn't made the time. Didn't realize it was because our entire stock is now straws."

"Ah." I pick up on her irritation. She'd scold me for not helping, but she's not in the position to, since this is still her responsibility. Not only does she do inventory more efficiently than anyone else, but for as long as I can remember, she insisted on doing the weekly stock checks herself. Da and I put this off because we hoped one day she'd be ready to come back to the pub. And in the meantime, he did his best—which left much to be desired.

But Mam's here, so that's a good sign. I take a couple of steps toward her and hold up the colorful bouquet for her to see. "For you."

"Oh, Danny. You—you didn't have to get these." She uses the boxes as support to stand up, and she takes the flowers. "What're these for?"

"For missing brunch."

"Thank you. They're beauties."

"June helped me pick them out." I recall standing in the flower shop with her at my hip and can't help but grin. "Not peonies, but close. Dahlias, she said."

Mam inhales the fragrance and gives me a weak smile before reaching over the stack of cardboard boxes between us and pulling me into a one-armed embrace. Sometimes I get the sense that she can't handle physical contact—almost like a hug from me reminds her that she can't wrap her arms around Michael. I wonder if I cause her pain by just existing, like I'm a living reminder of her other son.

I fetch her a pint glass of water to arrange them in until she goes home. She pats the petals and gives the bouquet one last sniff before returning to her spot in the supply room. Today must be a better day for her.

"Need help in here?" I ask.

"No. Usual tasks, that's all. Been a little behind, what with visiting Bri and all."

Aunt Brianna has needed more support with her ever-growing collection of farm animals, so Mam's gone up to assist. The trips have given her a break from the black hole of all-consuming grief.

"How's Cara?" my mam asks. "Bundle of nerves? Or you keeping her sane?"

"Both, I'm sure. This week's about as smooth as she and Yaz could've asked for. Some stressful moments, but manageable." It's June who came out of nowhere, who truly pulled my focus. "You're, erm, you're still planning on this Saturday, are you?"

"'Course!"

"Cara'll love to hear that. Da's going too?"

"He is," she says, her voice tighter, like she's holding onto something. "We wouldn't miss her day."

"Danny!" Da appears at the entrance. The bags under his eyes sag, and his hair could use a comb. "D'you work today?"

"Not back until after the wedding. I stopped by the house for Mam but found her here instead."

"Since you're here, perhaps—"

"Oh, stop with that." My mam bats at the air, chasing away his words. "It's his time off, let 'im have that much."

"Well." Da speaks that single word with exasperation, leading me to believe this isn't their first disagreement of the day. "We need him in here at some point."

"Are you blind to this? We should make other plans. What we need is someone to handle this when I'm gone."

"You can talk to me. I'm right here," I say, my voice blade-sharp. But what she said drains the fight out of me. "What d'you mean, when you're gone? Gone where?"

She and Da look at each other and then apart, both avoiding my question. The worst-case scenario punches me in the gut. "What's going on? Are you sick?"

"No, it's not that, Danny," she says, abandoning her post at the straws and wiping some hair from her face. "We've discussed it, and this...oh, love, this really isn't how I intended us to tell you."

"Tell me *what*?"

"This," my dad clears his throat. "This might not come as a surprise, but we...we've agreed we need some time apart."

I shrug at this non-news. "You've been up with Aunt Bri almost every other week. You two've been apart."

"We wanted to see how that time away from each other would feel." My mother fiddles with her rings, twisting her wedding band around and around. "And we think that's the way forward."

"So...you're divorcing?" The room shrinks around me, becoming too small for the three of us.

Mam shakes her head, and Da steps in. "Separating. For now."

"And when were you planning on telling me?" I whip my head to Da, who has both hands hidden in his jeans pockets. "How long would you let me go on believing this was all working out? Why didn't you tell me sooner?"

"We're telling you now."

My parents' marriage hasn't been perfect, but all along, I thought Mam was trying to process what she'd lost and make peace with the universe. Turns out, the time up at Brianna's was a test run for her new life. Mam needed a break. From the pub, from the reminders of Michael. From me.

"It's for the best." Mam sounds like she's reading lines from a poorly rehearsed play. "For everyone."

"It's certainly the easy thing to do."

"Aidan McCarthy." Da saying my name in that threatening tone makes me bite back any harsher response.

"Nothing about this is easy, love." Mam's voice shakes like a skinny blade of grass in furious winds. "Your da and I have fought for each other, and the most loving action we can take is to step away." Her eyes well up and the tears cascade down her face, which rips me in two. "I'm working to be better for you, Danny, I am. But we need to do what's right. For us both."

The air's become thick, almost impossible to breathe. Mam excuses herself to the bathroom while Da remains stock-still at the door.

"You should've told me," I say. Him not mentioning this until now is a betrayal of our fragile trust in each other.

"I wanted to." His raw honesty shakes me, like he knows how much this hurts. "But the decision comes down to me and your mam and no one else."

With an exhale, I grab my coat. He calls out, "There's nothing more you could've done, son," but I'm out and already tearing through the front door.

Somewhere along the way, from when Michael died to now, I've failed. There's no number of picnics together or amount of willingness to learn inventory or bouquets of pink and orange flowers that can change how my parents feel. This whole time, I've lied to myself.

I'll never be Michael. I can't go back in time to take his place in that car. And I'll never be able to return us to the life we lived together before he died.

I slam my front door shut behind me, shocking June as much as myself.

"Sorry," I mutter. "Didn't mean to frighten you."

"No worries."

She closes her laptop as I stalk into the kitchen for a drink of water. I almost don't have the energy to admire how adorable she looks, sitting cross-legged with a pair of tie-dyed socks decorated in cat drawings. I down half a glass and wipe my chin with my hand.

"You okay?" she asks.

"Not really."

June studies me with a neutral expression. She doesn't press for more information, but she creates the space for me to share, if I'd like. I've never met someone who has a sixth sense the way she does—who doesn't force what she wants or needs on anyone. She just lets them exist with her and open up on their own time. She did it with me on the way to Dublin after the interview, and she's doing it now.

"My, uh, my parents told me they're separating. I..." I scratch the back of my neck, remembering how awfully the conversation in the stock room ended, with Mam in tears and me storming out on Da. "They just told me, and I didn't—I handled it poorly."

"Well, yeah, that's understandable." She pushes her computer off her lap and hugs her knees. It's heartachingly cute. "I'm really sorry. That must be so hard."

I nod and redirect my attention back to my glass.

"Do you want me to go?" she asks. "I can give you some space."

"No. I mean, do what you like. I won't stop you. But it's grand, you bein' here." I clear my throat and process my thoughts out loud. "I thought I was doing everything right," I say to myself. "Doing everything I could."

"You are."

"Not enough, though."

"It's their relationship. It's…" June sinks deeper into the sofa, still balled up, but looser, relaxed. "You have to recognize that other people's bullshit often has nothing to do with you. It sucks, but you can do and be everything for your parents, and it still might not matter." I catch the earnestness in her voice—a sincere understanding behind every word she's saying. "Wanna go for a walk? Get some fresh air and clear your head? Four walls can suffocate you if you're not careful." She watches me and shrugs. "We don't have to. Just a thought."

I've a million things going on in my brain that I don't fully appreciate the gracious invite and how she's looking out for me. I gesture to her computer. "Don't you have to work?"

"I could use a break. Just salvaging this assignment if I can."

"How d'you mean?"

"Oh, it's boring." She waves her hand at her laptop, dismissing it. "Dealing with my editor, deadlines. Don't worry about it. A walk would be nice."

Once I grab my camera, I take us to one of my favorite spots to catch the sunset. A late afternoon drive together doesn't mean anything, no matter how much heat floods my chest when we pull into the driveway of a familiar sky-blue cottage. The paint's peeling more than I recall. I step on each cobblestone leading into the gated yard, which is protected by worn fencing and shrubbery. The ceiling of gray clouds makes the day feel later than it actually is, but I checked the forecast, and we should still have a solid hour to explore.

Mr. Flynn opens the door and passes me the key with a grunt. He juts his thumb toward the back of the house, as if I haven't visited his property before, and I thank him.

"Who's that guy?" June asks as we make our way down the hill. Before I can answer, she squints and points across the field. "Is that a castle?"

"That man runs the estate, and you need a key to get in."

"We're going to a *castle*?"

June looks like a child on Christmas morning, and her excitement gives me something positive to focus on. That we have to dodge piles of manure and mud holes on the route through the pasture doesn't lessen her joy in the least.

She pulls out her phone and begins typing with deft thumbs.

"Bored already?"

"Taking notes," she says.

"Thought you didn't want to talk about work."

"I don't. And I'm not. This is different. Maybe it'll find its way into another article one day, but for now I want to write memos so I remember."

When we arrive, she wanders around the property, trailing her fingertips against the stone structure. The dilapidated crest on the north side of the exterior stops her in her tracks, and every nook and cranny seems to fill her with a new wonder. Watching her, I almost forget why I wanted—needed—to come here. Room. Space. Time to think behind the lens.

"You're in some of my photos. Is that okay?"

"Sure. Let me know if I need to get out of the way. Don't want to ruin your pics."

"You don't. Look." I walk over, scroll through the photographs on my SD card, and hold one up for her. Her chestnut hair waves in the wind while one of her hands stretches out, reaching for the castle walls. June's face tilts upward, taking in the behemoth of ruins in front of her.

"That school's probably typing up that acceptance letter as we speak."

"You're talking like my brother."

"Is that a good thing?"

"He was the first person to encourage me to apply for the program. If not for him, I might never have envisioned any other life for myself other than what's at the pub. I almost feel like if I don't get back in, somehow I'm letting him down."

"He's kind of the reason you're sticking around too, isn't he?"

The breath in my lungs *whooshes* out of me. I've been lost, wandering with what I think Michael would want from me and what I imagine he would do in my position—two opposing forces—as my compass.

"He'd want you to be happy," June goes on, her voice cautious, like she can sense I'm processing something deep. "He knew how much you loved photography, but pursuing that can look a million different ways, not only through a degree. You've got the gear, you've got the eye. No one needs to give you permission to do what you love except you."

Her words hit me somewhere unknown, shaking my core. "I wish someone could just tell me what to do sometimes. Figuring it out alone is..." I hiss out a breath.

"Yeah." Her steps look heavier, like she's carrying a load on her shoulders. "I know what you mean."

We approach one of the ground-floor windows, which looks out over waves of grass. The cool gray tones of the stone contrast with the pastoral hills.

"We work with some freelance photographers at *The Edge*." She traces her finger along the edge of the weathered rock. "I could connect you to them, see if they can help point you in the right direction. If you set up a site and email some editors, I'm sure they'd love to have someone like you on their roster."

I chuckle and stuff one hand in my pocket.

"What?" she asks.

"Nothing. You have a way of...I guess, making me feel like anything's possible," I say as a smile inches across my face. "Thank you for suggesting I get outside. Some room to breathe is nice."

"Good." June leans into a window and smiles at the landscape. "This place is amazing. I've got a layer of mud on my boots, the weather's awful, and it smells like cow shit, but I'm having a great time."

"You'll have to come back to visit."

"Here?"

"No. Yes. I mean, Ireland."

"We'll see." She runs her bottom lip through her teeth. "I've liked getting away. Traveling. Wish I could do it more. You've been an outstanding tour guide."

My heart is a string, and the way that June turns and beams at me, dazzling and purely happy, ties me into a knot. Her gaze flashes down to my lips, and I swallow.

"I'd take you anywhere to see you smile like that," I say, barely loud enough to hear over the breeze.

What would you do if you had one of those moments coming up where you knew, you just knew, your life was about to change?

I don't want to live always wondering *what if?* but I really shouldn't do this. June must pick up on my hesitation, because she closes most of the space between us and lifts her chin up like she's giving me permission. I'm hit with the sweet smell of her hair and a hint of mint on her breath.

If I want to have no regrets, now's my chance.

We lean in, and our mouths meet in a curious, tentative greeting. Her lips on mine, so soft and warm, make half of me dissolve into the ground and the other half soar into the sky—all from the tiniest touch. I want to bury myself in this moment. With one hand, I cup her jaw, stroking her cheek with my thumb.

I've found heaven.

She pushes into me with intensity, and a delicious moan rises in her throat. I'd like nothing more than to coax every pleasurable sound possible out of her. She tugs on my jacket so our bodies fuse together, and our mouths melt into each other.

When we pause, separating the smallest amount, the air between us crackles with energy. Our breathing is in sync, and I press my forehead to hers.

"That was..." I swallow. "Unexpected."

"Good-unexpected?"

She's Cara's sister. She's not a relationship kind of woman. She doesn't even live here.

"Complicated-unexpected."

"Oh." She takes a step back. "Did I read things wrong?"

"No, I just...I've thought about us. This."

"Okay."

"I just haven't thought far ahead enough about what Cara might think about this."

"Cara?"

"I don't want her to feel odd about us getting involved. She's my closest friend and your sister."

"Right." June's expression changes, like a cloud going over her face, and she retreats another step. "If she and I weren't related, you wouldn't care?"

"Suppose not." I feel like she's asking a trick question, but I don't know why. "You wouldn't be here, though, would you? We wouldn't even be having this conversation."

She looks like I've just slapped her across the face. "You know, we should go."

"June, I just don't want to rush something—"

"No, you're totally right. We shouldn't have done that. Bad idea. I'd like to go now, please."

"We just need to make sure we consider...everything."

"I agree." She zips her jacket up higher, closing herself off to me. "And after considering everything, I want to go."

Somehow, I had the most perfect chance with the most perfect girl and obliterated it. I know June deserves someone dashing, daring—someone who'll take a real chance and not let thoughts get in the way. I wish that could be me.

We walk back to the Flynns, return the key, and without another word, we head home, where June goes straight to her room. Confusion eclipses the elation of our moment together, her face pressed to mine. If only I could talk to Cara about this, but she wouldn't appreciate me hitting on her half sister, I'm sure. That's got to be part of why June pulled away and established stronger defenses, and honestly, I should thank her for it. She made the right choice for both of us.

That's what I tell myself, over and over, before drifting off to sleep.

Chapter Sixteen

Juniper

"Where the heck are you?"

"Side street," I say. "Cute, right?"

"Yes, I'm loving this. Very cottagecore. Virtual tour, please."

I hold up my phone to show Lissie the parts of Ballygrá that have become regular sights for me this past week—a white church that can't be bigger than Aidan's house, the town's library with colorful lettering on the side, and a pastel bed-and-breakfast. I thought going on a walk would give me the chance to show my friend around town and tell her about the last few days. And also to get my thoughts straight after that earth-shattering kiss.

I can't stop thinking about it. It was one kiss, but no one has ever kissed me like that before—gentle and kind and without distraction. He looked at me like I was heaven and earth combined, and his hand was touching me so reverently that it almost felt wrong to wash that part of my face.

"Alright, your turn. Give me some much-needed New York."

"Same old, same old over here. Manspreaders galore on the park benches. Someone feeding the squirrels." Lis flips her phone's camera around to show me what is unmistakably Union Square. She points toward a sea of people and vendor tents. "The farmers market is super busy, and I'll probably stop in and spend half of my paycheck on some more of that organic honey."

"Worth it."

"Those bucket drummers are here somewhere, too. Oh! I didn't tell you." She flips the phone back to her face, fringy bangs popping out from under her knit hat. "I got a callback."

"What! The one with the boots?"

"The one with the boots." Lis and I break out in a happy dance, an act that instantly brings me closer to home and closer to her. I don't know if I miss New York or if I just miss familiarity and being in a place where life's less complicated.

After Lis tells me about the scene the casting director has requested her to prepare, she asks about me.

I've sent some texts, but I haven't told her about my conversation with Evvie. Or the kiss.

"You made out with him?" Her voice climbs an octave. "Why didn't you lead with that? Oh my goodness, tell me *everything*."

"We were at a castle," I say, and Lis lets out a squeal. I shouldn't be as excited about this as I am. "An actual, honest-to-god castle. It was like a scene from a movie."

"Is he a good kisser?"

"He is..." I sigh. "He is an exceptional kisser."

The memory of his lips on mine sends my heartbeat through the roof and stirs desire low in my body. All from a kiss. I'm afraid of what I'll be tempted to do the next time I run into him alone at his house. Getting tangled up with Cara's best friend would muddle an already murky situation, though. Aidan reminded me how complicated something between us would be. I only wish he'd waited to remind me after we let things go a little further.

"So you made out and..." She waits for me to fill in the blank. "Tell me more."

"Nothing more to tell," I say, ignoring my disappointment at not having anything juicier to share.

"June!" Lis loves the drama, so this must be killing her. She paces down the sidewalk, providing me with shaky, nausea-inducing video. "If a strapping young

Irishman takes you to a *castle* to kiss you, it should not lead to nothing."

"He didn't bring me there to kiss me." I roll my eyes, wishing I didn't have to point to the fine details that put a stop to us making out. "We happened to kiss, then he mentioned something about me being Cara's sister, and—"

"Weird."

"I freaked out."

She's my closest friend. And your sister. Aidan's words reiterate why I need to maintain a distance from him.

"When I'm with Aidan, I forget why getting involved with him in any way is a bad idea, or why I'm here in the first place," I go on. "For Cara and the article. Nowhere in the plan did I leave space for an Aidan. I've hid in my room almost all day to avoid him."

"Are you safe?"

"Oh, yes. He's kind and gentle and completely unlike the guys I'm normally attracted to. I'm just...embarrassed. We didn't just kiss, we *kissed*."

"That sounds great."

"It's not great, it's awful."

"Oh, I get it." Lis's mouth quirks up, and she wags a finger at me. "You like him. Oh my goodness—"

"Stop."

"You do! Aw, you haven't had a legitimate crush on someone in years."

"I do not have a crush on him."

"You can be honest with me."

"I am. Zero crushes here."

"This all makes so much sense. You would have jumped his bones if he were some rando, but you really like this guy, so of course you're looking for any reason to push him away."

"Fine," I say, lowering my voice. "I like him."

"Yeah, I know."

I like Aidan. A smile tugs at my mouth because really liking someone—really liking Aidan—fills my body with a fizzy sensation. My hastiness in demanding we leave yesterday squashes some of that fizziness, though. He must think I don't like him like that, and I probably scared him off, going all hot and cold on him. For all I know, he's avoided me today as much as I've avoided him.

"You should let him know how you feel."

"You're such a romantic." I try and fail to keep a neutral face while she grins at me. "I'm not going to tell him."

"You must. He likes you back."

"He—" I don't like how Lis is pointing this out, because it only reminds me of everything after the kiss—the quiet car ride, the avoiding eye contact like the plague. "In case you've forgotten," I say, willing my brain to stop thinking about Aidan, "I have other things going on."

I sit on the corner of a dilapidated roadside bench. Lis lets me talk, nodding her head as I tell her about what happened with Evvie, the new test at the DNA lab, and the results that will make this trip all worth it or a total waste. She paces up and down one of the pathways in the park, taking in every bit of information.

"So her mom wants you to lie until the wedding." Lis says. "You're okay with that?"

"It's more of a not-telling-the-whole-truth kind of situation."

My best friend chucks a doubtful look my way, and I wither under her disapproval.

"I know," I go on, "it's not much better. But Cara's juggling a billion things between the ceremony and her new restaurant. And she's so..." I can't quite explain how Cara's friends tore her heart out by ditching her, and how she acts like I've mended her back up. Telling her about what happened at the lab, as inconclusive as it all is, would devastate her. "We don't want to ruin the precious final days before the main event, and maybe for no reason."

"True." Lis removes her hat and lets her hair wave around in the wind. "But like, you're gonna be in this woman's wedding photos."

"I've already asked Evvie to talk to the photographer. She's arranging a round of formal pictures with every combination of family, so there will be plenty without me." I'll appear in some of them, but at least I can't single-handedly ruin all of her memories of the wedding. "There's no perfect choice here, and her mom is putting Cara first. That's a good thing, right? That Cara's mom is on my side?"

"Sure." She breaks eye contact and scratches a spot along her jawline—the dead giveaway that she's lying. "Better than her not being on your side."

"But?"

"No buts."

"I didn't call so you could bullshit me."

"I would never *bullshit* you," she hisses. Lis is a grown woman who I have only heard curse a handful of times, so she must mean business. "I'm trying to be gentle here because I...well, I'm worried about you."

"Why?"

"Because you're lying."

"If I find out the worst news possible, then I'll tell her," I insist. "It's a matter of timing. Waiting and hearing from the lab."

"I don't mean that. You're lying to *yourself*."

This knocks the wind out of me, but I play off the shock by making a *psh* sound. "Ridiculous."

"You're getting close to these people in such a short time, and if you're not careful, you'll set yourself up for heartache."

"I already told you, we kissed. Once. And yes, it was hot, but that's it. There's nothing more going on between us."

"I'm not just talking about Aidan here. I mean everyone. Cara, her parents, everybody." Lis looks directly at the phone camera so her stare cuts right through me. "I love you, okay?" I shift in my seat, because I always get a little uncomfortable when she pulls out the L-word. Hearing it, saying it—it makes my brain break out in hives.

"You've been there a week, and you're getting all swept up in this family," she continues.

"I'm not."

"I don't want you to get hurt. You're like a sister to me, and you're usually so careful with your heart, so I'm looking out for you."

My eyes sting. "I'm being careful, *mother*," I say with a playful jab to lighten the mood. My best friend's expression tells me she's not having it. "Okay, fine. I'll admit I've gotten a little carried away." Growing up, I kind of missed out on getting to experience a family. Real family. "But I can walk away from this anytime I'd like."

If I have to, I can. I know I can.

"Okay," she says, and we share a few moments of silence. She doesn't believe me, I'm sure, but she's made her case and doesn't need to say anything more. "Well, I'm glad you're having a good time. I love you so much."

I let a few seconds pass.

"Say it." She points at me through the phone.

"I love you too," I whisper. She's the only living person in the world I've ever uttered that phrase to, and I don't think I'll ever get used to saying it.

"And I miss you like crazy, and the trip sounds like fun even if it's kind of chaotic. But you coming back to New York with your heart ripped out would be the literal worst. You act all tough and have your guard up, but I see you. Secret softie."

My abrupt laughter fills the empty street. "Don't worry. I can handle it."

After an hour and a half of tying twine with name tags to wooden tea light holders and a sprig of dried lavender, I can't feel my fingertips. But the wedding favors look *spectacular*.

Cara's parents invited everyone over to finish up some of the handmade decor for the reception, so their home looks like a craft-supply bomb exploded inside. We're digging into DIY projects at the dining room table while Roger assembles some larger items behind the living room sofa. Yasmine and her family will arrive later, along with Aidan, and the prospect of being in the same room as him again has my stomach flip-flopping.

"Those are perfect," Cara says, lifting a candle holder up like it's made of gold. "I love them."

Winnie raises his head to see what's going on, and when he confirms no treats are involved, he returns to snoring by the china cabinet.

"They belong in a bridal magazine," Evvie adds. She's shown me lots of silent support tonight with tender pats on the shoulder and side-hugs. She knows I can only wait in a bizarre agony until my test results come through, so she's treating me with extra care. The special attention is like bubble wrap around my heart.

"What's next on the list?" I ask.

"Not too much in the way of crafts." Cara's pleased with herself, nodding in approval as she checks off one more item.

"I could use some help here," Roger says. "Mostly finished, but I need another pair of hands to put it together."

I head to the clear space behind the floral-patterned couch, where he's working on a photo booth backdrop. The frame is made of PVC pipes, connected by fittings and reinforced with some heavy-duty glue. He shows me all the pieces yet to be assembled, and we get to work while Cara and her mom dig out supplies to finish the centerpieces.

"I'm guessing that an evening of manual labor wasn't what you hoped for when you booked your trip here."

"I don't mind," I say as I knock one of the longer pipes into place. When I catch Roger's eyes, I give him a grin and decide to pull out some of the slang I've picked up. "It's good craic."

"That we are." He barks a laugh. "I trust Danny's showed you a pleasant time 'round town since you got here."

"Yup." I play it cool while my disloyal cheeks warm up.

"Good lad, he is. We lucked out that Cara's friend for life is someone like him. Being her stepfather means I watched him grow up too."

I guide the conversation away from Aidan, since I don't know how much longer I can think about him or talk about him without kicking my feet like a school-girl. "Did you grow up in town?"

"No, Dublin. M'parents ran a cleaning business, and I went into finance. Consistent work, reliable, but nothing special about it. Then I had a stroke in my late thirties, and that was a wake-up call." He holds his hand out for another piece of PVC pipe from me. "So I moved to Ballygrá on a whim. Met Evvie. Never looked back on the fast-paced city life, and it was the best decision I ever made."

"Did you know anyone here?"

"Not a soul. Since I could hold a job, my life had been: wake up, go to work, drink, and sleep." As he says this, I nod, relating a little too much. "So I thought to myself, Dublin's not going anywhere. Why not do something different? Perhaps I'd end up back in the same place. Perhaps I'd meet the love of my life."

Yasmine walks in the front door as Roger and I talk, three people trailing behind her—a couple about Evvie and Roger's age and a man who shares the same facial features as Yasmine. She introduces me to her parents and brother, and they all make their rounds of hellos, giving everyone a hug and a kiss on the cheek.

"Thank you so much for this," she tells me. "No chance we could do this without you."

"Alright, I'm here and ready to work." Aidan shuts the door behind him, and my heart skips a few beats.

"Saved the best task for last," Cara announces.

"Thank you for working so hard on this, babe." Yasmine stands behind Cara, wrapping her long tan arms around Cara's waist. "Oh, you really did, didn't you?"

"Wanna get it over with?"

"No." Yasmine groans. "But we need to."

"Seating chart it is."

"You've done that weeks ago, haven't you?" Evvie asks.

"We did, but see." Her daughter holds up a makeshift drawing of the reception and table arrangements. "We can't seat the O'Sullivans and the Byrnes together. They'd murder each other after what happened at the farmers market last month. And over here, we've got Johnny and Marie at the same table, but they broke up last week."

"How many times is that now?" Yasmine's mother asks as she rolls her eyes.

"On-again, off-again," Roger explains to me out of the side of his mouth.

"Alright, let's do this." Cara arranges some numbered sticky notes on the table, assigning Evvie and Yasmine's family to different ones. "Rodg, we'll need your help too, to make sure we don't seat any mortal enemies near each other."

"Backdrop's assembled, so I'm happy to." Roger walks under the archway dividing the living and dining rooms, stopping at the seat Cara's in. "Aidan, can you help June with decorating it?"

My knees morph into cooked spaghetti noodles. After avoiding Aidan for the past twenty-four hours, I can't escape him now.

And as much as I want to avoid him, I also don't. He looks cool and collected, the same way he did when he led me through the crowded pub in Dublin, and when he stood on the stage to tell that story. He's the complete opposite of how I feel inside, and his casual attitude only makes me want him more.

Aidan brings over a bag of long pieces of silk fabric and joins me by the PVC frame. "Looks good."

"Thanks." I know he's talking about the backdrop, but my cheeks still get toasty. "The genius of Roger, who came up with the plans and construction. I'm just the assistant."

This is the first time we're seeing each other since yesterday, and I can't catch my breath. We're far enough from Cara and everyone else that we could have our own private conversation, but also, what could I say? *Not sure about you, but my brain nearly imploded from that kiss. You know the one, right? The one I definitely haven't been thinking about nonstop since I saw you.*

"So how's all of this"—I wave to the bag of fabrics and then the freshly assembled frame—"supposed to go on this?"

"Easy." He takes one ribbon and ties it to the top of the backdrop, demonstrating how the delicate fabric should dangle and skim the floor. "It'll look sharp on camera with the different colors. Oh, hey. Your favorite." Aidan holds up a strip of woodland berry fabric and grins, and I'm pretty sure I turn the exact same shade.

"Can we talk?" I keep my voice low, although I doubt anyone else would catch our conversation. The discussion at the table hasn't reached explosive status yet, but they've hit a few colorful disagreements on who should sit where. You'd think they were engaged in a high-stakes game of *Risk*.

"I'm sorry about yesterday," he says, keeping his attention on tying the silks. "You don't need to explain yourself."

"Don't apologize."

"I shouldn't have put you in a position like that. I've thought about yesterday all day. To assume that..." Genuine worry has stitched itself into Aidan's brow.

"Aidan, you were a perfect gentleman." I touch his forearm and I might combust. "Really."

"Then...I don't understand what happened. You asked to leave so quickly after."

I think about the kiss, and my insides tug in opposite directions—what a perfect kiss and what terrible timing. "I got kind of in my head."

"Was the kiss that awful?"

"No." I laugh, loving how he knows what to say to take the tension out of a situation. "It definitely wasn't that."

"Good." Aidan seems to light up knowing that I most certainly did not dislike our kiss. He gives me a lopsided grin, and damn him for being so handsome. "Then what—"

"You two!" Cara's voice shocks me, and I let my hand fall from Aidan's arm. Cara walks over to inspect our waterfall of fabric strips. "That looks fab! Love this."

Aidan's heated gaze lingers on me, but no one seems to notice. While I'd love to continue this conversation, we can't. Not here, not now.

Everyone praises our work. They've sorted out the seating chart, and Cara ticks the last item on the list. All that's left is to gather in the living room for a celebratory drink.

"Here you go, dear," Evvie says as she scoots over on the couch to make room for me in between her and Roger. When I sit down, Roger puts an arm around my shoulder and squeezes. Whatever just happened at that backdrop surrounds my night in a warm glow, and sitting between Cara's parents grounds me in a space of safety and security.

"Thank you, everyone," Cara says as she holds up her beer. "So glad to have all that done."

"And thank you for the free labor," Yasmine adds with a smirk, sneaking in a pet for Winnie.

Roger balks. "I'll be on the lookout for my paycheck in the post, you two."

Evvie reaches over me to playfully smack his thigh, and I snuggle into the comfort of it all—being surrounded by these wonderful people. We lounge and talk and drink and laugh, and I ignore the creeping concern that maybe my best friend is right. Maybe I am lying to myself most of all.

Chapter Seventeen

Aidan

"Take care of her, will you?"

"I'll be fine." Cara kisses Yaz and hops into the front seat of my car.

"We'll be on our best behavior," I say out the window with my hand up in a solemn swear.

"And you," Yaz says, pointing at her future bride. "One, I love you, and—"

"Love you more."

"Two, don't let Naomi chew poor Danny up and spit him out. We need him on Saturday."

I groan and drive back to mine, where everyone will gather before the festivities. Naomi has always been the wildest of Cara's cousins, and a few drinks in, I'll have to protect myself from her wandering hands. I wouldn't want anyone getting the wrong impression.

"Ready for one of your last nights as an unmarried woman?"

"Absolutely," Cara says. "Can't wait to see my favorite people before this weekend. It'll be good, yeah?"

"The hen do?"

"No, the wedding. I've no doubt about tonight, it's Saturday I'm thinking of."

Cara can't mean she's considering backing out. But my unflappable best friend may have nearly reached her limit, and it's my responsibility to remind her why all this stress is worthwhile.

"You told me after your third date with Yaz that you would marry her," I point out. "There was never a question that you'd end up here, so how could it not turn out amazing?"

"A lot of ways, Dan. I still have plenty of time for a massive zit to pop up on my face. The food could taste terrible. It could rain. Gran will be there, so who knows what she might utter under her breath during the ceremony. This weekend is essentially hundreds of people coming to see me on one of the most important days of my life."

"It'll be grand."

"Thank you." Cara blows the air out of her chest. I've never seen her this nervous—she's normally so self-assured. "Not sure what I'd do without you. So what's happening tonight?"

"Surprise."

"Oh, c'mon."

I pinch my thumb and forefinger together and run them along my lips to zip my mouth closed.

"Christ. I told you to keep it simple. At least tell me you didn't go with strippers."

"How'd you know?"

"Danny!" She laughs and play-punches my arm.

Cara had the most nonchalant attitude toward her hen do—quite a surprise, since she arranged so many specific details for her wedding. I suspect she wanted to avoid inconveniencing me, but I'd do anything for her. She accommodates other people all the time, myself included. She deserves this night, especially after months and months of planning, and I stuck to her request and kept the plan as uncomplicated as possible.

When we walk into the house, June is teetering on the edge of a chair while taping up some balloons. She's gorgeous, even with the crooked hair part and a sheen of sweat forming on her forehead.

"Looks good." I swallow, my throat coated in sand. "The decorations."

"Thanks. You left the list out on the counter, and I figured setting up was the least I could do."

"I appreciate it."

She steps down and stares at me almost expectantly, but I've no clue what to say.

"You two're acting strange." Cara waves a pointer finger between the two of us as my heartbeat stalls. Am I that obvious? "June, be honest, is nudity part of the plan?"

"What?" She bubbles out a laugh.

"How about you stop trying to guess what I planned for tonight and just relax and enjoy? No exotic dancers. Promise. "

"Fine." Cara purses her lips into a little pout. "Seriously, if all we do is sit around and drink here, I'll be ecstatic. This is already such a special night." She waves at the minimal decorations and pulls us into a group hug, kisses me on the cheek, and then does the same to June before grabbing the last of the balloons to blow up.

I take a vegetable tray from the fridge while June sets out plastic cups for drinks. We maneuver around each other like we're dancing, with me clumsy and unsure of the steps. I'm trying to ignore this person who I simply can't ignore. There's a charge in the air between us, an electric shock waiting to happen. Deciphering flirtatious interactions has never been a strength of mine, and I need to remind myself that those glances, coy smirks, all of it—they don't mean that June wants a replay of the other evening, no matter if she liked our kiss or not. She said herself that she doesn't do commitment, so the flirtation might be enough to satisfy her.

As the first guests arrive, I push away visions of satisfying June the way I'd really like to. Elisa and Thom show up first—they work at the restaurant that employed Cara until she opened her own place. Behind them comes Marta, Cara's mentor from college, who has a cast on her right arm but told me that wouldn't stop her from attending. And then, of course, Naomi appears. She glides in and undresses me with her eyes, an uncomfortable move nobody misses except for Cara's other cousin, Ingrid. Ingrid is nineteen and disinterested in pretty much everything, save for her mobile.

"Okay everyone," I announce. "Before the drinking, we've got to gear up."

"Oh dear." Cara's elation overshadows the bit of trepidation in her voice as I pass out mystery bags. She opens up her tote and pulls out the attire with a delighted giggle. "Wow. Just...wow." She puts the eggshell-white boilersuit against her body. "Industrial chic. Is this Ghostbusters cosplay?"

"They've our names on them," Marta chimes in as Elisa wriggles the full-body suit over her clothes. "Such a nice touch."

Cara's is white, while the rest of us have—what else?—woodland berry.

"You said no typical hen party stuff, and while I know you would've been game for anything, these are, in fact, practical for tonight's activities."

With the driver arriving in ten minutes, everyone changes, and I top off the drinks. Elisa's suggestion of the boilersuits was genius, and I tell her so. They add the right amount of silliness to a night that Cara asked us not to take too seriously. And although they are built for utility, my breath still hitches when June walks out in hers. Somehow she makes a unisex work suit unbelievably sexy.

We gather in the living room, cups prepared for toast.

"Cara," I start. "You are exceptional. One of a kind. We are all lucky to know you and love you and watch you marry Yaz on Saturday." A few hushed *awwws* pass through the group, and even Ingrid stops her scrolling. "And while you might be a bit mad for opening a business and planning the largest wedding Ballygrá has seen this century, tonight is all about the craic." Cara covers her face with her hands in a poor attempt to hide her embarrassment. "We love you dearly. To Cara."

All of us knock our glasses together with a cheer.

With a mellow glow from the alcohol—including the shots Naomi insisted we all take—we make our way outside where the car pulls up. June goes to grab something from her room while Naomi lingers by the door, eyeing me like a lonely cat looking for attention.

"All set?" I ask, hoping to prompt her to the car, but she reaches out to give my biceps a generous squeeze.

"Whenever you are," she purrs. After taking in my blank expression, she cackles. "I'm joking, Danny. Don't worry, I'll keep my hands to myself, I promise. You're just so easy to tease, it's adorable. Can't help it. And you look downright dangerous in this whole getup. Don't you think?"

She directs the question not to me, but to June, who's emerged from the hall. Her eyes bulge wide, like she's witnessing a private moment between me and Cara's cousin. I might crumble underneath June's gaze, and I've no idea what to say to ensure she doesn't get the wrong idea.

"Isn't he a certified snack?" Naomi asks her while pinching my arm.

"Yeah," she says as a rosy hue floods her cheeks. "You're, uh, wearing the hell out of that jumpsuit."

Before I can process a response or react to the painfully gorgeous way she's biting her bottom lip, Thom approaches. "We're all settled in. Anything else to bring?"

"No," I reply.

"Alright then! Let's go have a helluva night."

The look on Cara's face when we pull up to the ropes course tells me I've done a smart job planning. She yelps with joy and bounces in her seat. "I've wanted to do this from the day they opened!"

"Thought you might go for it."

No more than thirty minutes outside of town is a private patch of land that someone purchased and turned into a high ropes attraction last year. The course zigzags through a lush canopy of trees, with intimidating platforms, cables, and nets hovering up high, but Cara adores thrills like this. The setup hovers at least ten meters above the ground, with an array of dangling bits and bobs. There are car tires, shaky ladders, and obscenely narrow walkways.

"This looks class!" Elisa remarks, keeping everyone's spirits high, despite the quiver in her voice.

"It'll be a little more interesting with this." Naomi winks and flashes the leather-bound flask in her bag.

"Anything for our bride," Thom says, swiping the container for a gulp.

Ingrid could not be more unenthused, smacking bubble gum while she's plastered to her mobile in the backseat. June looks the opposite, her gaze glued to the treetops in awe.

"Oh, wait!" Cara cries out as the van driver parks in the gravel lot. "Marta, what about your arm?"

"Don't mind me. I'll enjoy from the ground. It's your day, and like Thom said, anything for you."

"Could you take photos?" Elisa asks.

"Is that our instructor?" June points to the strapping young man headed our way, who looks like a stallion. My face falls in disappointment while everyone else watches him, their mouths hanging open. It's my luck we'd get paired with the fittest man in the country.

"Ooh, I will climb every one of his ropes," Thom says with a gasp.

Almost everyone erupts into giddy laughter as the muscular man opens the sliding door.

"Hello, and welcome to the County Kerry Ropes Course." His bold Aussie accent and movie-star smile hush the van in a heartbeat. "Are you the five-thirty reservation for Cara?"

We nod, and he thrusts a fist to the sky. "Right on. I'm Roddy, and I'll be accompanying you on the trials today. Let's get rockin' and rollin'."

After watching a safety briefing and signing away our lives with the liability waiver, we suit up in harnesses. Marta collects everyone's phones, much to Ingrid's dismay, and juggles them as best as she can with a cast. Roddy explains the unique challenges we'll face in the sky, starting with a skinny rope bridge, and then some more complicated ones, ending with a zip line. As a group, we ascend a staircase, which spirals around a thick tree trunk. When I reach the top platform, Marta looks like an ant down below.

"Okay, bride first. And remember what I said before: you're attached to a harness, so if you fall, you don't have to worry. We'll all laugh at you, obviously." Roddy recites his go-to script, but he does a decent job of painting the delivery with humor. "But once you've stopped swinging from side to side, I'll come out and help get you back up on the ropes."

Cara teeters across the narrow bridge of dodgy-looking wooden slats, and when she gets about halfway, Roddy motions for someone else to step up. Ingrid glides with the nimbleness of a squirrel, while Naomi wobbles and giggles every step of the way. Elisa waves down below, shouting for Marta to take her photo while she poses.

While adjusting her feet for the camera, Elisa missteps, and her body darts toward the ground. I can almost feel the rope as it jerks back up with an aggressive tug, leaving her bobbing and screeching while her legs wriggle and writhe.

"Ohmygod." June's hands fly to cover her mouth as she looks on, horrified. "Is she okay?"

"She'll recover," I say, giving June some comfort. "I'm sure it happens all the time."

"I'll be right there! Don't panic," Roddy yells, stepping into Superhero Mode. With lithe movements, he
clips himself into the safety rope with his carabiner and
jogs across the bridge to help her back up.

"Wait." Thom gives the rest of us on the platform a
sideways glance. "That's what happens when you fall?"

"Not as bad as it looks, I'm sure." I pat him on the
shoulder. "She'll be able to finish the course, no problem."

"I'm fine, I'm fine," Elisa calls out, sounding like she's
reassuring herself more than us.

"Oh, I will be *more* than fine," Thom says.

I follow Thom's eyeline to Roddy and Elisa. Roddy
is a regular Tarzan, wrapping his ripped arms and
masculine hands around her waist to hoist her up. She's
clinging to his body for dear life. When Thom's turn
to walk comes, he flings himself from the center of
the bridge. As Roddy assists him, I look toward June,
who has stayed mostly quiet since we got up here. Her
eyes have gone all distant, and I catch her muttering to
herself.

"Something wrong?" I ask.

"No. Maybe. Check back later." She looks at me like
a frightened rabbit.

"I'll be right behind you."

"Mhmm. Yup."

"All right, we ready and rarin' to go?" Roddy asks, floating onto our platform while clapping in anticipation.

Cara and the group *Woo!* from the other end of the bridge. June lets out an uneasy sound under her breath and takes three wary steps, like a toddler walking for the first time. Even from a distance, her knuckles turn white from their vise grip on the side ropes. Everyone cheers for her with each minor advancement, and halfway across, she becomes visibly more comfortable. Any major wobbles stop her in her tracks, but once she regains her balance, she continues.

The course progresses, and each section has Elisa pausing for a photo, Thom diving to require a rescue from Roddy, and Ingrid putting us all to shame. June must be dreaming of putting her feet back on the ground, and she takes twice as long as everyone else, but she looks pleased with herself every time she shuffles onto the safety of the next platform. After each round, she has these intensely red cheeks—perhaps from embarrassment, perhaps from sheer exertion—and I ignore how the sight makes my outfit tight in certain places.

We make it through all but the final rope bridge—a series of narrow dangling platforms that lead to the start of the zip line. Once June has gotten halfway,

Roddy gives me the go-ahead, but I catch up in no time. She's become a statue a third of the way from the end.

"Almost there," I speak softly so as not to spook her.

"I can't move my legs."

"You're doing great."

"Has anyone ever died here?" Her voice rattles. "I don't mean by falling. Just right here, this exact spot?"

"Unlikely."

"Okay, well I'm going to be the first then."

"How we doin' out there?" Roddy calls from the deck behind us.

"Um," I yell back, unsure how immobile June is.

"Please." June begs from between clenched teeth. "I need to get off this thing."

"Look ahead, and take tiny steps."

"I can't walk this on my own. The other ones, sure. But this one..." She makes a sound between a groan and a whine, and I'd wrap her up and carry her on my shoulders if I could. "This is impossible."

Instead, I take a hesitant step toward her, getting so close that my toes brush up against her heels. The shift forces her to tighten her death grip on the ropes and crouch down in fear. Below, Roddy's climbing up the stairs of the next tree to help from the other side. "We'll walk together." I place my hands over hers with enough pressure to say, *Don't worry, I've got you.*

The electric current of her skin hums its way up my arms and into my chest.

One vertebra at a time, she straightens, her back pressed against me and her line of sight glued on the grassy patch of earth below.

"Straight ahead," I whisper to her. "You've got this."

"Alright, Mr. Hero!" Cara yells, followed by an *ow-ow!* catcall.

"Me next," Naomi shouts, and they all laugh.

"Not helping," I call out to them, aware of how intimate June and I must appear, with me wrapping myself around her for protection.

"Is this a bad time to mention I'm afraid of heights?" She lets out a razor-sharp exhale and I squeeze her hands. "Ohmygod I'm so nauseous. It's probably a bad time."

"You didn't have to climb up here if you didn't want to."

"Wish you'd said that sooner. Everyone kept saying *anything for the bride*, and I thought I could handle it."

"You can. One step at a time." I keep my voice quiet and soothing like it's just the two of us and nothing else. "Don't think about the end, just get through this and know that I've got you."

We baby-step closer to the other end. I keep my breathing even and my steps in line with June's, like we're moving as one. I'm in tune with her, homing in on every movement of her body and every curve and line of her, and I'd love to rip this boiler suit off her and get more familiar with them.

"That's it." Roddy's outstretched hand comes into my sight line, and I look up to see everyone in full view of this private moment of physical peril. He reaches for June while everyone else has eager faces clocking our every footstep forward. The second June's feet hit the platform, they all burst into raucous applause. Sheepishly, she grins at them before looking at me to say thanks.

That undeniable pull from when we were at the castle roots me in place. I can't keep toeing the line with whatever I feel between us. Her body near mine has made me lightheaded, and I catch myself overanalyzing her every word and action with me. But I don't know what to believe, or what I've merely led myself to believe.

"Great teamwork there." Roddy claps yet again with pure pep. He leads us to the other side of the platform. "So how're we doing? Ready for something different? Zip-line time, baby!"

When we make our way down to the end, Cara stands near me as we remove our gear. She locks eyes with me, then darts her gaze toward June and back to me.

I shake my head, scowling. *Don't know what you're on about.*

One of her brows shoots to the sky, and my blood pressure spikes. Cara can see what's going on—she's known me for ages, and she knows what I'm like when I fancy someone. Of all the someones I could choose, I've engaged in a flirty back-and-forth with her new sister—during a time when I should be putting all my focus on Cara.

"Hey," she whispers and nudges me with her elbow, which brings me down to earth. She gives me a nod of approval with one hand in a fist, the thumb sticking up.

I pause, making certain I understand her correctly. "You sure?" I whisper back.

Yes, she mouths. Then, for good measure, she quietly adds, "Don't be an eejit."

"Thanks," I scoff. I roll my eyes at her, but my lips coiling up give me away. Cara's essentially given me her blessing—which means I need to talk to June, and I can't do it soon enough.

Marta returns our phones, and Thom and Naomi chat up Roddy. Cara and a few of the others go to check out the gift shop. Aside from Ingrid, who scrolls through her mobile on a bench as if this is any other day, we all seem to vibrate from the adrenaline.

"I'll never, ever do that again." June removes her harness and headgear. The helmet has given her this halo of frizzy, damp hair. "I think I'll be nauseous for the rest of my life."

"You did well. And you've got a little—" I motion to my head to mirror her.

"Oh. Thanks." As June uses her fingers to style the strands into place, her expression flips in an instant from gratitude to something else. Her eyes widen, and her face drains of color. "Oh god." Before I can ask what's wrong, she twirls around, leans into a nearby shrub, and retches.

Chapter Eighteen

Juniper

Aidan rattles off a drink order to the woman behind the bar and turns to me. "And what else?"

"Ginger ale, please." The promise of a bubbly, spicy soda calms my belly. After hurling the contents of my stomach into a bush, I feel better, but not enough to tempt the fate of my insides with any kind of alcohol.

And Aidan, of all the people from our group, held my hair back while I puked. Maybe I should thank my guts for turning me into the most unattractive human being in the world. Aidan can run off with Naomi or whoever he wants, because after getting sick in front of him, there's no way he'd want anything more intimate than what we've already shared. Aidan's probably the nicest, most well-intentioned man I've ever kissed.

He deserves better, plain and simple.

And yet, memories of his breath in my hair and his hands over mine muddle my brain. I keep having very stupid, very sexy thoughts about him. Like how, even in the equivalent of a worker's onesie, he is the hottest guy here. He's rolled up the sleeves, and the sight of his forearms alone is some twisted form of foreplay.

"What's everyone going to sing?" I ask, flipping through a notebook.

"ABBA," Cara replies without hesitation. She flips through the enormous songbook, which is so thick it could double as a lethal weapon, while Elisa and Thom peer over her shoulder. "Or Queen."

"Whitney Houston," Thom declares and races to scribble down his choice on the request paper. "The only appropriate answer."

The ginger ale makes me a new woman, and I find exactly the song that a night like this calls for. Meanwhile, a despondent man leans on a stool while belting out "Someone Like You" by Adele. His key is off, but the emotion plays across his face so viscerally that he appears close to tears. Onlookers, bathed in the bar's blue- and purple-tinted lights, sing along with abandon.

"Aidan." Naomi's voice has dropped a few octaves. "We should do a duet. 'Love Shack'?"

My ears perk up for his response. I don't have any reason to get jealous over how handsy Naomi is with him—besides, Aidan can sing a song with whoever he wants—but dread swirls inside me at the thought of him with someone else. Anyone else. I wish I could do our kiss at the castle over.

If she and I weren't related, you wouldn't care?

Suppose not. You wouldn't be here, though, would you?

Those words caused all my insecurities and concerns over the DNA test to bubble to the surface. I closed myself off to him, even though that's the last thing I want.

"Hate to break it to you." Aidan situates himself on a stool, so uninterested in karaoke that he won't acknowledge the notebooks' existence. "I'm no singer."

"Karaoke's not about talent," I say, inserting myself into their conversation.

"Exactly." Naomi pats him on his muscular thigh. "You need *passion*."

"And some alcohol, depending on how well you sing," Thom adds, lifting his wine glass up to the sky.

Our karaoke crew does not disappoint. Elisa and Thom win the crowd over with a gender-swapped duet from *Grease*, Marta defies her injury and dry-humps the stage in the raunchiest rendition of "Super Freak" possible, and Naomi settles on a drunk young stranger to join her for "Love Shack." And while Ingrid has kept her lips zipped tight for most of the evening, she makes us all look like amateurs while she belts out Sia's "Chandelier" to perfection.

After Cara finishes "Dancing Queen," the host calls up "The Future Mrs. and Company." I squeal and jump off my stool, spilling the last dregs of my ginger ale. While I am not made for climbing trees fifty feet in the air, I know how to do a night out right. "That's us!"

"Us?" Aidan's eyes bulge in surprise.

"A *group* song?" Cara looks like she might implode from booze and happiness. "Brilliant."

"Come on." I grab Aidan by the arm as everyone else heads toward the stage.

"You're really going to make me sing, aren't you?"

"I won't force you. But you are technically the 'and Company' part."

He digs his heels in and pulls me closer to whisper-yell over the crowd through his panic. "Getting up in front of people to tell a story from my childhood is one thing, but karaoke is another. I am *terrible*."

"Mouth the lyrics and let Ingrid do all the work." I shrug, backing away from him and toward the rest of our group. "Your call."

By this point, not only are Cara and everyone on stage beckoning him forward, but the entire bar has broken out into a chant of *Sing! Sing! Sing!* If he decides not to join us, the crowd might boo him out of the place.

He suppresses a smile and holds up his hands in defeat. "Anything for the bride."

Aidan follows me to one of the mics as everyone claps—and once we start, nothing could have prepared this tiny bar in Cork for the force that is all of us performing Spice Girls. It only takes a few notes into the intro before Aidan sings along, and by the second verse, he must realize that nobody will hear his singing voice, anyway. The entire bar joins the refrain for "Wannabe," belting out lyrics about lovers and friends.

Even without a single ounce of alcohol in my body, this has to be one of the most fun nights out I've ever had in my life. I forget about DNA tests and assignments at *The Edge* and all the complications that led me to Ireland. Instead, I enjoy being here, surrounded by people who are all here for the same person.

Cara dances around the stage, giving wet, sloppy kisses on the cheek to all of us, as the song concludes to boisterous applause. She's blissfully happy, and some corner of my mind wants to believe that's in part because of me.

"Thank you," she yells as she leans toward me. "This is honestly—"

She loses her balance and lands butt-first on the ground, which only makes her tip over with glee and giggles. She stands up and gives a bow to more thunderous claps before we exit the stage.

"Many thanks to that impressive group of off-duty mechanics," the karaoke DJ says. "If any of you need a tire change, just look for the uniforms. Now, next up..."

"Thissiz *the* most incredible night," Cara slurs. "Seersly, I love you all. So. Much."

Elisa tears up, so Cara dives in for a hug. She then pulls Naomi and Ingrid in while wailing over how pretty they are.

"Will she be okay?" I whisper to Aidan as someone sings about two lonely people living in a lonely world. Another patron walks by me on the way to the bar, and I scoot closer to Aidan, keeping my eyes on the stage and not on the long veins and solid muscles of his arms.

"I've seen her worse than this. She's a happy drunk. When some folks get plastered, they get angry or sloppy, but she'll just go 'round telling everyone how much she cares about them. It's like her, times a thousand."

"D'ye mind if I come back to yours, Danny?" she asks as she drapes her arm over his shoulders.

"'Course not."

I don't sense an ounce of reluctance on his end, although he peers at me for a millisecond. To hide any disappointment, I temper my expression. Not having the temptation is a relief, after all. I stow away thoughts of his fresh, cedary scent, the roughness of the scruff on his chin, and the Y-shaped scar on his left hand from my mind.

When we arrive back at Aidan's, Cara prances right inside like she's walking on clouds. I take some cash from my wallet to give our driver an extra-generous tip and head in to find Cara already curled up on the couch and snoring.

"G'night, you angelic wee angels, you," Cara murmurs as Aidan tucks her into his bed.

I place a full cup of water on the nightstand and float back into the hall, not without first looking around Aidan's room. He has a display of framed landscape images on one wall, all in black and white, and a plush velvet armchair in the corner. There's no trace of clothing peeking out from the closet, but some boxes spill out from underneath the bed. Boxes like he hasn't entirely unpacked, like he's halfway ready to go if given the opportunity.

We tiptoe into the living room, which is lit by a couple of dim floor lamps. I don't want to intrude on Aidan's space, seeing as he's the one who has the pleasure of sleeping on the couch, but I can't bring myself to turn in just yet.

"So..." He pauses by the kitchen island. "Safe to say you haven't found your new favorite hobby tonight?"

A loud laugh escapes me, and I muffle the sound with my hand.

"Don't worry," Aidan says. "She's out for the night."

"At least you spared me from the humiliation of Roddy saving me like some damsel in distress."

"Thom didn't seem to mind."

"True. You planned a killer party, minus the heights thing. Cara had a blast, and that's what matters."

"Thanks." Those gorgeous eyes remain locked on me. "Want a drink? We can talk about your speech. Or...if you don't—"

"Yeah, sounds good."

I grab my computer off my bed while he prepares some tea. Back in the living room, the kettle simmers in the background. Once I'm sitting on the sofa and have the document open, Aidan stands behind me. A flush of embarrassment courses through me while I review the notes I have so far.

"It's a work in progress," I say as I tilt the screen his way. After ten seconds, he gives up on reading over my shoulder and sits down next to me, our thighs touching and his arm on the back of the couch.

"Hm." He leans into the cushions. "It's good. Just..."

"You hate it."

"No," he says, chuckling. "The whole thing's very formal. There's nothing wrong with that, but—here, look at mine."

He slips his phone out of one of the many cargo pockets on his jumpsuit. I scan the note he's typed up, laughing at the sweet playground memories he'll share to open the speech. His words turn more vulnerable and heartfelt as he talks about meeting Yasmine for the first time and seeing his best friend find an equal partner.

"You have an unfair advantage with all this shared history." I hold the phone back out to him.

"Just speak from the heart. Doesn't need to be long. You're her sister."

"Half sister." That reminder chips away at some of my joy from the evening. I can't forget that I'm still in DNA limbo, even though life keeps happening, and this wedding date keeps approaching. "And not like half sisters who grew up together. New half sisters. How quickly can you really know someone?"

"Time can help form strong bonds between two people, but that's not the only thing. Sometimes you meet someone and you just...you're sure of it."

I stare at the half-written speech in front of me and hope that Aidan is right.

"With siblings especially, that's an unbreakable connection you have to another person, forever and ever," he continues. "Michael and I weren't the closest, him being six years older than me and all. We fought. I annoyed him to no end. But through all that, and even now that he's gone, I'm still his brother."

I close my laptop and twist my body to Aidan. He's mentioned his brother a few times before, but I don't have the full story. "What happened to him?"

Aidan leans further into the couch like the cushions could protect him. "Car accident. He got behind the wheel after drinking with some of his mates."

"I'm so sorry."

Aidan pauses and clears the thickness in his throat. "He's my brother. And if he were still alive and I were writing some best man speech for him, then I'd have as hard a time as you are now. You can be with someone for a few days, and those few days can be everything, or you can grow up with a person and witness their whole life and never really know them."

"You feel like you didn't know your brother?"

"No, that's not what I mean." He sighs and strokes some of the scruff on his jawline. "I suppose I looked up to him quite a bit, being the younger brother. And dealing with the aftermath of...all of it, I guess, I see him more as a real person. Flawed. This sounds awful, but sometimes I have this intense anger at what he did. He knew better. He had to. We run a pub, and he'd seen how alcohol could ruin people's lives. He didn't think to call me or get a ride with someone else. I love him, and I miss him, but I'm so fumin' at him for what he did." He rubs his eyes with his thumb and forefinger. "I sound fucked up, don't I? Angry at a dead man."

My heart aches at how he beats himself up. I can't relate entirely to his situation, but I've had enough therapy to recognize that what he's going through is complicated.

"Sometimes I think I'm kind of glad I didn't know my mom." I sigh and play with the flap of my leg pocket as my confession comes out. "I never had the chance to really find out who she was as a person. But because of that, I didn't have to see her in the throes of her addiction. I never saw her suffering. And I don't have to know what I lost either. Somehow that's a relief."

My voice has gotten thin, but admitting the ugly truth is liberating. It's like an invisible barrier has come down between us. Almost everyone expects my grief surrounding my mother to be one-dimensional, but the reality of losing someone entails so much more than sadness. I can't be honest about that with many people, but I bet Aidan will understand.

"It doesn't make sense," I go on, "but that's how I feel. Same with you and your brother. So no, you don't sound fucked up at all."

Aidan offers a grateful smile. "Thanks." He clears his throat again and changes the heavy subject to something easier to swallow. "Cara tells me you've time after the wedding. You should drive out to the coast."

"There's a minor detail that you're forgetting," I say. "I don't have a car. Or a driver's license."

"I'd take you. Drive you to see more of the country-side."

A road trip alone with Aidan is everything I need to avoid and everything I desire.

"As tempting as that may be, I don't know if I should go gallivanting around the country with a handsome Irishman."

"I'm handsome?"

I pause. "Very."

We both get impossibly still as we sit too close to each other on this couch.

"June, I'm a bit confused." He scooches away from me, and I despise the space between us. "We kissed, and then I thought you hated me. Now you're flirting with me."

I can see why he'd be confused—I'm confused too—but he's technically the one who put a stop to our kiss before. "You told me you weren't sure how Cara felt about things, and you're right. It probably would be, like, super weird for her."

"I wouldn't be so sure of that."

My head jerks toward him. "You told her?" They're friends, and he has every right to talk to her about me, but I wish he'd given me a heads-up.

"No. But Cara knows me well. I didn't have to say anything."

"Ah." Some of the tightness in my back dissipates. "What did you not say, exactly?"

He taps his knuckle against the arm of the sofa. "That I like you." It's the most innocent confession, but still, my chest goes all fuzzy. "But what about you? I can't tell if you like me or not, or if you just like the thought of me, or what."

"I do like you," I confess. This isn't some fleeting attraction to some guy I'll forget in the morning. Aidan is a fire, and I stand close enough to get burned. "How could I not?"

"I sense a *but* somewhere after that."

I pull my knees into my chest and curl into the corner of the couch for protection as I decide what to say.

But I might not be who you think I am.

But I might *be.*

But I don't know what to do with all these feelings I have for you.

"But I'm a mess," I manage.

"So'm I, in case you haven't noticed. My brother, my parents, school, the pub—everything." He laughs to himself. "I'm a wreck."

He chuckles again, and I can't help but smile.

"Yeah," I say. "You kind of are."

"We're complete disasters."

"You're right." My giggles grow, and soon, we're both cracking up, snickering and shushing the other person so we don't wake Cara. After some shared laughter, the energy in the room fizzles, and the only sound left is that of the kettle heating. Aidan smiles, catching my gaze from the corner of his eyes.

"I like you," he says in a voice so gentle and yet powerful enough to make my heart splinter. "A lot." Aidan looks at me like no man has looked at me before. I'm bare but safe, and maybe all the moments of my life were leading up to now. All the reasons to keep my distance dissolve into white noise, and all I know is that he's wonderful and unfairly charming, and I really, really want to kiss him again.

I shouldn't. But when his gaze flashes down to my mouth, we gravitate toward each other like two magnets.

Our lips lock, and this is a billion times better than I remember, because this time, I'm not holding back. I drink him in. My hands can't decide on where to roam, because I want to touch every perfect part of him at once. I settle on one palm resting on his neck and the other gripped around his biceps. He pulls me closer, and I hook a leg over his lap so I'm straddling him.

He smells spicy and warm and like he's been waiting for me his whole life.

"Is this a bad idea?" he murmurs into my mouth.

"Terrible."

"You're right."

"It's awful," I pant.

"Brilliant."

Before, our kiss was slow and careful. This? This is unknown territory. Our tongues explore each kiss with fervor, and oh my god, is he an even better kisser than I thought. He puts his mouth on mine like I'm the only thing in this world that matters. Thoughts escape me as I take in every part of his body. His stiff erection presses against my groin, and the pressure heats me up from the inside. I pat around on his back to find some kind of way to lift his shirt, because I need my skin on his, but we're both wearing jumpsuits. My exploration is redirected to his front, to his chest, which—*wow*—and I undo the top button.

The kettle chooses the worst time possible to whistle. Aidan lifts me off and races to the stove, but the noise has tugged Cara from her sleep. She enters the room with sleepy eyes and yawns.

"Oh, Dan, I'd love some tea."

I wipe my mouth and pull out my phone as a distraction.

"I'll bring it to you," he tells her, pouring hot water into the cups.

"Amaaaazing," she sings as she pads back into the bedroom.

"Here." He carries two teacups over, and I stand, taking one from him. His lips are swollen from making out, and his cheeks flushed, same as mine. "I should go play nurse and make sure she's okay."

Breathless and wordless, I nod. *What the hell am I doing? How am I going to say no to him?* The simple answer is: I can't. Logic means nothing anymore, and my head officially can't get through to my heart.

"I hope you sleep well, June." Then he brings his lips to my ear, warming them with an invitation. "And think more on taking that road trip with me, will you?"

Chapter Nineteen

Aidan

I don't need an alarm clock because someone walks in and slams my front door shut at—Christ, six in the morning?

"Nggh?" I blabber into my pillow as I crack one eye open.

"Did I wake you?" My best friend has many talents, but closing doors quietly is not one of them. I've little hope of returning to my slumber, but once I catch an intoxicating whiff of ham-and-cheese *jambon* pastries, I'm willing to forgive and forget.

"Why're you up now? And how?"

"Body's used to waking up at five," she says, carving out a spot on the couch by my shins. "Oof, my head."

"You have fun?"

"Best night of my life, just behind when Yaz proposed. The ropes course? Brilliant."

"Karaoke."

"Those outfits." She pats me on the leg since I still have mine on.

"Glad you enjoyed it."

"Thanks for letting me stay here. Hope I didn't crash a wild after-party." She waggles her brows at me.

"I don't kiss and tell."

Her breath catches. "You kissed?"

"Who's asking?"

"Me," she says, poking me in the ribs. "I'm asking."

"Let me eat my pastries in peace."

I grab one of the bite-sized pastries and glare at her, because there's no way I can hide this from my best friend if I tried. Her face bursts into sunshine, and she lets out a hushed squeal, shaking me into the couch.

I would've loved to jump into bed with June and explore her body more—and let her hands work more of their magic—but my kettle acted as a savior in some ways. June's still a guest in my home. If she wants to continue what we started last night, then we can, but I don't want to pressure her.

"Hey," June says from the hall.

"Shite, I woke you too," Cara says.

June's morning voice is subdued, but it could catch my attention from an ocean away. Even in a rumpled old T-shirt and sweatpants, she's a vision. She stands partially obscured by the shadows in the hallway, and her expression is bashful, like last night's emotional closeness was somehow more revealing than sex for her. I wish I could capture her in this moment with my camera.

She joins us in the living room, sitting down in the recliner at the end of the coffee table. I've never been able to play laid-back when it comes to love, so I pass her the platter of pastries and accidentally drop three. She eats while the bride-to-be gushes more about the hen do, and I relish every moment I notice June noticing me.

"I got us nail appointments for the afternoon, but before then, I was wondering if you'd help me assemble the welcome baskets. Putting those goodies together has taken me longer than I expected, but with you and Yaz, we should finish in no time."

"No problem," June says.

"All the supplies're at your place?" I ask.

"Mhmm. But you, sir, have done more than your fair share for this wedding already." Cara pops another *jambon* in her mouth and speaks through the flaky, cheesy goodness. "Consider today your day off. We're due for some girl time."

Cara's day-of coordinator, Stevie, appeared talented and attentive on paper, but she made it clear that she doesn't go on the clock until the day before the wedding. Aside from her occasional check-ins and advice via text, Cara and Yaz have been in charge until the sun came up this morning. Granting me a break from the madness just means time away from June. She already has so few days here, and if given the choice, I'd like to take all the time I can.

"What you could use," I say, "is some help with the baskets."

"What?" June asks through a *jambon*. "Afraid we'll gossip about you?"

"Yes. That's precisely what will happen." Both of them talking about me—the thought puts a smirk on my face. "Insufferable, you two."

Cara and June share a glance and giggle. Seeing them so in tune with each other opens something inside of me—like going through the house and finding a room that didn't exist before. It's new and different and nice, and it makes me want to fill that room with furniture, get comfortable, and stay awhile.

My best friend gets her way. The two of them depart after we've consumed every last pastry, and Cara texts me shortly afterward.

> CARA: Enjoy some relaxation! Big weekend coming up, and I've a feeling you'll need your energy!!!

This is followed by three lines full of winking emoji.

Restlessly, with nowhere in particular to go or anything to do until the rehearsal, I decide to pull the SD card from my camera, offload my work onto a hard drive, and jump into editing. June planted a seed of a decent idea. My days would look like this if I went freelance or started submitting my portfolio places. I've been set on restarting postgrad, but what if I just did the work that I loved to do? No more sitting around and waiting. And no more pub.

But I don't know what that would mean for Mam and Da.

I sift through photos from the other evening and admire what I captured. June's fresh footprints in the muddy field. June's hand dragging along the weary stone. June marveling at the massive half-destroyed castle in front of her.

Shite. My heart's in a freefall. The sensation terrifies me, and I love it.

The images represent some of my better work. I crop them, alter the white balance, and bump up the shadows to perfect the shots. At some point—minutes or hours later, I've hardly any concept of time when editing—my phone chirps again.

> JUNE: Behold, the bridal baskets!

> JUNE: Also these things are HEAVY. I am getting in a serious workout

A selfie of her smiling and holding a gargantuan gift basket fills my phone screen. A selfie. She hasn't sent me any photos of herself before, and I simmer with satisfaction knowing that she's thinking about me.

> AIDAN: Looks gorgeous

> AIDAN: The baskets are nice too

The second I hit send, I groan.

> JUNE: Wooooooow, that is perhaps the cheesiest text in the history of texting

> AIDAN: Admittedly not my finest

> AIDAN: Sure I can't help out over there?

> JUNE: You're under strict orders not to enter the premises

> AIDAN: Fine, I'll keep working on these

I send her a picture I'm editing, and she replies with a string of colorful emoji.

> JUNE: Omg this is soooo good

> JUNE: You really should let me introduce you to some of my photog friends

I take in a fortifying breath. There's no harm in a simple chat with them. My fingers hover over the screen before I type out a thumbs-up.

AIDAN: Sure, ty

JUNE: Of course

She sends me another photo of her, this time without a colossal wedding basket. The sight of her smiling coyly at the camera, only for me, makes me catch my breath.

AIDAN: I can't wait to see you again

Thinking of her has made my pants impossibly tight, so I adjust myself and stare at my computer, willing myself to get more edits done. Not a chance. This erection won't go away, especially if all I'm doing is looking through photos of the woman I'd like to pin down on my mattress.

I need a cold shower, or a release. Leaning back in my chair, I close my eyes and let my hand drift south while my imagination drifts to what could've happened last night. June felt so good, so right, pressed up against me. My strokes are slight and tentative at first. I've spent so much of my time denying myself these thoughts of her. But my grip becomes firmer, and I speed up, remembering the way her breasts nestled against my chest and how her breath caught in her throat after I latched onto her hips and pulled her against my hardness. I haven't wanted a woman—truly wanted someone—in such a long time, and I stroke with that yearning, burning a bonfire inside me. *Oh, her mouth.* What dirty words I'd love to hear pass through that perfect pair of lips as I get acquainted with every part of her, as I learn what makes her scream into the pillows, as I—

Groaning like a wild animal, I come before the rest of that blissful scenario can play out in my head.

I take the cold shower and remind myself to keep it together. June hasn't given me an answer about the road trip I proposed, so last night might be all we'll ever have. I need to be okay with that and get through the next few days while acting normal and not like a thirsty teenager.

Luckily, when I arrive at the wedding rehearsal, Stevie leaves no room for distraction. She knows her stuff and runs the event like a naval officer, so all my attention goes to where to stand, what to hold, and when to walk. None of it whatsoever goes to daydreaming about removing all of June's clothing with my teeth.

"You." Stevie points to Yasmine's brother and best man, Joseph, who stands opposite me and across the aisle. "Two steps in. And you two. Move half a step and get closer." She points to me and June. When we don't close the gap to her satisfaction, Stevie grabs my shoulder and pushes me forward until June's botanical perfume overtakes me again. I need that scent on me, on my bed, in my car, and on my every belonging. My cock presses up against my fly just being close to her.

Stevie marches around, and once she seems satisfied with her work, she circles one fist in the air. "Cue music!"

The string quartet picks up where they'd paused, and the brides appear at the entrance.

"You're making it hard to focus," I whisper behind June, to which she chortles. Stevie shoots us both a look of death.

"I could say the same about you," June says once Stevie looks back at Cara and Yaz, who have chosen to walk down the aisle hand in hand. "I keep thinking about last night, and tonight, and what you and I might get up to after all the rehearsal stuff."

"Yeah, no clue." I grin, envisioning our mouths together again. "You'll have to enlighten me."

"Sure," June says as she leans back, almost close enough for me to bury my face in her silky hair. "I've got some ideas."

We file out of the coach, and a few groups of people chat while others disperse to call dibs on telescopes. My vision takes its time adjusting to the blackness, which grows gradually less intense. The brides already gave us a rundown of what to expect—grab a drink, follow the pathway with red lighting out to the guides with the telescopes, and don't use your phone.

June nudges my arm with hers. "It's official. We survived the dress rehearsal."

"Stevie doesn't mess around."

"No joke," June says and takes a sip of her wine. "Good company too. At least on my side of the altar."

"Same."

Some people head down the path, and June leans toward me, resting a hand on my upper arm. The move wouldn't seem all that out of place in the daylight, but being shrouded in darkness makes it somehow more personal.

"Okay, I'm really going to need your help here," she says. "Meeting a bunch of Cara's family and friends in the pitch dark is more than a little intimidating."

"How 'bout you tell me first if you and Cara talked about...well?"

"About what?"

"You know."

She sniggers and brings her warmth closer. "You're blackmailing me for information shared in confidence."

"I've a right to know."

"I told her we kissed. Nothing more."

That takes me by surprise, because what we did wasn't *just* kiss. A kiss and nothing more sounds innocent and forgettable.

June tugs on my arm to make me keep up with her pace. "I didn't want to share every detail. I kept it classy. But she is beyond excited."

"Sounds like her."

Cara's selfless. On a weekend that's all about her, she still musters up joy for others.

"Now," June says, "will you help a girl out?"

"Right. Who've you met so far?"

"Aside from Evvie and Roger—"

"And Granny."

"Right, and Granny." She shudders at the mere mention of Cara's gran. "Everyone from the bachelorette. But there are so many other people here."

"Well, those two back there singing by the liquor are Evvie's sister, Auntie Nola, and her husband Connell. They know how to get the party going." I turn from them to face a bickering older couple. "Cara's granny is over there with her granda, doing what they do best. And over there," I jut my chin out straight in front of us, "are Yasmine's godparents, Lena and Antoni. They're sweet."

I rattle through a few more people I can identify by silhouette or sound alone, and then we mingle with godparents, cousins, more aunts and uncles, and other folks who I've known from growing up close to Cara.

We move as a unit down the pathway, and enough red light shines to illuminate her profile. She's beautiful. We're afforded more privacy in the dark, so I can enjoy our time without getting self-conscious. There's no wondering who might see us walking so closely, or what they might think of us arm in arm. Cara knows something's going on—and presumably she's told Yaz—but I'd like to keep every nosy neighbor in Ballygrá out of our business.

As we approach one of the closer telescopes, I inform June that stargazing in the Kerry International Dark Sky Reserve is some of the best in the country. "Not a lot of light pollution," I say, admiring the expanse that overflows with waves of glinting stars. "Look."

"The sky here is bigger than any sky I've ever seen before, if that's possible." Her head tilts straight up where a blanket of midnight blacks and navy blues fold together, freckled with silver dots as far as the eye can see. "And the stars. There are billions of them."

We stop at one of the telescope stations, and the attendant proudly announces that we will get a glimpse of Alpheratz, the brightest star in the constellation Andromeda. June and I take turns examining the glowy, blue halo only ninety-something light-years away.

"Hey you two!" Cara approaches us from behind. "June, you've already met Granny, but I also wanted you to meet my granda."

"What's that?"

"Granda," Cara accentuates her words so he'll hear better. "This is Juniper. Granny met her the other day at the dress fitting."

I can hardly hear Granny's "hello" over the sound of sheer delight that escapes from Cara's grandfather. "Oh! This is Juniper. Orla, this is Juniper."

"Yes, love, we met." Her voice sounds like brittle plastic, but she attempts a partial smile to greet us. Beyond that, she remains silent and keeps to herself. Cara's granda pats June's hand while saying sweet sentiments, like how lucky Cara is to have found her and that she's part of the family now.

"Enough about me," June says, and I sense something strange in her voice. Hesitation? Concern? She must be more nervous than she let on, having to meet people in close to zero visibility. "Are you excited for tomorrow?"

"We very much are."

Granny titters out a cutting laugh.

"Orla," Cara's granda mumbles. "Remember what we agreed—"

"I'm *aware*." She straightens. "I'm allowed concerns, though. When you dream of your little ones or their little ones getting married, you…you hope for the best life for them."

"This is the best, Granny," Cara says with an unsteady voice. "I'm beyond lucky."

This won't go anywhere good. But her gran showed up to the dress fitting and to this, and she'll have her reserved seat in the front row tomorrow. Somewhere in her heart, she's happy about this match. She just needs to keep her mouth shut long enough for her grandchild to get married.

"Orla." I step in to ease the situation like I've done countless times before. "Have you peered through the telescope over there? Let's go have a look together."

Granny releases her grip on her granddaughter's arm, and Cara whispers a *thank you* my way.

We turn to make our escape, and I guide the ticking time bomb that is Granny elsewhere—anywhere away from my best friend. Her gran shakes her head in a feeble back-and-forth. "I really hoped for a real wedding for her. I really did."

"You've got to be kidding me." June's voice, ordinarily breezy and light, stops us in our tracks. Try as I might to lead Granny elsewhere, she's glued her feet to the ground.

"How can you say that about your own granddaughter?" June goes on.

"It's fine," Cara says, letting out an uncomfortable laugh.

"No, it's not," June says directly to Granny. "Why do you act like this?"

The old woman gasps, scandalized. Shite, this is bad.

"Cara is one of the kindest, most incredible people I've ever met. She's your grandchild. Don't you love her?"

"'Course I love her," Granny spits out.

"June, I—" Cara attempts to butt into the conversation, but June keeps going.

"Then why are you letting your own issues and hang-ups stand in the way of an amazing relationship with her? She's marrying Yasmine because Yasmine is wonderful, which you'd understand if you ever talked to her or treated her like a real person. She makes Cara *happy*, which is a lot more than anyone can say about you."

Her tirade happens like a car wreck—it's too fast for me to intervene, and it's painful even though I'm not directly involved. June hasn't yet grasped their knotted-up family dynamics, and a smidge of second-hand embarrassment comes over me. If she'd just let me whisk Gran away, we could return to normalcy for the wedding weekend.

June notices the extra attention from some nearby clusters of guests. Unaffected, she straightens her posture and clutches Cara's elbow. "Come on, let's go."

Cara doesn't budge.

"June," she speaks through a set jaw. "How...how could you say that?"

Granny and Granda turn their backs, facing each other in a tense yet hushed quarrel.

"That's my gran."

"She's being awful, and you—"

"You...that was out of line. You insulted her."

"She insulted you. And Yasmine."

"You can't talk to her like that."

"You're mad at *me*?"

"Yes. Just—" Cara doesn't let June finish. "Just go. I need to clean this up. Go, *please*."

Their conversation ends, and Cara goes to soothe her grandparents. As she ushers them down the path, I'm left with a stunned June. She looks smaller, like she's shrunken into herself, and she waits until the last of the guests who witnessed her outburst go back to their telescopes and discussions.

"I can't believe this," she says.

"Cara's relationship with her granny isn't always the easiest to navigate," I offer. "Granny's...critical. Evvie's talked to her many times about her attitude, but she lacks a filter."

"Why didn't you say something?" Her words cut like paper. June crosses her arms and faces me head-on, her appearance made more menacing by the red lights around us.

"What?"

"You let her grandma talk to her like that all the time. You're her best friend. Or supposed to be."

I don't know where she's going with this, but I lower my tone. "Which is why I wanted to take her gran off to do something else. If you'd let—"

"So you can ignore her comments, as usual? She needs to know what she's doing is wrong, but instead of standing up to her, you were more than happy to remain silent, like you always are, and then I look like the bad guy."

"That's why you're upset?" I keep my voice steady, grinding out each word. "Rather than worry over what people think of you, why not think about what Cara needs?"

"She needs someone on her side."

How bonkers that she's turned this onto me. What more could I have done? I relied on a tried-and-true method of handling Cara's gran. Progress with her granny happens at a glacial pace, but she is coming around, slowly but surely. I'd love to set firmer boundaries with her, but Cara's assured me that this is how she wants it handled.

"You don't get to drop in here and tell people what they should do or how to help their best friend of nearly thirty years. Family is complicated, June. Nothing you'd understand after a week being here."

I despise myself the moment those vicious words come out. I'd swallow them back down if I could, choke on them, but it's too late—they've blown up everything between us.

June takes a step away, and when I reach for her arm, she retracts it like I'm covered in thorns. "No," she says in a trembling voice as she backs up. "Don't touch me." She slips away toward the parking lot and into the empty night.

Chapter Twenty

Juniper

I slink out of Aidan's house on quiet feet in the faint morning light. After our fight last night, I called a cab and shut my bedroom door to the world. Today, I'd like to avoid him as much as possible, which might end up easier than expected. If my hunch is correct, I'm not just going over to Cara's apartment to remind her to grab extra hair pins before we walk to the salon together. She's pissed and probably needs to tell me I'm no longer a guest, and definitely not maid of honor.

And that's fine. It's fine. I'm mad, but it's totally, completely whatever Cara wants because today is her wedding and I won't ruin the day any more for her. *Just go,* she had said. The echo pounds in my head.

But if Cara decides she's upset enough that she wouldn't like me there, then she can at least tell me to my face.

On my walk to her place, I huff and shoot off an annoyed text to Lis.

> JUNE: Hope your Friday went better than mine did

> JUNE: I yelled at Cara's grandmother last night and fought with Aidan and everything is awful

Less than ten seconds later, Lis's name appears on my phone as an incoming call.

"Why are you awake right now?" I ask.

"Crappy date tonight."

"I'm sorry."

"It's all good. I'm on the couch eating junk food and watching *Real Housewives*. But when friends message friends about smack-talking grandmas, it doesn't matter whether it's after midnight or who's fighting on TV, you pick up. Spill."

I relay every infuriating comment Cara's grandma made at the dark sky reserve.

"She's the worst," I say. "Like, a heinous woman to her core. But everyone carries on as if her behavior is normal. They'd rather let her go on treating her own grandchild like she's a mistake."

"Oof, that's rough."

"I blew up at her." When I don't hear any response at the other end, I continue. "And I could have been more subtle, sure. But I'm also the first person who's willing to say what needed to be said. Someone needed to tell her she can't get away with that kind of behavior, right?"

"Mm."

That doesn't sound like an enthusiastic yes at all.

"Do you think..." Lis pauses. "I don't know, do you think how you reacted might have something to do with your relationship with your grandmother?"

"W-wow." Her question makes me falter. "Didn't know I'd be going to therapy right now."

I'd hoped for a laugh from her, but I get silence instead. I feel like I'm staring into a mirror without makeup on, and I can spot each and every flaw.

"Look, her grandmother sounds like a nightmare, I'm with you there. But her grandma isn't *your* grandma. And could they all use some better boundaries? Yeah, probably. But if the truth is your goal here, and I mean this with love, there is still the question of your DNA test. You haven't exactly been forthcoming about that."

I didn't expect her to say *that*. The words suck the confidence out of me.

"You can't compare that with her grandma's snotty comments," I say.

"No, but that should show that sometimes stating the raw, honest truth doesn't make for the best choice." Lis rustles a bag, and the methodical crunch of a potato chip fills the line. "What happened is embarrassing, but—"

"I'm not embarrassed."

"Okay, fine. Did Cara ever tell you how to handle her grandma?"

"No, but—well, once, a little. At her dress fitting, she told me..." *Constant positivity.* Those were Cara's exact words.

And yesterday I acted the total opposite.

"And if you're so sure that she doesn't want you at the wedding—which is a little dramatic, but okay—then why are you walking over there right now?" Lis asks through a mouthful of chips. "Protect your peace and give her space, if that's what you're so sure she wants."

"I can't *not* show up."

"Why?"

"Because I'd upset her, and...I don't want to."

"Again, why?"

"Because!" I yell. "Because I care about her." I let my own words sink in. "Shit."

"Mhmm."

The gravity of last night has pulled me down to earth, and I know one thing for certain: I owe Cara an apology.

I hang up with Lis once I get to Cara's doorstep, and I knock. Then I knock again. "Cara? It's me."

She doesn't open the door, so I pull out the spare key she gave me the day I arrived. The space has three times as much room with all of the wedding supplies gone, which is a good sign, but Cara isn't home, which is a not-so-good sign. Calling her cell goes straight to voicemail. As if the universe aims to taunt me more, Evvie sends me a text to ask if Cara and I would bring an extra comb.

If Cara's not with her mom and she's not here with me, then I have limited guesses of where she could be. Rather than worry Evvie, I call Aidan and feel a tug when he picks up.

"Have you heard from Cara at all?"

"Mmm, sure," he says in a morning voice so rugged and rough I can picture myself curled up beside him in bed. "Sent her and Yaz a text to say congratulations and I'd see her soon."

"But have you actually talked to her? Anytime this morning?"

He must sense my panic, because once I explain what's going on, he arrives minutes later. Aidan has the nerve to look incredible, with his hair the perfect amount of wild and sexy while he wears a simple jeans-and-T-shirt combo.

"Should we call the police?" I ask him. "What if she's hurt? I'm not sure what to do, and I think this is all my fault."

"How is this your fault?"

"Because of last night, obviously."

He shakes his head. "We'll find her. For all we know, she and Yaz planned some secret rendezvous today before the ceremony. She doesn't have a car, so she can't be far."

"Right."

"June, I'm—can I just say, I'm sorry about what I said last night. I didn't—"

"This isn't the time," I say and swallow down the knot in my throat. "Let's find Cara."

Our plan involves phone calls and texts to her close friends and family. We mention nothing that would raise the alarm, but after we get through the shortlist of guests Cara knows best, we have no leads.

"She didn't talk to you?" Aidan rubs his temples when I tell him no.

"Not since last night. Did she say anything to you?"

"Not much. She seemed down. Deflated. And she..." He winces. "She said she was glad to have her place to herself. Said she needed some time alone."

Ouch.

"Well, if she wanted time alone and she's not at home, then she could be literally anywhere else. That doesn't narrow down our options."

He drums his fingers on the kitchen table. "It actually might." His words perk me up. "I've a place in mind."

We leap into the car for a short drive, and then he parks and leads me to the far side of a hill. The ground squishes underneath my feet from the dew, and sunshine pokes holes through a veil of gloomy clouds.

"Why would she come here?" I ask, dubious that she'd abandon the comfort of her apartment for some random patch of grass.

"Remember that sheep I told you about? The place he stashed all that loot? It's where I used to come with my brother sometimes as kids. She and I came here too. Not since ages ago, but if privacy was what she was after, this is where to go."

I think back on our first conversation ever, back when he was just the cute bartender. We round the tree-covered corner to find Cara sitting on a rock and staring at the slow-moving creek. My knees almost give out from the sight. She's okay. She looks up and lifts one hand in a sad wave as we approach.

"What are you doing?" I blurt out, relief seeping into my bones.

"Needed to get away." She shrugs. "Away from Granny, away from Mam who's fussing over every detail. This was the only place I could think of where they wouldn't come looking for me." She picks at some moss. "Stevie's messaged me thirty times this morning. Thirty! I haven't replied, but now I'm scared to because I've no idea what she'll say. I just needed..." She sighs and looks up at us. "I needed space."

"Cara, I'm sorry I was such an asshole yesterday." I clear my throat, but my apology still comes out rushed and fierce and full of regret. "And if you want space, I will go right now, but I had to apologize. She's your grandmother, and she loves you, and you've had your whole life with her so you understand her so much better than I ever will. I should never have said what I said to her."

I hold my breath, waiting for her to scream at me or tell me to leave for good.

"Did you realize," Cara says as she shakes her head, "Gran's barely ever talked to Yaz?"

"I...um, no."

"Ten words tops. Guess that's kind of on-brand for her, isn't it?"

"Maybe a little." A weak chuckle escapes my lips, and I sit down next to her and rest a hand on her leg. "I'm sorry. Both for how she treats you and Yasmine, and for yesterday. I thought I'd make the situation better, but I hurt you more, which I never, ever wanted."

"Why should I go through with the wedding if she's going to act like that?"

"Are you having second thoughts?" Aidan's question treads carefully, but I hear the rising concern in it too.

"Not about Yaz. Never about Yaz. But we've got hundreds of guests at some stuffy golf club with all the frills. More flowers than the entire world buys on Valentine's Day, a horse-drawn carriage, and a cake that looks like a geode. Like an actual rock, like someone smashed it open. And I don't know why anymore."

"Because you want to celebrate," I say. "To share your special day."

"Pffft." She slumps and sets her elbows on both knees. "We planned on eloping. Doing a ceremony with the closest relatives and that's it. My gran's the whole reason we're having a wedding this size. She said we couldn't have a real wedding anyway, so why bother?" Her lower lip trembles like a child holding back their big emotions. "We're not allowed to get married in a church, so I thought if we went over-the-top and extravagant, that maybe it would be real."

"Why didn't you say as much?" Aidan asks as he kneels down in front of her.

"It's humiliating having my own gran acting this way."

"For her," I say. "Whether she realizes that or not."

"I hate that Yaz and I have to prove something with what we wear and all the photos and the meal. I'm too scared to stand up and set a boundary with Gran, and I don't want to do it if it won't make a difference anyway."

"Cara, you *are* having a real wedding." I squeeze her fingers tight. "Not because of the size of the venue or what flowers you have or your rock cake. That stuff doesn't matter. Take it or leave it. Spend the whole reception drinking too much champagne and dancing if you'd like to. All that matters is that you're marrying the love of your life today. That's real."

I have no clue where these words of wisdom are coming from. What do I know about family or about love? But the comments have softened Cara's face, and her hand pulses against mine in thanks.

"You're the best sister I could've asked for," she says, and I'm hit by a surge of anxiety mixed with hope. Half sister or not, I care so much about her.

"You can go run off with Yaz, and I will head to the venue and let everyone know," I say, straightening my back to act like the rock Cara needs now. "If that's what you want, you should do it."

"That's the worst wedding task ever."

"I'd do it for you."

She giggles. "Thank you. But you're right. Everyone's there and waiting for us, we've planned the whole day out already, and the money's spent. Might as well enjoy the party then."

I rub the hem of my jacket between my forefinger and thumb. "If you don't want me there, I understand."

"Are you mad? 'Course I want you there." Her swift, certain reply lifts the two-ton boulder resting on my chest. "I'm aware the whole situation with my granny is shite. I am. But if you intended to help me, all you had to do was ask how."

"Understood. Guess I owe your grandma an apology too."

"She's been such a nightmare, I don't care anymore. I'm serious," Cara says, a smile growing on her face as the three of us laugh. "Besides, my mam talked to her again last night. Set her straight, I think." She sighs. "This might not have been what I envisioned for my wedding day, but I am glad you'll be there for me."

She hugs me once more and then ropes Aidan into the embrace. My heart does a somersault to feel him so close, one arm against my back. On our walk to Aidan's car, I send a text to Evvie telling her we'll get to the salon right away. At the top, I see an email notification that sucker punches me square in the gut.

The lab.

Dear Ms. Martin,

My name is Juliet and I am an analyst at Double Helix Labs. I'm reaching out regarding your on-site test with us, Vial ID 55835521. After a thorough review, the results differ from your original specimen, Vial ID 01830058. Below is a sneak peek of the updated genetic matches tied to your account.

Very Distant Matches (Fifth Cousins and Beyond): 02
Distant Matches (Second, Third, and Fourth Cousins): 00
Close Matches (Immediate Family, Close Relatives, and First Cousins): 00

Your results, including a full ancestry, ethnicity, and health report, will update in your account within 24 hours. These numbers may change as more people test with Double Helix Labs.

Send a friend or family member an invite, and they will get 30% off!

I have passed this new information to

the associate assigned to your account, and as a courtesy, you will receive a phone call from them within three business days. They will happily answer any questions you have.

We at Double Helix recognize the immense amount of trust placed in us by our customers. Thank you for choosing Double Helix Labs!

Warmly,

Juliet Garcia, they/them/theirs Senior Data Analyst, Double Helix Labs

My world has flipped upside down. All of my hoping and dreaming and wishing was for nothing. I actually thought Cara was my family, and all that does is make me the most pathetic person alive. For almost two weeks, I've been living a life that was never mine.

Aidan starts the car, and Cara calls my name before she slithers into the backseat. I force my feet to squelch through the mud, one after the other, and I order my body to sit down and buckle my seatbelt.

"Alright then," he says. "We've got a wedding to get to."

Evvie gnaws on her cuticles during our hushed conversation in the hall. "That lab," she says with a shake of her head. "I'm going to write them a letter. It's not right, what's happened."

"I can't tell her before she walks down the aisle."

"No. Not tonight, either. She leaves tomorrow morning, and that would spoil the trip."

"So I wait until she comes back?" My stomach ties itself into another knot at the prospect of keeping this quiet any longer.

"Shite," she mutters under her breath. "I've no clue, love." She unwraps a mint, her hands shaking as the wrapper crinkles open. "I support you, no matter what you think's best. We've found ourselves between a rock and a hard place, haven't we?"

I like her use of *we* to imply that we're in this together. She's on my side, and she knows Cara better than almost anyone, so that means something. "What would you do in my position?"

Her lips twist as she thinks. "After she gets back. Not the best timing, but now is worse. This wedding's the only thing on her mind."

I nod, envisioning that scenario. *Hey, turns out I'm not your half sister. Congrats on the wedding, enjoy your honeymoon!* I can't do that. This is her day, and she has hundreds of people vying for her attention. I should wait until we can discuss this one-on-one.

"We'll make a plan, you and me." Evvie pats my back and gives me a side-hug. "We'll get everyone together and tell them. Cara first, then everyone else who needs to know. Sound good?"

I run my teeth along my bottom lip and nod.

"For now, we carry on for her sake," she goes on. "But we'll find the right time. This will all work out."

"Thank you." I wrap my arms around the person who's become my lifeline in guiding me through this.

"There you are," Aidan rounds the corner to get us. "Evvie, Cara was asking for you." Rather than follow Evvie back to the bride, Aidan hooks an arm through mine. "Hey."

"Hi," I say, disentangling myself.

"Can we please talk?"

My guts twist as I wonder what Aidan will make of my revised test results. *Cara first, then everyone else*, Evvie said. While my mind keeps picturing the worst-case scenario, maybe—*maybe*—the change won't matter as much as I'm dreading. My heart latches onto that.

"I am so sorry for what I said last night," Aidan says, his voice low and sincere. "It was a shite way to respond to you."

"It's fine."

Besides, he was right. I know nothing about family. I blink up at the ceiling to clear my vision.

"First I straight-up told you that timing doesn't matter in a relationship, then I turned around and threw it in your face. You mean a lot. To Cara, to her parents, to—"

"Time to go." Stevie's stern voice orders us both down the hall. I don't want to keep a woman like her waiting, so I hustle to get in line for the procession.

This whole day is happening at warp speed. I've had a couple weeks here in Ballygrá in my own little world. A fantasy. And this morning reality hit me with an open palm to the face.

Cara waits in the back, looking even more like an angel on earth than at her fitting. She's done her hair half up and has added some pearl jewelry to the ensemble. With a final emotional embrace before we line up, she whispers, "Love you," into my ear, and I muster a sad smile.

I walk past the elaborate bouquets of roses planted down the aisle, and I catch Evvie's eye. *This will all work out.* Maybe she's right. Cara's the nicest person I've ever met. She'll understand.

I grasp that last inkling of hope with everything in me.

The ceremony and reception are exquisite, but I don't allow myself to get too swept up in them. I don't clutch my flowers closer listening to Cara and Yasmine's emotional vows. I don't share a knowing laugh with Evvie when Roger weeps like Niagara Falls. I don't wonder why my cheeks hurt and then realize it's all the involuntary smiling from seeing two people hopelessly in love. My emotions remain in check, even when it's time to stand in front of 250 people and speak from my banged-up heart.

"Hi everyone. I'm Juniper. Most of you haven't heard about me before because, um, neither had Cara until a couple weeks ago." The crowd of well-dressed friends and family murmur a laugh that ups my confidence. "Because of that, I don't have any fond childhood memories to share or embarrassing stories from her teen years. Sorry to disappoint you. All I have is these past eleven days."

The best eleven days.

"I've been asking myself a lot lately, how quickly can you really know someone?" My thoughts stumble when I make eye contact with Aidan, whose advice shaped exactly what I'm saying now. I clear my throat and look in a different direction.

"I consider myself an independent person who's been on her own for a while, so when I came here, I sort of figured that Cara would find all the things that are wrong with me. All the reasons I don't belong." I grab my glass of water and take a gulp that echoes through the speaker system.

"Cara should have every reason to want to push me away—the new person who appears two weeks before her wedding. And she could have. But from the second I got here, she opened up and gave me a home."

A home I never had before. My heart is being wrung out in front of hundreds of people, and I'm the one squeezing and twisting it. I sense warm wetness on my cheeks and swipe them clean. Something soft brushes my palm, and Stevie has materialized by my side with a tissue. *What a woman.* I collect myself and go on with the speech.

"I once heard a quote, and I can't remember what it was exactly or who said it, but it went like this: Home is people and not a place. Cara does that for others. She creates a home for them." Through a stream of tears that only Roger can rival, I turn to the brides. "I've known Cara a brief amount of time, but I see the relief and love in her eyes when Yasmine walks in the door. When she carries plates to the dinner table. When they walk hand in hand down the street. Yasmine gives Cara what Cara gives to everyone. These are two people who are kind and generous, and who give to each other just as much as they give to others.

"So, to Cara and Yasmine." I hold up my champagne and take a breath, hoping the last bit doesn't come out as garbled and incoherent. "Wherever you go, whatever you do, whoever you meet—may you always have a home within each other."

This shatters my heart. I've faked my way through the speech, but standing up here and talking about these past few weeks only reminds me of what I'm losing.

I fake a smile for the first dance, and I push food around on my plate during dinner, since I have zero appetite. At least all the attention is on the brides, and I can blame the multiple times I well up on the emotions of the day and not on the storm inside of me. Once the brides cut the cake, the DJ welcomes all the guests to the dance floor, and I use this opportunity to escape the revelry. I swipe a bottle of champagne and burrow myself into the loveseat in the bridal suite to drink and feel sorry for myself. The half sister who never was.

"There you are. Didn't catch you after—hey, what's wrong?"

Aidan enters, and my mood lightens for a second until real life drags me back down. I'm tragic and teary and drunk, and I don't want him to see me all mascara-streaked and puffy-faced. With his jacket off, sleeves rolled up, and tie loosened, he looks even more attractive than during the ceremony, which shouldn't be possible.

"Christ, was it because of yesterday? What I said?"

"No," I snort. "Although you weren't wrong."

"I was, June." He kneels in front of me and sets a hand on each of my thighs. "Please let me fix this."

"You can't fix this."

"I'll do anything."

"Aidan, it's not you. You couldn't do anything if you wanted." I take another swig of sparkling wine, which tastes more like water, and wipe the trail that dribbles down my chin. Then, with an unceremonious sigh, I slump back in my seat.

"Talk to me," he says as he studies my face.

"I get this close to getting something good. And not just *something* good, but like, everything." I gesture to the entire room, my arm sweeping around while a little bubbly sloshes out of the bottle I'm holding. "What I never got to have in my life. And I just..." My eyesight blurs. "I'm an idiot."

"You'll fly to New York, but you can come back anytime."

"I should never have come here. Agreeing to be the maid of honor, kissing you, all of it—I don't deserve any of it because—"

"Stop. You have to stop." His words come out firm and uncompromising. "You've set out on this mission to punish yourself, to tell yourself about the life you shouldn't have, but why?" His hand finds my chin, and he waits until my gaze locks on his. "You deserve so much goodness, June. In less than two weeks, you've brought joy to Cara, to the O'Sheas. To me. And simply because that's the way you are."

"But you don't know who I really am."

"Oh, I don't? I know you're brave for coming here in the first place, and strong because you've had to be strong your whole life, and you clearly don't see how much other people admire you. You're stubborn as hell. You make life fun, even mundane stuff, and you find funny moments in the strangest of situations. Your laugh is the most perfect sound." Aidan shuts me up with a kiss as I'm about to interrupt him. "So why? Why shouldn't you be happy too? Why shouldn't you be here? And why," he says, touching his forehead to mine, "shouldn't you just say yes to coming on a road trip with me?"

"Aidan."

He uses the pads of his thumbs to wipe away some more of my tears, all while wiping more and more of my resolve away too.

"I know what it's like to think you don't deserve something," he says. "But you do. So let's set it aside

and have the best, most extraordinary time. Let me—"
He catches his breath. "We can play pretend a little
longer. Forget that you'll hop on a plane and fly away
from me. Let's have these last few days together."

I didn't expect Aidan to beg me to follow him around
the countryside. He doesn't understand what's going
on, but he doesn't demand an explanation either. He
wants to ignore the inevitable future as much as I do.

Let's have these last few days together.

Evvie said we would make a plan, so maybe this can
be part of the plan. I shouldn't tell Aidan about the
lab results before I tell Cara anyway—of all people, she
deserves to hear it first. And since I'm staying at his
place, I can't avoid him.

"Are you sure?" I ask.

The corner of his mouth quirks up. "Is that a yes,
you'll come with me?"

I'd like to die inside of his green eyes—just lay down
and wrap myself in them and call it a life. Lust, I can
handle. But the fizzle in my belly when I think of him
or see him or touch him—I've never felt that for a man
before.

Aidan kisses me again before I whisper, "I'll go anywhere with you."

Chapter Twenty-One

Aidan

"This should do it." June holds out a basket with quite an impressive haul. Crisps. Red licorice. Peperami. Soft drinks. Cheese strings. Haribo.

"Christ."

"What?"

"You shop like a sugar-deprived five-year-old."

"We're rationing these for today and tomorrow," she explains, with the cutest hint of bashfulness. "Besides, this is classic road-trip food. We need the essentials."

Content to accept defeat, I take the shopping basket. She throws in one more item—a chocolate bar she claims is also necessary—and we check out.

At least her mood has lifted since last night. Throughout the wedding and reception, I never stopped noticing her and how she looked cheerful and sorrowful at the same time. In the back room, I didn't need her to tell me anything more. She's grappling with something dark and painful, something she tried to use as an excuse to push me away—to push everyone away.

So I held her hand as we lined up for the grand exit, waving sparklers to the lucky brides as they boarded their getaway car. Just like their honeymoon, or minimoon, or whatever it's called, this trip with June could be a onetime thing. It might be all we get for a while, or forever. We haven't talked about anything beyond these next few days, so I'm going to savor them.

"Now," I announce once we've both settled into the car. June's already opened a stick of Peperami. "I thought today we'd travel around the Ring of Kerry and explore one of my favorite scenic drives. How's that sound?"

I've mapped out a route that gives June some highlights of the South-West, like Killarney National Park this afternoon, a sunset by the western coast tonight, and then a drive up the coast tomorrow morning. We've enough room left for spontaneity, but hopefully I planned the road trip of a lifetime for her.

"I'm intrigued. I expect full commentary on the history of the country and landscape as we ride."

"Please review me on Tripadvisor. Five stars."

June hasn't cracked a smile yet today, but this elicits a honey-sweet laugh from her. It's like the first peek of sunshine on a gloomy day. "I will."

I admire the little glint of gold in her irises before putting the car in reverse. After twenty minutes of driving, every rolling hill we ascend or tight curve we round has June craning her neck left and right to take in all the views. Large looming mountains are on either side of us, and just as we reach the top, the landscape bursts wide open with fields and rivers and stone bridges.

"This," I explain as we get out of the car, "is the top of the Gap of Dunloe. These ranges on either side of us are MacGillycuddy's Reeks and Purple Mountain."

June types into her phone, her thumbs flying across the screen, but her attention doesn't once veer from the view. "Aidan." I could bathe in the sound of her saying my name. "This is incredible. Like the most amazing place I've ever been. Do you come here all the time? Because I'm pretty sure if I lived here, I would visit this exact spot every day."

"You're a country girl now?"

"With views like this, I'd manage." She pauses, smiling at our surroundings as she tucks her phone away.

"I've kind of always viewed living in New York City as a badge of honor. I could look back on my upbringing and say my childhood was worth the pain because I ended up succeeding in the hardest city there is to succeed in. Leaving almost feels like failure or something."

"People change. Lives change."

"I'd miss New York if I left, though. Subway commutes and teensy apartments and all."

"The good old American dream."

"Yup," she snorts. "But if I moved somewhere else, I'd be starting at square one with finding a job. I keep holding out, hoping for a promotion from my boss. And I'm close. Or I was, I guess."

"Why are you so loyal to that place? Your editor sounds like a piece of work."

While I don't know the man well, I've heard enough about him to know I don't like him. Anytime June mentions the assignment, she seems stressed out. I've overheard some of her conversations with this man too, and she turns into someone who speaks in stilted sentences and apologies. That's not June.

"I need the job whether I like Ethan or not. And at *The Edge*, I've got some seniority. Sometimes interns get bumped up to some of the more exciting positions, and I don't cover what I'd like to all the time, or much at all, but it's consistent work." She kicks some chunks of gravel. "Okay, I guess it's not the best job ever."

"Work for someone else. Anyone else," I suggest, practically begging. "Or go freelance, like you were telling me. Travel the world while you work."

"Like I'd hop on flights to different cities around the globe and report back?"

"Why not?"

She seems to flip this idea over and over in her head. My chest seizes at the thought of her globe-trotting every week and living a full life while I stay put at the pub. Not that I've any right to concern myself with that. We're only ever bound to catch each other at the occasional O'Shea family get-together.

"What about you?" She turns to me as we stroll back to the car on the side of the road. "Think you'll leave Ballygrá?"

"Christ, I hope so. But not in a go-and-never-look-back kind of way. I'd come back for my mam and da, for Cara. But I want to make a life, and it won't happen there."

She opens the passenger door and uses the car frame to prop herself up, leaning her elbows on the roof. A gust of wind dances through her hair, and she attempts to brush some strands out of her eyesight.

"That was the plan once, with Dublin." I meet June's face, and something as simple as her gaze makes my pulse quicken. "My ex put such urgency into making it happen that I had to stop and think about what I wanted."

"You want to do things on your own time."

"I do," I say with a nod. "And Dublin wasn't my dream to begin with."

"What is your dream, Aidan McCarthy?"

"Know that my parents are in a stable spot. Then take the camera on the road."

"Well," she says, standing a bit straighter. "Maybe I'll see you there."

"Maybe."

"I've only met your parents a couple times, and they give you a hard time, especially your dad, but I can tell they love you. They would hate to have you stay and be unhappy."

I tuck my hands into my pockets. While I've not much choice now, for the next few days, I get to live a different life. A kind of dream where June doesn't have a flight back to New York, and I'm not tied to Ballygrá indefinitely.

"That said, I'm glad you didn't move to Dublin." She speaks with a quiet tenderness. "At least long enough so I could meet you."

"Me too."

She flashes another one of those smiles that makes me forget how to breathe.

I nod at the expansive route of greenery in front of us and say, "Let's get going."

Driving around with June almost makes me forget that she'll leave a few days from now.

I try not to think about that.

Instead, I focus on the road and on our journey. I know the routes well enough to drive them backward and blindfolded, but we're moving slower than I anticipated. June requests that we stop at every outlook along the way. I don't mind, though, and quite like hearing the awestruck gasps she makes. Once, when she thought I wouldn't pull over, she reached out to rest her hand on my arm, almost begging me to park.

From that point onward, I pretend not to notice each outcropping on the roads I'd driven thousands of times before.

During another one of our hundreds of stops, we stand on a cobblestone bridge over a trickling creek, and June snaps a photo. She examines the screen more closely and shakes her head. "There's no way to capture this. Even when the photo looks amazing, I can't compare what's on my phone to the real thing." She turns to me, failing to suppress a girlish grin. "I really appreciate you driving me around. I'm having a horrible time, obviously."

"Me too. Downright horrendous."

We both laugh. She takes in the hills surrounding us, and her eyes land on mine. They linger there for one, two, three seconds, until she breaks contact and holds up her phone.

"Here," she says. "We should get a photo together." And just like that, June wraps her arm around my shoulders as if we've taken selfies dozens of times before. She fits next to me, and her head nestles into the space below my jaw and collarbone as she squeezes my shoulder. Daring to indulge in as many of these moments as possible, I reach around her waist to tuck her in closer.

After the photo, she blindsides me with a kiss—her mouth meets mine while she clutches the collar of my jacket with one fist. Before I register her delicate lips, her playful tongue, or her chest pressed up against my body, she pulls back with stitched brows. "You're going to make us miss the sunset."

We dash down the road in fits of laughter, chasing each other and sneaking in kisses, oblivious to the confused sheep on the side of the road.

When we get to the car, one of the right tires looks saggy. The vehicle leans to the side like it's had one too many drinks, and a quick investigation reveals a constellation of glass shards firmly embedded in the tire.

Shite.

In an ordinary world, I'd pull a spare tire from the boot, which has just enough room for a spare, and twenty minutes later, we could head out. Except earlier this year, I'd used the spare and never quite got around to buying a *spare* spare tire.

"Minor problem." I explain the issue, hoping June won't find me a complete imbecile for not handling this before a road trip.

"Is there a cab company we can call?"

"Sunday night'll be tough, all the same." We're in the middle of the countryside, with not another car in sight in either direction, and calling someone back home to pick us up would take a couple hours both ways. "We'll have better luck finding a place nearby to ring from. There's a bed-and-breakfast roughly a kilometer and a half that way."

I'd hoped we'd have time to get to the coast for a sunset in all its glory, with rusty oranges and reds bleeding into the land and sea. I can wave my original plan goodbye, but I quickly realize that's the least of our worries. A low rumble roars in the distance, and I scan the horizon to see angry, ominous clouds.

More thunder churns through the air, this time louder and longer. "That weather's turning bad fast."

June grabs her purse and slams the door shut as she shoots me a devilish grin. "Guess we'll have to move faster then."

We get a steady jog going, but right when going back to the car proves a bit more hassle than forging ahead, buckets of rain pour from the sky. Raindrops pelt us like tiny bullets, and those monochrome clouds have swept in with a vengeance. After another bend in the road, I spy a row of oak trees with yellowed leaves. One's tall enough to offer some protection from the downpour, although the damage has been done—with each step, my socks squish in my boots, and cool water drips from my hair down my neck.

June runs underneath the tree behind me while using her handbag as a shield from the elements. I'd planned for this to be the trip of a lifetime—instead, I've just about ruined the day, all because I preferred to use my car's boot as camera gear storage.

"I'm so sorry," I yell over the rainfall. "This was not what I had in mind."

She uses my arm to steady herself as she's overcome with fits of laughter. Our situation has played out like a comedy of errors. We've had our sunset plans interrupted, discovered a flat tire with no help in sight, and gotten caught in a rainstorm that's penetrated every article of clothing on our bodies. I shove the idea of a flawless getaway aside and instead enjoy June's laugh, which is so hearty her cheeks become plump and pink. Her joy fills me up, and I have to laugh along with her.

Thunder cracks again, causing her to jump, let out a shriek-laugh, and then cozy up toe-to-toe with me. Desire growls inside my chest, a visceral part of me I can't keep at bay anymore.

Our laughter subsides, and we're breathless and sopping wet and grinning like fools. The scenery around me blurs out of focus. No more thrum of the rain, no narrow road, and no biting wind. My world shrinks to me and June and the air between us. My best friend's sister. Someone I can't stop thinking of. Someone who won't be visiting for much longer.

I try not to think about that.

Reaching up, I wipe away a thick clump of hair that has glued itself to her smooth cheek and trace her jawline. The simple gesture is happiness and heartache in one.

June nuzzles her head into my palm, and I know she feels this too. I'm not dreaming. Whatever's going on between us, it could be more than some fun, more than a good time. It promises to be confusing and messy and imperfect, but it will be ours.

"I want you," she whispers, and those three words race through me. Her eyelashes flutter open to reveal two brown universes, laser-focused on my lips.

Lifting her chin, I press my mouth to hers and melt into the ground. The kiss goes slow and careful at first, but after one, two, three, the desire becomes palpable between us. She clasps the nape of my neck. My arm slinks around her, bringing those delicate curves closer into me.

She tastes like red licorice and hope.

As our noses and cheeks and chins mesh together, I know nothing else except wanting her.

Chapter Twenty-Two

Juniper

"Need a lift, you two?"

Our lips dance together a moment more before Aidan nods to the truck driver with the worst timing in the world. I'm tempted to wave him along, but we really could use the ride. Aidan has kissed the sense out of me, so I don't know how long he stands there holding the passenger door open for me before I crawl in.

Sitting in the middle seat, a supercut of my time with Aidan plays in my head like an old film. The glow of streetlights as we walk by the river in Dublin. His hair at the wedding, slicked back and more tame than his usual lion's mane. His eyes lingering on me. His smile.

God, his smile.

I haven't had a crush this bad in a long time. I've liked guys I've taken home before, but I would never have willingly spent hours and hours with them on a road trip or made out with them like my life depended on it.

As I admire some stray raindrops on his jaw, I wonder if I should tell him about the DNA test. I also wonder if that truth would put an end to this trip. Probably. Would he contact Cara too and ruin her honeymoon with the news?

No, I can't do that. I have to stand firm with what Evvie and I decided. I'll tell Cara once she's back. As for Aidan, he made it clear that the plan is to enjoy these next few days with no strings attached. We'll play pretend, then we'll face reality. *I'll* face reality.

So is this a ridiculous crush? Yes. As far as ridiculous crushes go though, I don't mind having one on a guy like Aidan.

We arrive at a tiny cottage down the road and thank our quiet driver, who cruises off. A chubby woman wearing a paisley apron opens the door and motions us inside. She welcomes us while another gentleman grabs towels from a skinny closet.

"Oh no, not much chance of a service truck out here this time on the weekend. My husband'd take you himself, but he's got a finicky back. Drives more'n half an hour don't treat him all too well."

"Don't want to trouble you," Aidan replies.

"Why don't I set you up with a spot for the night, then?" she asks, her eyes gleaming like we're the first guests she's ever had.

"That'd be sound," Aidan replies.

Their bed-and-breakfast is a modest home with a single room they rent out. Our host provides us some oversized loungewear while our own clothes dry, and she sets two extra spots at the dinner table for a steaming-hot meal. She talks while we eat, and I nod along with the stories our generous hosts share. My mind is all over Aidan, though—in particular, our sleeping arrangements and how well this couple soundproofed their walls.

She leads us down the hallway once we finish eating. Family photos dot the hall, with both grainy black-and-white pictures and more recent colored pictures, along with a gold crucifix at the center of the display.

"Here you are. Adjust the heat over here with this knob. Towels're in the bathroom, but if you need any more, then say the word. Anythin' at all, let me know."

She scurries out and closes the door, which leaves Aidan and me alone, facing the full-size bed at the other end of the room.

It's a rather narrow bed. I must have done something admirable in my life to have earned this.

"I figured this was a tiny B&B, but I didn't realize quite how small," he says.

"Hope you don't snore."

"Like a sawmill."

"So," I say in such a wavery voice that I don't know if he'll hear me. A moment passes before we dive into each other's arms, giving in to the pull between our bodies. I want to explore every sinewy line of him, starting with the firm plane of his chest. He's trim and in shape, lean yet strong—and I could sink right into him.

"Is this okay?" he asks against my lips.

"Better than okay," I breathe back. Although I'm not exactly sure what he means—the kissing, the sharing a bed, the touching? The answer is a resounding *yes, yes, yes* all around.

"I've been thinking about this ever since you walked into the pub."

Aidan breaks our connection long enough to remove the baggy shirt Mrs. McNally loaned him. Hypnotized, I run my finger across his bare chest and stomach, admiring the smooth, taut skin. I stop as I reach that tantalizing spot below his belly button, where a trickle of dark blond hair leads down to an already visible bulge in his pants.

"May I?" Aidan gestures to my sweatshirt. He's so gentle with me that it breaks my heart. Wordlessly, I lift my arms above my head for him to remove the top, and as he surveys my half-naked body and bare breasts, he expels a heavy sigh.

I return to his embrace with another urgent, burning kiss. His skin against mine induces a shiver that travels up my spine, and if merely touching him has that effect, then what will something more do?

His mouth trails down my neck to my collarbone and then to my left breast. I moan softly, biting on my lips to prevent the sound from carrying further than this bedroom.

Nothing matters anymore. Nothing except this man in this room with me.

He sucks on my left nipple, and I throw my head back to the ceiling in pleasure, dragging my fingers through his hair. With a flick of his tongue, he switches to the right while I guide one of his hands into my roomy sweatpants. When he touches me there, right at my center, we both seem to short-circuit. A string of expletives leave his mouth, causing me to laugh, but he shuts up fast when he caresses me. He moves at a delicious, slow pace, enough to satisfy me in this moment while also making me crave the next moment and all the moments after. His mouth finds mine again. I lean until the backs of my legs rest flush against the dresser, loving the pulses of heat and tension growing from his touch.

"Why weren't we doing this all along?" I pant. What he's doing has me so wet already that I'll climax soon, but I have to have more. I fumble around on his hips for the waistband of his pants. "These. Off."

He obeys and removes them in a swift move. The sight of his erect cock is enough to make the crucifix in the hallway blush. His thickness dips up and down, and a vein tracks all the way from the base of his shaft to the tip. I can think of a hundred different things I'd like to do with his dick, but I start with taking him in one hand, and I stroke up and down his length. His look darkens and fills with a desperate longing.

"I have a condom," I say as I reach for my purse on the nightstand.

"Not yet. I need to taste you," he pants, and the sheer lust in his expression is enough for me to give this man whatever he demands.

He tugs off my sweatpants and, in one deft movement, kneels in front of me and hooks my leg above his shoulder. His tongue writes the most filthy words on my inner thighs, and I wish he'd put his mouth *there*, right in the middle where I'm longing for him the most. Aidan skates his lips over my clit, and every inch of me becomes more awake and more present than ever before. I've never really lived until he latches onto me, nipping and sucking at a steady pace.

"That's so good," I whisper. "Right there."

An electric, buzzing sensation builds at my center, and Aidan doesn't back down. This man seems to be on a mission to make me come from oral alone, and he's doing a damn fine job.

His mouth sets the rhythm, humming a gentle vibration while he buries his face into me. With my hands in his hair and his name on my lips, I gasp into the darkness. My body shakes as pure euphoria takes over and eliminates all thoughts from my head except *holy shit*.

Aidan tracks kisses up my hips and torso, my breasts, and my neck. His erection presses into my leg, and a whole new desire makes me salivate.

"I want you so badly, June."

"Please. Fuck me."

"What's that now?" He smirks against my lips.

"I need you inside of me," I beg.

He picks up the condom but keeps his gaze trained on me as he rolls it down his length. "If I have to go one more minute without feeling every part of you, I'm going to lose my mind."

"Then hurry up." I smirk at him.

He doesn't bother dragging me to the bed. Instead, he lifts my butt onto the dresser, spreads my legs, and moves into me.

"Oh my god," I say with a growl. He hasn't even gone all the way in, but the pressure of him inside me makes me burst at the seams. He retreats to his tip, then pushes in a little deeper, repeating the move until he fills me to the hilt.

For a second, I can't do anything but hold the edge of the dresser for support as Aidan takes me completely. I drink in every detail of his face, from the roughness of his five o'clock shadow to the shape of his mouth. Our eyes meet, and that lopsided grin of his pulls me in for another all-consuming kiss. Gripping my hips, he drives deeper into me, and I bite back from screaming his name.

"It's been so hard today keeping my hands to myself," he says, breathless.

"You don't need to, Aidan. I want you all over me."

"Then we'll never leave this room."

"Good." Our breathing synchronizes, the sound of our inhales and exhales filling the space. "I want more," I say, and he responds with a thrust that knocks over a metal picture frame on the dresser. He squeezes my left breast, and I let out an audible moan.

"You're a loud one," he says playfully, lips hovering over mine.

"You're the one rattling the dresser."

"I can go slow," he says, leaning his weight deeper into me to steady the jangling sounds of the furniture. He pulls back at an agonizing pace that makes me clench tighter around him. "That better?"

I use my legs to bring him back inside me and we both exhale. "Again," I beg him. He withdraws as his warmth, his hardness, and his touch nudge me closer to the edge. I'm teetering on the precipice of an orgasm that I've longed for since our first kiss.

This time, he doesn't wait for my legs to do the work. He pushes his length back into me, building up my release even more.

"Look at how hard you make me," he says as he retreats another time. "Feeling you so deep drives me mad."

I watch his length poised right at my entrance, and I whimper as he pushes in again—an overwhelming sensation that goes from the top of my head to my toes. "Aidan."

"I like that. I like you saying my name when I'm inside you."

"Bet you'll like it better when I come."

"You're probably right," he says with a chuckle. "Tell me what you need."

"Faster."

"Don't know if this dresser will keep quiet."

"Forget the dresser." I put my hand on the back of his neck and bring him in for a kiss. "Fuck me," I say against his lips.

He moves quicker, building up momentum as we share breaths. A sensational heat builds in my lower belly, and I look down again to see him hammering in and out of me. "Yes, Aidan," I sigh as he takes me to the point of no return.

Hundreds of thousands of stars are all I see, like a celestial explosion in the night. My body floats, and in between breathy inhales and exhales, I manage a single word: his name. While I've found some kind of heaven on earth, his pace picks up. Aidan grunts as quietly as he can, face twisted in ecstasy. When he's done, we collapse into each other, and he places one soft, wet kiss on my shoulder.

We sit folded together with him breathing into my neck, both of us depleted of energy. He speaks my name into my skin, and I wish I could carve that sound into my memory forever.

I follow the wholesome smell of freshly baked bread and smoky bacon into the kitchen. Aidan helps Mrs. McNally at the stove, and Mr. McNally pours me a coffee before I snag a seat at the dining table.

"Mornin'!" Mrs. McNally looks chipper and in her element with an apron on and utensils in both hands. If the dresser gave anything away, she seems unaffected. "We've some fresh fruit here, there's yogurt, and the bacon'll be ready soon. How d'you like your eggs?"

She fries up the rest of breakfast while Mr. McNally talks to Aidan about the people he knows in Ballygrá. Aidan sneaks in a smile my way, which makes my insides flutter.

Last night was amazing. Being pressed up against the dresser and wrapped up with Aidan was some of the hottest sex I've ever had. But I'm now at a complete loss with how to act around him. That day-after panic that ordinarily propels me in the opposite direction from a guy after we sleep together hasn't set in, and instead, I'm looking forward to another day of road-trip mode.

But a different panic has made its way into my thoughts. Aidan is so *good*, and I'm lying to him. After last night, that knowledge sits heavier in my heart.

I never intended for this situation to snowball. The lab revealed the error at the worst possible time, and I haven't found the perfect moment to set things straight without everything unraveling in my hands. Forget *The Edge*—although I did email Ethan to request another extension so I could sort out a new angle. That's a fire I'll have to put out once I return to New York. But involving Aidan now would only make him complicit in this mess the same way Evvie is. I hate not telling him who I really am. *Be yourself*, Lissie had said. But being myself will merely rip me away from Cara, her parents, and Aidan.

Aidan carries on with Mr. McNally, but his foot finds mine. The touch tugs me from my negative thoughts and grounds me back at the table, his presence like a prescription drug that silences my nagging interior monologue. Watching him eat breakfast is an erotic act. That same mouth was on me, those hands left no part of me untouched, and I selfishly crave the attention again. By the way he catches me noticing him, he must know he's driving me crazy.

Mrs. McNally lines up a rental car for us, which arrives right as we finish breakfast. Aidan calls a towing company to get his own vehicle to the mechanic in Ballygrá, and once he's done, we check out to hit the road.

"I'm going to miss that dresser," I say to him as we settle into the front seat.

Aidan leans over the cupholders and kisses me like not being able to do so during breakfast had been some kind of a Herculean task.

This man. I might leave this place with a bit of a bruised heart.

I cup his jaw and throw him a sly smile. "So where to?"

"Would going back to my place to have sex in every room in the house be an appropriate answer?"

"Absolutely."

Aidan kisses me again. "I promised I'd show you Ireland, and I want to. Besides, we never got that sunset of ours."

"I can't say I'm not disappointed."

"Don't worry. I'll make it worth your while."

He drives toward the coast, and we're blessed with what Aidan admits is unusually nice weather. The crisp blue sky is dotted by dainty puffs of clouds, behind which the sun occasionally hides. I claim the role of navigator, which means that at every intersection, I point the way we should go, guided by nothing other than my sheer curiosity. We're lost but right where we should be—exploring unknown gravel streets together, filling up the tank at run-down gas stations, and finding quiet hideaways overlooking the unceasing waves of the Atlantic.

And, of course, we pull over on the side of the road for more than one make-out session, plus an unexpected and satisfying quickie in the compact backseat.

As promised, Aidan parks near a quiet harbor in time to catch the sun going down. The stone wall by the street, which winds to the water's edge, makes an excellent place for us to sit, our feet dangling above dancing strands of grass. The sun inches down toward the three dots of islands in the water, and the light casts a ghostly golden glisten on the waves.

I shiver, and Aidan drapes an arm around me.

"I can't believe I leave in a couple of days." As I speak to him, I keep my eyes on the hypnotic ocean rippling in front of us. "Two weeks have gone by so fast. A lot has changed since I first showed up." I tap my heel against the wall, which releases a few pebbles that fall to the ground.

"I wish you could stay longer."

"Aidan," I say as a knife twists in my heart. "That's not—"

"I know. Your home is New York, and I live here. But anytime you want to visit, you can. You should. And when you do, you can stay as long as you'd like."

I search his face and find a fragile earnestness that steals my thoughts.

"What?" he asks.

"Nothing. It's just..." For the first time, I have something to lose, and that terrifies me. I steel myself with a breath, then look to the horizon. "You know how my mom died when I was young? I was four. And then my grandma—she kept to herself, except for the rare moments when she gardened. Otherwise, she was locked up in her room smoking Camel Lights and left me to fend for myself."

"Did she hurt you?"

"Nothing physical. Lots of swearing. Insults if I didn't do chores around the house correctly, stuff like that. She'd forget birthdays. That's not such a big deal, but when you're a kid—"

"It is a big deal."

"Anyway," I say, sniffling. "She's still alive. At least, I haven't gotten the call that she's not. She's probably...I mean, she must be so bad by now. But I can't see her. I can't."

"You have to take care of yourself."

"I got so burnt out on being a liability." I run my teeth over my bottom lip. "But that's why I left the system as quickly as I could. Got a gig at the local florist to save up money, emancipated myself at sixteen, and never looked back." I turn and take in the blurry form of him next to me. "So it means a lot that you'd ask me to stay. Nobody's ever asked me to stay before."

He pulls me into his chest, and I bury myself there, letting myself cry in a way I haven't before, like enough tears will take away the pain and sadness of my childhood. He strokes my hair, giving me silent support. I pull back and marvel at this man in front of me, who makes me feel safe and protected and cared for. And maybe even loved.

The thought sends my heart free-diving.

His sage-colored eyes beckon me for another kiss. We settle in, side by side, as the sun dips below the horizon and darkens the world around us.

Chapter Twenty-Three

Aidan

After driving farther north up the coast, we happen upon a quaint coastal hotel south of Galway and check in. The management has leaned heavily into the whole seaside theme. Seashells sit on the dresser, ocean-inspired art of boats against a vibrant sunset grace the walls, and every piece of furniture is painted cerulean, seafoam, or turquoise.

"They sent us champagne." I nod toward the desk, where the neck of a bottle juts out from an ice bucket. Two tall glasses stand at attention by its side.

"You sweet-talk that woman at the check-in counter for this?"

"I have a way with the seventy-five-and-up crowd."

She crows with laughter.

With the expert hands of someone who's worked too long behind a bar, I remove the cage and cork so the bottle only hisses upon opening, and I pour two glasses. "What're we toasting to?"

"Well," June taps her chin in thought while closing the distance between us. Her mouth is so close I can almost taste her. "An incredible trip?"

"An irresistible navigator."

She brushes her lips against mine, and I don't care about the champagne or the toast. All that matters is that I'm wrapped around her finger.

"Mrs. McNally's dresser," she says.

"We should thank it for its service." I pull her closer by her hip and take a quick survey of the room. "Maybe tonight we'll make our way to a bed?"

"Guess we'll have to wait and see."

"Not sure," I say in between a line of kisses down her neck. "Not sure I can wait."

We ditch the glasses and dance over to the mattress in a tangle of limbs. Removing her clothes is a holy experience, and I worship each body part until we're skin on skin. She has teardrop-shaped breasts with pert rosy nipples, thighs I want to glide my hands up and down all day, and a luscious patch of brown hair between her legs where I'd happily bury myself. Her fingers roam my chest, shoulders, and back with fervor.

She presses her hips into my leg, and the warmth of her center makes my cock ache.

I trace my tongue across her collarbone and finally onto the pink peak of her breast. Her breath cuts the air when I pull it into my mouth, rubbing it in circles with my tongue while massaging the other between my fingers.

"You're gorgeous," I say in a ragged breath against her chest. I lay down a line of kisses from her breast up to her neck and to the corner of that coy smile. "Can I go down on you?"

"You can do anything you want to me."

I travel down her torso and situate myself between her legs. I'll never tire of this view. Her lips are swollen with anticipation, and her center already looks silky wet.

June tastes sweet and sour, like an irresistible piece of candy I can never stop sucking on. While I nuzzle harder into her, she gasps and groans with each new tilt of my head and flick of the tongue. Her legs shiver, and she whispers a guttural, "I'm close," so I wrap my arms tighter around her thighs.

When she comes, both of her hands scrape through my hair, pulling me closer with every shockwave traveling through her body. It's a glorious rush. I wait there, content to spend the rest of the night admiring

June from that angle, and then I hear her breathy voice again. "Condoms. Shit, I don't have any more."

"Got some at the petrol station earlier."

She props herself up on her elbows to look at me, her face full of mirth. "Aidan McCarthy, are you seducing me?"

"I sure as hell hope so."

June watches with hooded eyes as I roll protection onto my cock, pure hunger resting on her lips. She acts like I'm the sexiest man alive, and all I want is to make her come undone once again.

As I slide into her, my mind goes blank. June's warmth surrounds me, and every *Yes, Aidan* from her mouth gets me harder. She grips me close, pulling me as far inside of her as possible, and I rest my thumb between us to rub against her clit with each forward push.

"That feel good?" I ask in between breaths.

"It feels *phenomenal*." Her teeth clamp down on her bottom lip until a loud, pleasure-filled groan escapes.

"I love hearing the sounds you make. So sexy."

"It's because of you. When you're so deep inside of me like this, I can't help it." She moans again, and I latch onto her neck. "I love that."

"I'm going to miss this so much," I say.

"Me too." Her voice cracks. "Gonna miss this so much."

"Hey." I pause and search her face to find her eyes shimmering, which takes me from turned-on to concerned. "Hey, I'm right here. I'm right here, June."

"I know. I-I'm sorry."

"What's wrong?" I pull out and scoot next to her on the bed. "Did I do something?"

"No, it's me. I just..." Her eyes catch mine, and she smiles, like that could conceal her obvious pain. "Stuck in my own thoughts."

"That's fine." I toss the condom aside and lay down, my head propped in one hand and the other hand resting on her waist. "Do you want to talk about it?"

"I'm going to miss this." Tears pool in between her lashes. Quieter, she adds, "I'll miss you."

An ache shoots through my chest because I know what she means about missing a person before they're gone. I sense it, too. Tonight is one of our last nights together, and our last night alone. In a couple days' time, she'll board a flight back to New York. Back to her life. And what then?

I can't wait around on this or leave us up to fate. I won't.

"What if I visit you sometime?" I splay my palm on her stomach.

"I mean, I'd love that, but..." June traces an infinity symbol on my arm. "I don't know."

I catch a flicker of fear in her, enticing her to pull away. I'm not having it. "Why?"

"That sounds so serious. You planning a trip to see me."

"All it means is I like you, and I hope to see you again." I hold my breath, hoping I haven't overstepped my bounds here. Hoping I haven't misread this situation entirely. "Unless you don't want to."

"No," June says. She rolls toward me, her brows forming a V-shape. "That's not it at all."

"Well, that's fortunate for you. I am Cara's best friend, so you won't get rid of me that easy."

June doesn't respond and instead worries her bottom lip so hard she might bite right through it.

"Do you have a holiday coming up?"

"Christmas."

"Before that," I say.

"Thanksgiving? That's in like a month."

"And?"

"That's so soon. Flight prices must be astronomical."

"Don't worry about that." I reach out and trace my thumb across her cheekbone. "I'm not dreaming this up, am I? Us?"

"No, but—but why the rush?"

"I *like* you." I don't dare say the other L-word, but it sizzles in my mind and disappears like steam from a coffee cup. "You leave in two days, and I'm going to be devastated. Let this pitiful man buy a ticket to see you."

"You should wait until prices go down."

"I've already looked," I confess. "I can manage them. C'mon." I plant a kiss on her shoulder. "If you can give me a real, honest excuse why I shouldn't purchase a flight right now, then I won't do it. But if not, then missing each other won't be so miserable when we've got this to look forward to."

My heart pounds its way out of my ribcage as I wait for her to respond.

When she says *okay*, I almost don't hear the word, but it sends a current of energy through me. I climb on top of her and burrow kisses into her neck. She releases a low laugh, and I wish I could play that sound on repeat. She appears happy, if a bit tentative. I probably came on strong with wanting to buy a transatlantic flight to visit her in less than thirty days, but she's smiling to herself.

Our kisses go from playful to deep, meaningful, and passionate. We're both still naked, and the feeling of June's breasts pressing up against me reawakens my cock. Her leg links around me, the heat between her still feels slick, and I run my finger down her center. She hisses when I slide two fingers in and stroke her from the inside, and her eyes flutter closed.

Reaching to her side of the bed, she paws around until she grabs another condom. I love watching her roll it onto me, almost as much as I love how she climbs on top of me and lowers herself onto my erection with a satisfied grunt.

"Christ."

"Now's not the time for prayers, Aidan."

With a smirk, I say, "With a view like this, it might be."

I rest my hands on her hips, following how her body rocks back and forth against mine and using my strength to grind her harder on top of me. Her breasts sway with each movement, and I pull her toward me so I can capture one of her nipples in my mouth. I suck my way up her neck until we're face-to-face, molded together and breathing each other in.

This doesn't mirror the rushed, lust-filled heat of yesterday. We move in a sensual push and pull like ocean waves. This is desire—for each other, yes, but mixed with something else. Perhaps the hope to be careful with each other's hearts.

June's eyes lock on mine as her mouth falls open.

"I'm right here," I say, hushed, coaxing her toward a climax. "I'm here with you."

"Aidan."

Her head nuzzles against me when she comes, shaking and quivering until she collapses. My own climax ramps up like rays of light shooting in every direction, and involuntary shudders of release work their way through my body. We hold each other in stillness, almost as if the night could last forever if we don't move or say anything.

I think this woman will be the end of me.

After we clean up, neither of us has the energy to put our clothing back on. June rests her head in the crook of my shoulder, and I guide a few stray hairs behind her ear.

"I wish I could stop time," she says against my chest.

"You're in luck. We can." I get up and dig around in my bag. When I hold my camera out to her, June smiles. "Stop time. This is how I do it."

"I'm a phone camera person."

"Here." I settle in next to her on the bed. "It's easy."

She grips the Nikon, framing a shot of our feet poking out at the bottom of the sheets, the rest of the room in the background. I talk her through the aperture and shutter speed dials, and she clicks the shutter with a grin.

"Can I take a photo of you?" I ask.

"Sure." She tucks herself further under the comforter. "Not for anything dirty, I hope."

"No," I assure her. "You look gorgeous, and I want to remember this moment too."

As I point the lens in her direction, I preserve her perfection indefinitely—the graceful curves from her toes to her hips to her waist. I pull the camera away to inspect the image, and the sight of her makes me have to catch my breath.

"Okay, I might have lied. I might save this for something dirty."

She shrieks and tosses a pillow in my direction. I dodge while lifting up my camera for one action shot. The shutter clicks at exactly the right time. Hair tousled. Wide smile from ear to ear. And most importantly of all, with me.

Selfishly, I'd love to keep June all to myself, but we ought to get back to Ballygrá. We can't spend the next twenty-four hours together, just the two of us, as much as I might like to. Cara and Yaz return this afternoon, and Evvie's arranged a dinner for June's last night in town.

One more day. June leaves in one more day. The only shred of knowledge making that more bearable is knowing I'll get to see her only a few weeks from now.

I take the drive back at a luxurious pace. No need to rush, as long as we get back by nightfall. We stop in some towns along the way to eat lunch and wander through bookshops and boutiques. I pull off to the side of the road for photo stops too, although it's a toss-up whether June peeks at the scenery or puts her hands on me. The hire car has less room than my own, but I'm impressed with the creative things we can do in such a compact space.

We get back to my house and have a chance to shower, break in my bed, and shower again before heading over to Evvie and Roger's. My mind has turned to mush. I make a dedicated effort to stop thinking of how June took the whole of my cock in her mouth half an hour prior, and how her tongue made magic as one of her fists worked up and down my shaft.

June knocks on the door, her hair still damp and skin still flushed in a post-orgasm glow.

"There you are!" Roger welcomes us inside. "No Cara and Yaz with you?"

"No, they said they'd come separate."

"Hi love," Evvie says, kissing June on the cheek and then me. "I invited your mam and da as well. They got here a few minutes ago."

I haven't talked to them much since our last chat when I ran out. With the wedding, I barely saw them long enough to say hello, but I noticed how they spent the night talking to other people. I don't understand why they'd bother showing up here together if they want to go through with this separation.

"Lovely to see you again, June," my mam says, pulling her into a hug. June greets both of my parents, and I can tell they like her by their ear-to-ear smiles. I ignore their covert side-eye in my direction—I'm sure Mam would kill to know precisely what we got up to these couple of days.

"What would you both like?" Roger asks.

"Don't trouble yourself," I reply. "Back in a sec."

When June and I reach the kitchen, she turns to me. "When will Cara get here?"

"Anytime."

"Right. Right, okay." She gnaws on her lower lip. "Your mom's sweet."

"Wasn't expecting either of them here. Not the both of them." I grab two glasses from the cupboard and set both on the counter. "Acting as if they're a happily married couple who're gonna tell jokes and go to dinner with each other and pretend like nothing's wrong. Unless they've changed their minds. If not, then they're living a lie."

"Yeah," June says, rubbing her thumb on the mouth of the green glass. "Your parents are doing their best. I'm not trying to diminish what you're feeling, but they're showing up how they can for you, even if their relationship has become complicated."

I grumble, not willing to admit that she's probably right.

"They love you enough to put aside their bullshit and be here together. That's special. Doesn't make the situation any easier, but it's something."

Reaching down for her hands, I intertwine mine with hers to pull her in close. I move to give her a swift, soft kiss, but she reaches up to my chin and entices me with the promise of more. It's the kind of time-stopping kiss that feels like a hello and a goodbye in one. Passionate, yearning, and bittersweet.

"June, can you—oh." Evvie walks in on our intimate moment. "Would you help me with some of the dinner prep?"

"Sure." A pinkish blush spreads across her cheeks while she washes up in the sink. "I'm not as impressive of a chef as Cara, but I'll do what I can."

"Thank you, love. Danny, message that daughter of mine and see where she is. Thought she'd be here by now."

I text Cara as I wander back into the living room.

"...plays with shadows, I'm impressed. Every single one has such character. Ah, here's the pro." Roger has his point-and-shoot camera out again. "Was telling them 'bout your Instagram."

"Oh?" I almost drop my seltzer. Roger's twice my age, and he has an Instagram. And he's somehow found me on there?

"You came up as a suggested profile the other day. Gave you a follow. Interesting stuff."

"Thanks." I'd prefer to talk about pretty much anything else at this point. Photography and my family don't mix.

"Y'see this?" Roger holds up his phone to my da. To my surprise, he doesn't scowl. Instead, his eyebrows jump up to his hairline, and he nods in such a way I think he might actually be impressed.

"Clicked through to your site, too. Looks grand. 'Click here for booking information.'"

"What're you booking?" my da asks.

"That's—I'm still working on that. The template had that, but I should change the site, for sure."

I'm saved by my mobile.

> CARA: Here

> CARA: I need you to come outside

> CARA: Now

I count my lucky stars for the excuse. When I head out to the driveway, Cara's leaning with her bum against the car, and Yaz stands right by her side. The scene looks off, tense. They're not the types for big, dramatic arguments, but whatever's going on, they don't look happy.

"...too much of a coincidence. Who else by that name would work there?"

"I agree," Cara says as Yaz recrosses her arms. "But, *why*?"

"That's why you'll go in and ask her."

"Everything all right?"

Yaz sighs and takes a step back, encouraging Cara to talk to me.

"No, not really."

"Did something happen on the honeymoon?"

"Minimoon. And no. Just—here, you best look at this."

I sidle up next to her as she pulls up an email on her phone. It's a newsletter from a site that sounds familiar.

"That's June's place?"

"Yeah. Scroll down," she says, impatient enough that she swipes down the message for me and presses the URL in the newsletter with heated conviction.

The headline reads: "DNA EXPOSÉ: FAILED DNA LAB RESULTS AND THE BROKEN FAMILIES LEFT IN THEIR WAKE." I don't know what I'm looking at, or why.

"Keep going," Cara instructs. "Read that sixth paragraph, two sentences in."

After finding the exact spot she mentioned, a familiar name stands out.

Juniper Martin, one of our employees here at The Edge, recently encountered her own genealogy grief after a faulty DNA test result from Double Helix Labs. Robert Edwinson, a former lab technician there, said mistakes such as this happen infrequently but can't be ruled out completely. However, the rate at which he encountered them at Double Helix was ultimately one of the reasons he looked for employment elsewhere.

In ordinary circumstances, when labs catch these issues early, they're easily undone. However, after first contact, they can create complicated scenarios.

Such is the case with Juniper who traveled across an entire ocean to meet her supposed half sister. "It's my life, and it involves real people," she said. "People who I do [now] care about."

I read and reread those few paragraphs, paralyzed. June's words from the other night ring in my head. *You don't know who I really am.* She didn't mean *this,* though. She couldn't mean that she came all the way here to trick Cara.

To trick me.

"Did the lab reach out to you?" Yaz asks Cara.

"I don't think so, but I didn't pay much attention to my phone these past few days."

"But why would she hide this?" I sputter, reexamining every interaction I've had with June since she arrived. I know her.

Don't I?

"We need to get to the bottom of this," Yaz says in a way that's both diplomatic and unyielding.

Cara's face turns hard, and she looks toward the house. "There's only one way to find out."

Chapter Twenty-Four

Juniper

"What's this now?"

I turn to see Cara standing at the entrance to the kitchen, holding up her phone.

My world screeches to a halt. A minute ago, I hatched a solid plan with Evvie—I'd pull Cara aside, we'd sit in her childhood bedroom, and I'd be honest with her. She'd have questions, which I'd already prepared responses to, and she might be understandably upset. But I held onto the hope that she would understand why I didn't tell her sooner.

So Cara's glower trips me up, and I know, I just *know*. I'm not sure how she found out—the lab must have sent her an update—but my secret is a secret no more.

"I can explain."

Aidan appears right behind her, looking at me in a way he never has before. Helpless, wounded. So much so that I sense my heart tugging toward him.

"I'm scrolling through my emails, and I click on an article and this is what I see." Cara possesses an angry fire and a forceful determination in every movement. Overcome with nausea, I take the phone she's offering me and discover a familiar website on the screen. The headline punches me square in the gut.

"What the hell?" I mutter. This was not what I pitched, and this isn't my story. How in the world did Abby, a new intern, write some explosive hot take based on my life?

"Your name is in there," Cara says, pointing to the phone. "Right there."

"How did you get this?"

"I subscribed. It was in this morning's newsletter."

Of course. She's a wonderful, supportive human being who assumed I was her half sister. And now she and Aidan and everyone have found out the truth through an article on a clickbait website.

"I'm sorry. I was waiting for the right time."

Aidan crosses his arms, and his disdain for me has me gasping for air.

"I was!" I go on. "When the lab reached out to me, they weren't sure if the results were just off."

"So you *lied* to me." Cara snatches the phone from me and directs her pointer finger at my heart. "To all of us."

"Love, listen." Evvie steps in, but Cara's own mother can't salvage this wreckage. "She told me, but she got word right before the wedding. You were overjoyed to find out about her, to have a close girlfriend, a half sister—"

"You're joking." Cara runs both of her hands down her face in exhaustion. "You didn't think to mention that some woman's been pretending to be my half sister?"

"I wasn't pretending," I plead. "The whole time I've been here, I really did believe we were related."

"I doubt that."

"It's true." My heartbeat bangs like a drum. "I mean, I *hoped* we were related." I'm close to begging her to listen to me. "The DNA lab believed the results were fine, but they had to make sure. I retested about a week ago, and I found—"

"A week?" Aidan exclaims.

We've attracted the full crowd now, with Aidan's parents and Roger all filing into the kitchen. Even Winnie lifts his head from the dog bed to see what's going on. Everyone's expressions pierce me with all the questions

I've asked myself over the past few weeks. *Why didn't I just tell them? Why am I even here?*

"I waited until I was sure, which ended up being the wedding night, so—"

"She figured it was best not to trouble you amidst all the wedding prep," Evvie says. "Surely you can understand that."

"Mam, *enough.*"

"I wanted to tell you, but also..." I look at them all, and my heart sinks to the very bottom of my chest. "I guess I didn't too. You were so wonderful, all of you were." They're slipping through my fingers, like I'm grabbing at sand. "I got swept up in being around all of you. And then you asked me to be your maid of honor, and I tried to say no, but you insisted so—"

"So this is my fault?"

"No." I take a step toward her, but she backs up like I might turn her to stone if I get too close. "I expected nothing more than to come here and become friends and see you get married. I didn't plan that you would treat me like—like—"

"Like a sister," she spits out. "Because that's what I thought you were."

"Love, if you're to be cross at anyone, be cross at me," Evvie says.

"Oh, I am. I'm not some child you have to protect. I'm a grown woman. If I behaved like this to you, hid some secret from you because I said it would be better for you—which is absolute shite—you'd be furious." Cara shakes her head in disgust, making me wish I could dig myself a hole to crawl in. "And you. I invited you here. I confided in you. I asked you to be the maid of honor at my wedding. Except you've been a stranger all along."

My eyes prickle. "I'm still me. I've been me this whole time, just—"

"No," Cara says as tears form. "I can't trust a word you say."

She storms off, with Yasmine right behind her. My breathing has gotten shallow, and I think my body's gone numb. I yell out another desperate *sorry*, but it doesn't matter. Everything's spectacularly blowing up in my face, all at once and in slow motion.

"She's off to her room," Evvie says. "I'll talk to her." But once she goes and Roger follows her, that leaves me with Noah and Sarah McCarthy, and their son, who looks like I've crushed him to a million tiny pieces.

"I'm so sorry," I rasp out before he runs out the door. I call out for him and follow him into the front yard. "Aidan, please."

"Why didn't you say something?"

"I came this close to confessing everything to you."

"Yet you didn't."

"I couldn't tell you and not Cara. I needed to talk to her first, so I waited." I appeal to Aidan's loyal side—the man who puts others before himself. "I planned on telling her and then you and everyone today, but that fucking article ruined it."

"June, you can blame your workplace for how much you hate your life, but don't blame it for this, too. This is down to you and no one else."

The words slice through me. "You're right. Please look at me. I agonized over this. I'm not saying what I did was right, but what would have happened if I'd spoken up?"

He scoffs and throws his hands to the sky. "No point thinking about it."

"Everything would have changed. Everything. Even with the results in limbo, Cara never would have asked me to be her maid of honor. Maybe I wouldn't have even had a place at the wedding anymore. You and me—"

"And your article. Not much to work with there, I suppose." His voice catches, and the sight of him in pain because of me makes me feel like I'm suffocating. "D-doesn't matter what you intended, you fooled everyone. You fooled the town, all the guests at the wedding. You fooled..."

His last word goes unspoken. *Me. You fooled me.*

I swipe at my cheeks because they're soaked with tears. Only hours ago, he was inside me and whispering devotions onto every inch of my skin, but now Aidan looks at me like I'm scum on the bottom of his shoe.

"You got what you wanted. You could make believe, go back home, and have your story, and what do any of us matter?" He straightens to stand even taller above me. "What did I matter?"

"Aidan. I'm more myself with you than I've ever been."

He turns to walk away.

"I'm serious," I continue, tears blurring my vision like an impressionist painting. "Cara and I might not be related, but I am everything else that you know about me."

"I don't know anything about you! You showed up two weeks ago, but you haven't been you."

"Time doesn't matter. You said that yourself. Two weeks, two years, who cares? What I told you, about my mom, my grandma. Work. My dreams. That's real. You can't honestly believe you know nothing about me."

He exhales and shakes his head to the sky. I leaped at the chance to have a family, to belong, so much I ignored that I never really belonged here.

And now I'm losing all of them.

"You don't pick and choose when to be honest with people." He musses up his hair in visible frustration. "That's not how 'real' works. You're either all in or you're not."

"And I've been all in. I swear."

"No, you haven't." The volume of his voice rattles me. "This isn't a healthy way to begin a relationship. Or what—whatever we were doing. You need to trust the other person. And not just in how they make you feel good so you can talk to them about your whole life, but in their actions. I've spent time on people before who...who lie. I'm done with that."

I set a hand on his forearm, and a bright hope pulses through me when he doesn't pull away. "I fucked up here, I get that. But with you, I was the most honest I've ever been. So much that it scares me."

He seems to consider what I say, giving me some dangerous confidence before he releases himself from my grasp and scratches his neck. "C'mon."

"What?"

Through a shaky breath, he says, "I'm going to take you back to mine to pack, and after that, I never want to see you again."

"I swear, I told them to redact your name, Juney."

Ethan has taken zero responsibility for what's happened. He doesn't care that he took my personal story and donated parts to someone else's news-breaking byline.

"This is so screwed up," I say.

"I'm sorry you feel that way. We've changed you to Anonymous Source, if that helps."

"It doesn't. The damage is done."

"You can still write your piece, the personal narrative side of things. That might pair nicely with this investigative one. Which is blowing up, in case you were wondering." He waits for me to reply, but I'm too angry at his excitement about page views to say a thing. "I...I really am sorry how it all went down," he says, with something that sounds like empathy. "But we had to push this one through."

Turns out, I'm not the only one to deal with an algorithmic error, which was the lab's elaborate way of saying "software bug." The editor in chief at *The Edge* discovered some serious internal issues with Double Helix Labs through dating the CEO. It's why she finagled free kits for everyone, to get closer to the product. It's why Andy sounded so inexperienced—he was. The lab had a wave of new hires to manage the mounting problems they encountered with testing and matching.

So for her hard-hitting piece, Abby worked undercover. While I knew her as an intern, she was a seasoned journalist with years of experience and not a single dog-photographer-profile piece to her name. She included my information because Ethan, in his oh-so-helpful way, relayed some of my notes and our conversations to her. In helping her, he disregarded me.

During the editing process, the note to leave my name out of it was lost, if Ethan even did ask for that in the first place.

I've been a pawn in someone else's game.

"To be fair, I sent you an email update," Ethan says.

"I attended a wedding! A wedding I gave a speech at. A wedding where I'm in the *pictures*."

"You're getting a little emotional right now."

I fight the urge to scream. Instead, I hug a pillow to my chest, hoping I don't tear the thing to shreds.

After Aidan drove me back to his house, I packed my bags, and he arranged for me to stay at a bed-and-breakfast for the night. He despises me so much that he can't stand having me under the same roof as him. Every piece of furniture in this room, every wall, and every inch of carpet is some shade of pink. The owner said she rarely gets guests, so it's where her granddaughter sleeps when she visits. I'll spend my last night in Ballygrá in a Barbie doll fever dream.

"I wish you'd called me," I say. "Anonymous Source or not, I deserved to know."

"I never forced you to take this piece."

I snort a laugh, because while he didn't explicitly tell me I had to go along with the story, he made it clear that if I killed the article, I'd pay for it with a resignation.

But the most frustrating part of all of this is that he's also right. I called him because blaming him and blaming *The Edge* hurt less than admitting I'm the one to blame.

Me.

If I were smarter or braver or better, I would have pulled Cara aside the second I got the call. I wouldn't have waited for the perfect time because the perfect time would never happen. And while saying something sooner would have ripped the O'Sheas and Aidan away from me, the truth is I don't deserve the joy of a family. I never deserved someone as good as Aidan, either. I shouldn't, not for a glimmer of a moment, have allowed myself to believe otherwise.

Ethan tells me he expects me back in the office later this week, and I hang up before he says goodbye.

The double bed squeaks when I lay on it, and I don't have the energy to sit upright. I push my duffel onto the floor with a thud, and some of my clothes spill out. At Aidan's, I packed my belongings in a rush, not bothering to fold anything, so the inside of my duffel was an explosion of outfits and toiletries. He sat at the dining room table, head low and avoiding eye contact at all costs.

When I entered his bedroom to grab a few final clothing items we'd flung around that afternoon, my tears threatened, but I sucked them down. The smell of Aidan planted itself in my memory—that powerful woodsy scent that makes me long to slide my fingers through his hair and straddle him.

I'll miss that smell.

My phone rings, and my heart races with the anticipation of Cara or Aidan calling. Instead, Lissie's name and photo pop up, filling me with an intense longing for New York. A desire to get as far away from here as possible.

"How are you?" she asks before I can say hello, and her generosity makes me well up again. "I got off my shift like two minutes ago and saw your texts. Holy cow."

"She's never going to speak to me again."

"I'm sorry, June. Oh my god, I wanna hug you so hard right now. What can I do? Do you need me to come out there?"

"No. That's silly." I sniffle into a tissue. "If I can pry myself out of this bed tomorrow, I'll be on my way home. What I could really use is a machine to go back in time and listen to you and tell Cara about that phone call. Then I wouldn't be in this mess. I'm a moron."

"You're not," says Lis, calm, kind, and certain of herself. "You are a smart person who made a not-so-smart decision. Which then turned into a huge destructive snowball. There's no way you could have guessed this would be the outcome."

Lis. Even after I've done something despicable, she still sees the good in me.

"Do you think Cara asked you to be her maid of honor just because she thought you were her half sister?"

"Yes. I wouldn't have gotten an invite if that weren't the case."

"Okay, that technically is true, but she didn't have to ask you to stand in her wedding. She did that because she likes *you*," Lis says. "She had a bunch of crappy friends who were terrible to her, and then you show up, and you're fun and you're cool and you're the best type of friend someone could have."

"You have to say that because you're my friend."

"I don't. Listen to me—are you listening? You are a gem of this earth. I love you. I love how you text me when I'm not back at the apartment by a certain time and how you always buy an extra-unripe banana at the grocery store because the green ones are my favorite. You are a ride-or-die kind of gal, and Cara's smart and picked up on that immediately, so of course she was jazzed to get to know you and have you in her wedding."

"She hates me, and I can't blame her."

Lis sighs. "Have you talked to Aidan?"

"He hates me too." The mention of him makes me wish I could sink into the floor. I deserve every bit of his disdain. "We fought, and he dropped me off at a Malibu

Barbie Dream House-themed bed-and-breakfast. He's made it clear that he wants nothing to do with me."

"It's okay to be heartbroken."

"I'm not—I'm not heartbroken."

"Okay, okay. But you spent every waking moment in Ireland with him, so I'd understand if you're hurting over that too."

My reflex to dismiss her hunch and move on doesn't kick in. I've had my fill of pretending, so I go for blunt honesty instead.

"I like him. A lot. More than I've ever liked anyone. But that doesn't matter."

"It could."

"We knew each other for two weeks. So what."

"Do you remember Where's Waldo?"

Where's Waldo is a nickname we gave to a man Lis met, as she described it, one heavenly night in Hell's Kitchen. The two of them spent the whole evening walking around the city, talking and laughing and talking some more. It was one of those magical New York nights that she said played out like an art film.

"I don't believe in the one that got away," she says, "and he never called, so clearly he wasn't the one. But I think about him sometimes, and I will for a long time."

"That's you, though. You fall in love, and you fall hard."

"Maybe it's you too, with him. There's some people you meet and they just make an impression on you that lasts forever."

I made an impression on Aidan, but it's not the one I meant to.

Chapter Twenty-Five

Aidan

I can't sleep. June haunts my every thought, and I toss and turn the whole night. I still smell her on my pillow, so I doze on the couch instead, unsuccessfully.

When I get up the next morning, I set one goal for myself: don't think about her. The June I know doesn't exist. So I'll do whatever I can to forget her—to forget the beauty mark on the left side of her neck and the jingle of her laugh and how her fingertips are always a little bit cold and need warming up.

June should be at the Dublin Airport by the time I head over to the pub for my afternoon shift. Not that I'm thinking about her.

I grab my camera and head to the one place in Bally-grá where I can be alone. As I round one of the willow trees at the grove, I'm evidently the man with the worst luck in the world. Of all people, Mary's here, sitting in the same spot where June and I found Cara the morning of her wedding. I'd turn and make a quick getaway, but she spots me. She waves my way while holding onto a flower with half-plucked petals.

She shakes her head in disbelief. "Of all the places."

"Nice to see you, too."

"You shouldn't sneak up on a woman like that."

"I didn't sneak. Didn't figure anyone'd be here." Kicking a few pebbles toward the stream, I slide my hands into my pockets. "Where's Heath?"

"Headed back early for work. I'll go back in a couple days. Some time with the family and I'm ready to scream. Mam nitpicking. Da glued to the telly. It's nice to escape." She contemplates something and then scoots over to make room for the both of us. "Wanna sit?"

Mary and I don't know each other anymore, but she's also not a stranger. Deep in my heart, I'll always care about her, so I stroll over and have a seat.

"Strange, sitting here together," I say into the excruciating silence, and she chuckles.

"Look at us." She knocks her shoulder into mine. "I miss this spot."

"How's Dublin?"

"Different, but nice. I needed more to keep me busy, and between work and friends and Heath, there's always something. I'm happy there."

"Glad to hear."

"How was the wedding?"

The wedding. I will forever associate Cara's big day with June. Memories of watching her from across the room, how adorably nervous she was for her speech, and holding her hand for the sendoff. Will I ever reach a point where Cara mentions June in passing and I don't care?

"Grand."

"You could make an effort here." She heaves a sigh. "I shouldn't be surprised."

"I'm the most predictable man in the world, aren't I?"

She scoffs. "That's classic you, going for self-pity."

"It's not self-pity, you've just said yourself—"

"You're *always* the martyr."

"Yes, I played such a victim after you cheated on me."

"I needed to talk to someone, and he was there."

"How convenient." Rage boils inside me. "My brother did die, so forgive me for not being there for you."

"I never said not to grieve Michael. But we moved back here together, first for a few weeks. Then months. Then more months. What happened with your parents was consumin' you, and if you're not careful, you'll wake up your da's age, runnin' that pub."

I can't quite argue there. The blinders on my situation have come off, and I reflect on those last few months of us. She put her life on hold and moved back here, and she attempted to get me to find light at the end of the tunnel. In some ways, I understand her seeking emotional support from someone else, even if I don't agree with it.

"I am sorry." Her apology comes out gentle and sincere. "For everything."

I pinch the bridge of my nose, then lean forward with my elbows on my knees. "Me too."

She crosses her arms from the chill, and I'm near-blinded by the glimmering diamond on her left ring finger.

"Shite," I say. "That's a rock if I ever saw one."

"I—" She fiddles with the ring which looks to be one size too large. "He proposed this weekend."

"Congrats," I say, and an honest happiness for her bubbles up in the background of my heart. After what we went through, I'll always want the best for her.

"Thanks. Complete surprise, but a good surprise." Mary twists the ring around her finger in circles, clearly still getting used to it. "What about you? How's your girl? You two looked smitten at the florist."

"It's nothing."

"You may as well have pasted on googly eyes. I stopped by the pub Sunday looking for you, and your da told me you'd taken her on a trip. Anyone can piece that one together."

"I offered to show her around. Trip was rubbish, though."

It was the best three days of my life.

"I'm sorry."

"Me too."

"You seem a bit down about it."

"I'm grand," I lie.

Mary toys with a hole in her jeans and turns to me. "My mam said it seemed soon. The engagement. On paper, I guess we are moving fast. But all the things that felt so uncertain before for me, with Heath, they make sense. I can't marry him fast enough." She meets my eyes and shrugs. "When it's right, it's really right."

"I'm getting relationship advice from my ex-girl-friend."

She laughs and nudges me with her shoulder. "A friend."

I look at my feet, despondence taking over me. "I'm not a very good judge of what's right anymore."

My parents come to mind—how they struggle with each other each day, and how I've failed to help them pick up the pieces of their marriage through the heaviness of grief. Nothing with them feels right. And I think of June, or the June I thought I knew. Maybe I ought to have given her an honest chance to explain herself, but I can't. Not after seeing how she hurt Cara, and not after her lying, over and over to me. What happened between us turned into something so wrong, and I'm not sure how to get past that.

But the alternative—getting over June—sounds impossible.

"Don't overthink it," Mary says.

"It's what I do best."

She snorts a laugh and gets up, kicking the tip of my shoe. "I should head back. Catch you later."

"Congrats again."

"Thanks. I hope you get what you're after." She walks a few steps and throws the last words over her shoulder. "And if it's right, don't let it slip away."

I don't get any decent shots, which doesn't surprise me one bit. If I'm not ruminating over the talk with Mary, I'm failing miserably at my goal of not thinking about June. Before too long, I head back to work for another thrilling shift at the pub. I wipe down the already clean-looking bar top. Glasses are stacked, the register's set. Whoever closed last night deserves a raise.

Two muffled voices come into earshot—one with a familiar ring and the other one new to me. They grow louder, climbing up the basement stairs that lead to the larger supply room.

"There's another of these down there that needs to be brought up," my mam's voice instructs. "Oh, Danny. You're here already."

"I'm on every Tuesday."

"Yes, of course. Wasn't sure if you'd be coming in on account of..." Her voice grows quieter as she becomes more and more unsure of what to say. "If you need the day off...or you need some time for yourself, then—"

"I don't."

"Well," she says, squeezing me on the shoulder, "s'good to see you."

A buff gentleman walks toward me and places a case of wine on the counter. "Hey there, I'm Oscar."

"Aidan."

"Thanks for covering for me the other night."

This is the lad who got food poisoning. What he lacks in common sense, he makes up for in sheer brawn. His handshake alone dwarfs me, and he could lift me over his head with one arm, easy. Still, his affable smile and warm demeanor leads me to believe he'll do well slinging drinks.

"Since you're here, Oscar can switch between shadowing you and popping into the inventory closet to work with me." She hesitates. "He's training as our new general manager."

"You're the general manager," I blurt out, as if she forgot.

"Oscar's got plenty of experience as a GM."

"So've you."

Her hands fall to her thighs with a soft slap as her irritation gets the best of her. "Let's have a chat in the back," she offers. We step into the office, and I shut the door behind us.

As I chew the inside of my cheek, I rummage through every question I have. *Why are you doing this? Why have you given up trying?*

"I didn't want to bother you while you were off," she says. "But I planned to tell you this week."

"So the separation means everything? Not just from da but from the pub as well." *From me*, I almost say, but I bite my tongue. "You've plans to stay with Aunt Bri again?"

"Not sure yet, Danny. We still care about each other. And nothing stops us caring about you. But neither of us wants to be unhappy."

"I knew you were sad. Didn't realize you were unhappy."

"I don't know what I am most days." She clasps her hands in front of her. "Losing Michael has been—" She chokes on the words before powering on. "The death of a son has...well, it's about killed me."

I exhale and wish I could pace, but the confines of the back office suffocate me. "The other day, I realized I forgot how his laugh sounded. No matter how hard I thought of him, it wouldn't come to me." That devastating realization kicks up the dust of emotions like they're fresh—the despair, the hurt, the anger. I rub my head a few times to calm down. "I'm hurting too."

My mam slumps in a chair. She shifts left and right on the cushion, like she can't quite get comfortable, and then finally rests both hands in her lap.

"I'm wrecked from holding it all together," I admit, taking the seat next to her. "I'm tired of trying to keep what's left of our family together. Of being the parent, having the weight of us three on my shoulders, and knowing I can't carry enough. I just want my mam."

"I know, Danny. I'm so sorry. No one needs to mention how I've been failing spectacularly with this whole motherhood thing."

Hearing her admit this cuts like a knife and also stitches the wound. She's trying her best, and it's not been enough, but at least she recognizes it.

I glance around, and oddly enough, I wish Da were here. As much as my da and me fight, he's a rock I can weather the storm with, even if he's a pain in my arse too. I can count on him.

"Michael is everywhere to me. I see him every place I look in this town." She twiddles her thumbs, one chasing the other chasing the other. "He's walking down the road to visit mates of his. He's dropping by the house, looking for leftovers. And he's at the pub most of all—pouring pints, wiping the counter, clapping along to the live music." She faces me for the first time in our entire conversation. Her cheeks shimmer with tears. "You say you can't remember his laugh. But there must be something wrong with me, something broken inside, because I just can't move on from losing him."

"But you haven't lost me." My voice is hoarse. "You've a son right here in front of you, but I may as well be invisible."

"Oh, sweetheart. I see you, I see..." She pulls out a hanky and runs it under her nose. "I see everything you've done for us. But I don't think this is something we can rush."

My mam looks broken. Like all the fight has gotten sucked out of her. If I could be furious with her, I would. All this time, I assumed she was dwelling on Michael and not allowing herself to move on. But I'm starting to understand that it's not because she doesn't want to—it's because she can't.

And the same way my ex pushed me, I've done the same with Mam. Deep inside, something cracks, because maybe taking shifts at the pub wasn't me doing my folks a favor. For good and bad, doing that kept me close to Michael.

"We've changed." My mam reaches up to a locket around her neck and worries it with her thumb. "All of us have. Your da and I are trying to figure out how to move forward, and that means life'll look different, that's all."

I absorb what she's saying, nodding along. "It's strange. I've been hanging onto the one thing that I thought would keep him alive and keep us all together."

"What're you hanging onto, love?" Her brows furrow in genuine concern.

"This. The pub."

"Oh, you." Her head bobs with a knowing nod, like she suspected as much. "You're a good lad wanting to do right by your family. Nothing wrong with that."

"I hoped if I gave you both enough time, we'd...sounds daft now. We'd go back to normal. Just...back to before."

"Perhaps your da and I aren't the only ones who need time."

My vision becomes muddled, and my eyes burn with realizing what I've been holding onto. "I miss him."

"Me too, love." She lets me rest my head on her shoulder as tears slide down my face and onto her shirt. We sit like that until the wave of sadness washes over, both of us sniffling less and less.

"Don't fret yourself about." Mam musses my hair. "You'll have us, always. But you've got so much life left to live that you shouldn't be afraid to let go of the past and chase after your future. You heard from uni?"

"No." Confusion ripples through me, and I whip my head to her. "How'd you know?"

"Cara let slip at the wedding. One too many champagnes for the radiant bride."

I chuckle to myself. "Doubt I'll get in."

"You're too young to be so cynical." Mam scoffs and grabs both of my hands in hers. "I'm going to tell you something your father should have said a long time ago."

"What?"

"We're lettin' you go from the pub."

I roll my eyes. "Hilarious."

"I'm serious, love."

After studying her face, I can tell she's absolutely serious. Her mouth rests in a straight line, and her eyes urge me to go. But my previous lofty plan of striking out on my own—the one June convinced me I could achieve—seems like an impossible feat.

"We want the best for you, and we agree it's not here at the pub."

"You've discussed this?"

"Of course," she chuckles. "He loves you and wants you to be happy. And Michael, he would too."

I stumble over my own thoughts before blurting out, "But what am I supposed to do?"

"Anything." She cups my face, a palm on each side. "Live life. Who knows, that camera of yours might lead you somewhere. But whatever you choose, only come back when you need a fresh pint."

Chapter Twenty-Six

Juniper

"Can I get anything for you, dear?"

The bed-and-breakfast owner doesn't know what to do with me. I declined any offers of tea or coffee or food, and when she gave the gentlest reminder of my checkout time, I handed her my credit card to pay for another night. My flight was supposed to depart tonight, but I couldn't bring myself to leave. Not with all the damage I've caused.

But neither Aidan nor Cara will answer my calls or messages, so I'm at a loss.

Lis has acted as my personal assistant and rescheduled my departure. She's an angel. Lis said she doesn't understand, but she respects my desire to wallow and lick my wounds. Beyond that, though, she's threatened to come out here and drag me onto the next plane herself.

Another light tap on the door pulls me from my trance.

"Thank you, Mrs. Doyle, but I'm fine, really."

"June?" The voice is soft and kind. "It's Evvie. May I come in?"

I smooth out some stray strands of hair on my way to the bedroom entrance and catch sight of myself in the mirror. My eyes have puffed up to the size of grapefruits and my nose is red from rubbing tissues on it.

When I see Evvie standing there, fists clasped in front of her body and eyebrows scrunched together in concern, something inside of me snaps. All of the worry and stress and melancholy of the last two weeks pour out of me in the form of hot tears and runny mucus. Evvie wraps me up like a delicate flower she adores, and we stay that way for a few minutes until my sobbing subsides.

"I'm so sorry, love," Evvie whispers into my ear. "I thought I was doing the right thing."

"It's my fault."

She can take responsibility for her somewhat ill-advised guidance, but I can't blame her. Evvie didn't make me do anything against my will. I did this, not her.

"I feel terrible," Evvie says, "because I asked you to continue the lie."

We settle onto the bed, with me lying down while Evvie perches on the edge. "Here." I pull the photograph of Cara's father from the depths of a notebook, and the act is like pulling a knife from my abdomen. "Don't need this anymore."

"Oh, love. I—"

"The photographer got photos at the wedding? Ones without me, right?"

"He did."

"Good. Cara hates me."

"She doesn't hate you. She's confused and hurt, but any of her anger, well, most of that's directed at me, and rightly so." Based on the hesitancy in her voice and the way she keeps rubbing her palms together, they must have had a nasty argument. "You were making the most caring choice."

"I should have told her sooner. No, I wish I'd gotten the results sooner. Then I wouldn't have traveled here." I swallow to keep another breakdown at bay. "Doesn't matter. Thank you for coming. Cara won't pick up. Aidan won't pick up. What a stupid choice to stay here, but I...I couldn't leave. I couldn't. I don't know why."

I fiddle with a decorative tassel on one pillow and sigh. At least I've reached the point where tears won't come—I've cried my quota for a long, long while. Evvie clicks her tongue and rubs my arm up and down.

"I think you do," she says. "You need to talk to her."

"How?"

"Have you tried leaving this room?"

I glare at her, wondering where the soft, sweet Evvie went. "I'm not in the mood for tough love."

She takes one of my hands in hers and holds it tight. "I'm sorry for what's happened. And I'm partly responsible—you can't say otherwise. I need to help you make it right, so you *must* talk to Cara. She's hurting as much as you. And listen to me when I say this, people make mistakes. But it's what you do after that mistake that matters. You have to try."

Mrs. Doyle appears with a tray of teas and cookies. She clearly wants to snoop—she loiters longer than necessary for someone intending to drop off a small afternoon snack. With a polite smile directed my way, she closes the door behind us. Not knowing what is going on must be eating her up inside, though, and when I mention this to Evvie, we giggle despite ourselves.

"You and Cara together remind me of me and my sister." She grins, and that fills me with enough warmth that I can't help but do the same. "Nola and I were so close growing up. Borrowing clothes from each other. Doing each other's hair. Staying up late and talking 'bout boys. But for a while, when we were in our twenties, we fell out. Barely spoke for years after."

"At the wedding, you both seemed so...I don't know. You're like best friends."

"We are, but we've had rough times. As we've gotten older and had kids, the tension calmed down between us. But we once had the biggest fight. Horrible. Said words we couldn't ever take back, too." She traces the floral pattern on the comforter with her forefinger. "Save for an odd call on the holidays, we didn't talk."

"What changed?"

"That's the thing. A few years go by, we're enduring a holiday dinner together, and my da locks us in a room and says we need to sort ourselves out or no Christmas pie for us. At first, we didn't acknowledge each other. But when we finally got to talking, we realized how small our problems with each other were compared with how much we loved each other."

"Cara won't ever forgive me for this." The immediate sting of my actions might go away one day, but not for months. Years. Maybe never. "What I did is pretty hard to salvage."

Both with Cara and Aidan.

"We also don't have an entire lifetime of memories together like you and your sister," I continue. "She'll be happy to get me out of her life as quickly as I arrived."

"No. I know her. She's upset, the way she found out and all. But she wants to talk to you. She'll listen." Evvie pats my leg and offers a regretful shadow of a smile. "Perhaps you don't believe me or don't trust I know her best interests after this, but—"

"That's not it." My chest aches to hear the doubt dripping off each of Evvie's words. I grip her hand and squeeze, guiding her attention to my face. "You wanted the best for her. You're a good mom. Anyone would be lucky to have you as their mom."

Her eyes glisten as some tears form. "I don't make the right choices all the time, though. And you, you've been good for her. You came into her life when she needed a friend, and you treated her even better than that. Like a sister. I'd hate to see that all go away."

Cara welcomed me like her own flesh and blood the moment I stepped into the restaurant. I basked in the glory of having a family and let her right past my defenses as a close girlfriend and a sister. As someone to confide in and get close to and love.

She loved me being here too.

"Okay," I say, bracing myself with a deep breath. "So what do I do? Unless you're going to lock us up and threaten us with Christmas pie, I don't see how I'll get her to listen to me."

Evvie tuts and waves at me. "You don't need to wait for me or anyone else to get the two of you in a room together. Don't waste time like I did." She strokes my cheek and plants a doting kiss on my forehead, and I feel like the child this bedroom belongs to. "You became close in a way where time didn't really matter, wouldn't you say?"

Lis and Aidan said the same thing—that sometimes those brief relationships can mean the most. But it's up to me now if I'm going to let that all slip into the past, or if I'll try to save us.

"Sooner than you're ready, talk to her. And talk to him, too."

The mention of Aidan makes my cheeks heat to a thousand degrees.

"I watched that lad grow up, and I've never seen him as happy as these last couple of weeks."

"What should I say?"

"The truth."

I manage a weak smile, and when she opens her arms, I fall into them. "Thank you for everything."

"Of course, dear." She pats me on the back. "You always have a home, and a family, here in Ballygrá."

"We're closed." Cara points to the sign in the window and arches an eyebrow at me.

"Can we talk?"

"Talk?"

"Um. Yes?"

"Alright, then," Cara declares, leaving the cafe door open enough to poke her head out and not an inch more. "Talk."

After my conversation with Evvie, I sank into the bed to pity myself some more and ponder her advice. *She wants to talk to you. She'll listen.* My intuition believes her, but Cara's expression, full of disgust, tells me otherwise.

But I have to try, and this is my only chance. I brace myself against a gust of wind, crossing my arms for warmth. The sky spits rain onto my face.

"Can I come inside? I feel awful, and—"

"You should."

"I do. Please."

"Don't you have a flight to catch?"

"Talking to you is more important."

"Well, I'm working."

"I can help."

Cara thinks this over, and much to my relief, she makes room for me to scoot inside. "Fine. Got some deliveries yesterday that I need to put away and I'm behind."

The lingering scent of cinnamon and butter doesn't relax me, but at least I'm here. I'm inside. She's willing to be in the same room as me, so maybe she's willing to listen. Evvie texted that Cara would stay late at the restaurant playing catch-up with work, but she didn't push beyond that. She'd made her case earlier, and she left the final decision up to me.

Cara ushers me to the inventory closet, and I follow obediently, two steps behind. Stacks of boxes litter the floor. I tiptoe around a few packages, some of them already sliced open to reveal their contents: napkins, condiments, and cleaning sprays. She sets a box cutter in front of me and points to some discarded cardboard.

"Break those down."

"You've got every right to be mad at me."

"I don't need your permission to be upset," Cara snaps. I wish with all my might that we could go back to how we were before—friends, almost sisters. But we can't. We can only move forward, and I'm going to have to push us there with all my strength.

Cara jams some rolls of paper towels onto a wobbling shelf, and while she doesn't speak, her jerky, rapid movements tell me all I need to know. She's furious, but she's also in pain. I see myself in her—the kind of person who pushes others away when they're hurting.

"I was going to talk to you about the call from the lab."

She flashes me a look that says *I don't believe you.*

"At first, they didn't have any answers," I go on. "They wouldn't until I tested again, so I sort of hoped the lab was just going through a formality and we would be fine. And with the wedding and—"

"Your article?"

"Yes, with that too, I pushed the other outcome from my mind. When I thought about mentioning it, the time never seemed right." I channel the frustration with myself into slicing through some of the tape and dismantling the boxes.

"I had a right to know too. We were matched falsely, both of us."

"You did." My hands tremble from the nerves, and I steady myself with a breath. "I clung to the dream scenario, and I just couldn't let go and face the truth. I told myself it was to make your life easier, and at first, it was. Had everything come back normal, we would have had a good laugh about it. But then...it was like I shoveled a hole for myself and couldn't climb out." I sheath the box cutter and reach into my pocket. The paper I retrieve has a few fresh crinkles that clash with some of the more worn ones—spots where the note creased open and closed and open again. "I'm sorry for everything. For not being honest, for the way you found out. But," I say, offering the sheet to Cara, "I meant this. Every word."

She unfolds the note, and her entire face softens when she registers that I've given her the maid of honor speech. Her mouth quirks in an almost-smile, but she doesn't grant me its full radiance yet. She folds the paper and looks up at me like she's deciding whether to toss me to the curb or hug me. "That was a real shite thing to do," she says. "You made me feel like such an eejit. I let you into my life without question. So desperate to have good friends again, and a half sister?" Her bottom lip shakes. "I guess I hoped it would be true too. So much that I overlooked how you and I don't look alike."

"Not even close," I say with a rueful laugh.

"And Mam knowing about it too. That hurt."

"She was looking out for you."

"I wish you'd been honest." She rests a hand on one shelf and cocks her hip.

"Me too." I swallow so loud I swear the sound echoes. "But I care about you. I love you," I say, and my cheeks warm at the vulnerable confession. "As a sister, even if I'm not. And as a friend."

She absorbs what I've said, breathes in and out, and then exits the room. My chest deflates. More hot tears build up, and I swallow back a sob as I grab my jacket. What I did to Cara has made our relationship irreparable, and I need to get out of here before I collapse.

As I race toward the door, Cara reappears with a bottle of wine and two glasses.

"W-what's this for?" I ask, wiping at my eyes as she pours me some, the ruby liquid swirling in the glass.

"For friends. For sisters."

My mouth hangs open in wonder. We aren't unsalvageable. That dream scenario could be mine.

"Love you too," she says, clinking her glass against mine. "And there's no limit to the people I love, remember?"

I barrel into her with a hug, sloshing some wine out of my glass. "Thank you," I mutter into her hair.

During one of our first conversations, we sat in a booth at McCarthy's Pub, and she told me this. Cara doesn't throw those words around as an affirmation when the mood strikes—they represent her and how she lives. She opens herself up to people completely. She gives second chances. We'll need some time until we're back where we were before, but we can start building back at least.

So we start. We laugh and put inventory away and drink and cry because we laugh so hard. I tell her how I'm not sure what's in store when I return home and walk into *The Edge*, and how it's the first time in my life I've thought of doing a job at any other publication or living in any other city. She makes me promise not to leave New York until she's at least gotten to visit for New Year's Eve in Times Square. Cara tells me all about the minimoon as she swoons, recalling, with that sparkly kind of newlywed bliss, all of the fine details—the boutique cliffside hotel and the starry night skies.

"And what about you and your grand tour?" Cara asks.

"I shouldn't have gone. Add that to my list of bad ideas."

Cara and I sit on the floor of the inventory room, buzzed and struggling to clean up the rest of the empty packaging. She taps my foot with her own.

"As your friend, and as his, you should do something about that."

I hide behind my hands. "Oh god, I violated some kind of girl code, didn't I? Sleeping with your closest guy friend."

"Please. I'd never let a man come between us. Even Aidan, who I adore. I'm not his keeper, so if he goes and falls in love with some crazy American girl, then he can. Honestly, he should. I think people should always choose love."

My posture tightens at the mention of the L-word. Of course, it was too soon for love with the two of us, but maybe we could have gotten there one day.

"But you hurt him. Danny's got a serious thing for you."

"Not anymore." I down the rest of my wine and snatch up the bottle for more.

"How he feels won't disappear overnight. He and I have been friends for ages, and when he's got it bad for someone..." She swirls the remainder of the wine in her glass, looking at it like it's a crystal ball. "Can I make a confession?"

"Sure."

"I found the air bed a couple days after you arrived. I didn't mention it because you two seemed cute together."

I narrow my eyes at her. "Sneaky."

"Forgive me."

"C'mon." I dismiss her with a wave of my hand. "You don't need to ask forgiveness for that."

"I don't mean for the mattress." She flashes a scheming grin before swallowing the rest of her wine.

The front doorbell jingles, and an all too familiar voice calls out for Cara. "Back here!" she yells. My world moves in slow motion as the steady sound of footsteps nears.

"Sorry, took longer than expected. I—" He stops in his tracks at the sight of me. "What're you doing here?"

Aidan has stolen my breath by showing up and walking in the room. His hair appears slightly roughed up, and some end-of-day stubble has grown in. He looks weary, which I'm a little happy to notice. That means he hasn't been living his best life since yesterday.

But that's because of me. Because I'm the last person on the planet he wants to see.

"I'm, uh, on a grand apology tour," I say, letting out a self-conscious chuckle.

He doesn't laugh, and he doesn't ask questions, but Cara skates around the awkwardness. She shoos us both out of the back room and says she'll finish putting items away in the morning. We walk outside and wait for her to lock the front door.

"You're heading that way, aren't you?" she asks me in a cheerful voice. "Drop by the cafe tomorrow before you head off, yeah? Say goodbye properly." She hugs me and kisses me on the cheek. "Danny, can you walk June home? I can't keep Yaz waiting any longer."

This was apparently not a request but a demand, because Cara jets off on her two feet before Aidan has the chance to say no.

He looks at me in the dim light of the street lamp for the first time since he showed up, and I see the betrayal reflected back. Neither of us moves, but I wish I could reach out and hold him with my whole being. I've missed him in the last twenty-four hours—the kind of longing for someone that overflows, like my feelings are a faucet that won't turn off. I don't know what comes next for us, and the uncertainty makes me sick to my stomach.

"Your room decent?" he asks, avoiding eye contact with me.

"Yeah. Very pink."

He nods.

"I'm sorry," I say, my voice straining.

"You've already said that."

"And I'll keep saying it if the apology will bring me back to you somehow." I take a tentative step toward him and could scream with happiness when he doesn't retreat. As I grab his hand, the sensation of his skin is electric. My thumb travels over the hills and valleys of his knuckles. "I hated the thought of losing you, but what I did made me lose you. If you would give me a second chance...at anything? Friends? Or people who text occasionally?" I let out a halfhearted laugh at my own words, but they don't prompt any response from Aidan. "I'll take you any way I can get you. My life is better with you. I'm better with you."

Aidan stares at where our hands are clasped together, and my heart beats a million times a minute. As he processes what I've said, I silently make every offering possible to the universe. *Please. Please give me this one thing.*

"I want to." Aidan clears his throat and gives my hand an apathetic squeeze. "Everyone in my life's weighing in with their own opinions, and Cara's made up with you, and maybe I should too." He shakes his head and releases my hand, sucking the breath from my lungs. "But I can't. I've so much going on right now with my folks. Maybe school, too, I don't know. You've really...I need to focus on me, and I know how I am with you. Not focused. Not thinking clear. I have to worry about what I need and what I want."

"And you don't want me?"

"Christ." He runs a rough hand through his hair. His sad eyes meet mine. "Not like this. I've been lied to before, and we have to start again from the beginning, and I...I just don't see how that's supposed to work with us. What, with you in New York and me here?"

"We can text. Call. Or FaceTime."

"June." He sighs, and I know I've lost him.

"Okay," I say, withdrawing as I wipe away the hot tears trailing down my cheeks. As I turn, all I want is to put as much distance between him and me as my feet will allow.

"Let me make sure you get back safe."

"I'll be fine," I call out, even though I am anything but fine.

"Goodbye," he calls out, and in between my heavy steps, my heart breaks.

Chapter
Twenty-Seven

Aidan

The cursor hovers over the Upload button. For what feels like the thousandth time this month, I make sure all the photographs are there, all edited properly and all in the correct order.

Someone knocks at my door, and I minimize the window as Cara enters the house.

"Danny, I've brought us dinner!" she calls. I catch the sound of paper bags rustling, and the scent of rosemary and roast chicken lures me straight to the kitchen.

"No Yaz?"

"Not tonight. Has to work late but sends her love."

"That's a shame."

"Ah, come on." Cara hugs me and kisses me on the cheek. "Your mind's on leftovers and nothing more. Can't fool me."

I pop one of the roasted potatoes in my mouth with a mischievous grin. We set the table, and as Cara scoops out food onto my plate, I salivate. I spent the whole day editing photos, so I forgot to eat lunch and I'm ravenous.

"Send in a response yet?"

"No," I reply.

Last week, I received my acceptance back into university. They want me. If I accept, I'll enroll in classes for the spring semester.

"You at least tell your folks?"

"They're glad." I spear some greens with a fork and pop them in my mouth, satisfied. "Said they support it."

"Your own mam fired you, so I'd hope so. I'm sure she's pleased that it wasn't for nothing."

"Christ," I say. "That's harsh."

Being unceremoniously let go from the pub unlocked something for me. For ages, I'd been the youngest Mc-Carthy—Michael's younger brother, Noah and Sarah's son, the presumed future owner. Now I'm just a man who stops in for a drink. The resentment has dissipated, and the expectations have been lifted from my shoulders. The pub still reminds me of my brother, and it always will, but the memories are more joyful now.

"Submitted work anywhere?" Cara asks.

"Soon."

Not clocking in at the pub means I've had more time to plan shots and loads more time to edit. Not that I've *done* anything with all those photos yet. While I've found some publications open to working with free-lance photographers around the world, I freeze when I sit down to upload a sample of my work. I've gone through the motions countless times, but I never hit that last button.

"How's married life?" I ask, hoping to deflect the attention her way.

"Paradise," Cara says with a blush. "Celebrating one month today."

"I forgot. Congrats."

"I don't expect anyone to remember except Yaz."

"Still, a month."

"I know," she says, pouting. "The wedding already feels like ages ago." She grabs my empty plate, and I follow her to the sink so we can clean up. "Have you given any thought to New York?"

My whole body stiffens. Cara hopes I'll join her and the O'Sheas for their New Year's trip—a New Year's trip to visit June. Cara doesn't know I've got a much sooner trip purchased that I'm agonizing over, unsure whether I should cancel the flight altogether or...what? Show up at June's in some grand romantic gesture?

The plane takes off tomorrow.

"I won't join. I shouldn't."

"Who says? Besides, that's not what matters." Cara playfully bumps me with her hip. "What matters is if you *want* to."

Want to? My heart says yes, of course I want to see June. I can't get her out of my head. Her laugh, her scent, her touch—all of her has stayed with me. One of the reasons I've added so many new photos to my portfolio is because I'm afraid of what will happen to me if I don't keep busy. Cara's continued messaging her, daily, I think, and I've thought of asking a million times how June's doing. The temptation to text her, call her, or hop on that plane in twenty-four hours—I can hardly fight it.

My head, though...my head tells me no.

"I admire that you've moved past what she did. I do. Even if I might like to see her, she wouldn't care. It's been weeks. What we had is done."

"But you want to?"

I furiously scrub a bowl clean, ignoring my best friend's question.

"Did you read her piece?"

"I don't want to—"

"Christ, you're impossible." Cara sets a dish on the dish rack and turns toward me, scowling. "She made a mistake. June didn't tell you or me or anyone because she liked us too much. There are worse reasons."

I focus on the dirty dishes, keeping Cara's reasoning at bay.

"You're being an eejit," she goes on.

"I know!" I exclaim, accidentally dropping a bowl in the sink. "Christ, I know." I rub my forehead with the back of my wrist, and Cara places a hand on my back. "I've spent the past month waking up every day wondering why I'm like this. And with each day that goes by, she's forgotten about me more. But what I want, I can't have. She said so herself—she doesn't do long-term stuff. And what I want with her..." I pick up the broken ceramic pieces and chuck them into the bin. "Going to her and making up so we can be just friends...see each other on holidays, or send the occasional text. I can't handle that."

"Danny." Cara snatches one last dish and rubs it dry. "I don't think she wants to be just friends."

Cara shows me her mobile, displaying an article in *The New York Times*. An article written by June.

"She did this for their *Modern Love* section. Would you read it?"

I take in a big breath, aware that these words could eviscerate me.

After a lifetime of loveless family and loveless relationships, I discovered love of more than one kind in a matter of only two weeks.

And then I lost it.

Luckily, I found that some love can be broken and put back together, piece by piece. Unluckily, once some other love shatters, it may lie on the ground of your memory forever, with no chance of repair.

June's writing stuns me. She's far better than that shite website ever gave her credit for. As I read about her experience, her words grip me tight and won't let go. They're vulnerable and they're heartbreaking. Even though I'm already plagued with indecision about whether to cancel my flight, this article has made the choice even harder.

I continue through her piece as she details what happened, but she focuses on what's happened since then too. She's going to therapy. She's experimenting with mindfulness—meditation just stressed her out, but she's enjoying yoga. She's getting to know folks in her building and reminding herself of what it's like to build trust in a healthy way with new people.

I'm an incredibly imperfect person. I convinced myself I didn't want any kind of love, but once I got a little of it, I wanted it all and lost sight of the very concept of it. So I'm learning how to have compassion for the wounded woman who went to Ireland with her defenses up, as misguided as she was. She's left me with a lot to process and a lot to miss.

What I did was wrong in so many ways and to so many people. To be given a second chance at sisterhood is one I want to deserve, and I'm doing my best to earn it, every day. I will carry that love with me the rest of my life.

And as for the man whose trust I betrayed beyond repair, I fear I'll never see him again. The thought hurts in a way I never realized was possible. But the love he gave me—I'll carry that for the rest of my life too.

I read the entire piece three more times, over-whelmed by the rawness and realness of it. My chest swells with pride because she had grand dreams of writing for more prestigious places, and she got one of the most prestigious of them all. As I hand the mobile back to Cara, that frustration and fury over what June did has washed away, and something else has taken its place.

Fear. Because what if I'm too late?

"What June wrote—that's not the way someone writes when they want to text now and then. 'The love he gave me'? And you're mad about her still. I can tell."

I lift a brow in her direction, not willing to verbally deny what she's said.

"Whenever my phone buzzes, you look over my shoulder to see who's texting. Which is rude, by the way." She shakes her finger at me in fake fury. "You haven't touched the guest bedroom, not even made the bed, since she left, probably because the sheets still smell like her. It's disgusting. And when I mention June, no matter how hard you try to look all angry and upset like you'll never forgive her, there's this light in your eyes. This kind of hope." Cara rests her hands on my shoulders and gives me a gentle shake. "You might be fooling yourself, but you're not fooling me."

Chapter Twenty-Eight

Juniper

The grocery store is insanity. There are carts every-where, stuffing and cranberry sauce flying off the shelves, and checkout lines that wrap around the aisles. I should have taken Lis's advice and not waited until the day before Thanksgiving to get the rest of the items on our list.

The burnt-out man behind the cash register swings each item through the scanner, and they beep one by one. He checks his watch and yawns.

"Sixty-five forty-two."

I give him a credit card, and I dig through my purse for a few reusable shopping bags.

"I'll need to see ID with this. No signature."

"Sorry. Wrong one." I switch that one out for my personal card. "Here, use this, please."

I roll my fingertips over the elevated numbers on my new business debit card. When I returned home from Ireland last month and went back into the office at *The Edge* for the first time, Ethan didn't bring up what happened. He sped right into the upcoming editorial, told me what he was looking for in pitches, and assigned me a few pieces with scandalous headlines to entice readers to click.

So I did what any sane, reasonable person would do: I quit. *And* I reported Ethan to human resources. I didn't realize how toxic the workplace was until I walked out that final day, free from Ethan's disgusting comments, Nancy's unreasonable demands, and all those obnoxious listicles.

Lissie has guided me through the freelance life, more than happy to share the wisdom she's gained from working countless odd jobs alongside acting. She advised me to open a separate bank account, and depositing that first check was a surreal experience.

When I step outside, the chaotic holiday foot traffic irritates me less than it used to. Everyone's prepping for some time off work and to see family. Maybe I'm extra sentimental because I know that feeling—the excitement of seeing family. I can hardly wait for a month from now when Cara and everyone will fly in for New Year's.

Well, almost everyone.

I hop on the train and, in order to not think about Aidan, I build a to-do list on my phone. Tomorrow, Lis's aunt will come over, and we'll lounge around and eat nonstop, so we've got to create a cooking plan. Ordinarily, I'd have Friday and the weekend off from work, but I have two assignments due early next week, so I should finalize those.

I've worked hard, sending out pitch after pitch, with a lot of them getting accepted. But the self-employed income hasn't blown me away. Fortunately, one of the former editors at *The Edge* reached out to me when she saw "freelance" listed on my LinkedIn. She founded her own site focused on design and architecture in the last six months, and while that wasn't my beat at *The Edge*, she said she always admired my work ethic. When she asked if I would like a reliable twenty hours per week of writing copy for the business, I jumped at the opportunity. I not only get a steady income, but I have a boss who won't call me by some cutesy nickname. Along with my other freelance work writing lifestyle articles and covering events across the city, I earn more than any paycheck from *The Edge*, and I'm infinitely happier. The subjects I cover vary, but I suppose that's one thing I can thank Ethan for—the ability to craft a compelling story about literally anything.

As I haul the groceries off the subway, my phone pings.

> **LIS: Where are you??**

> **LIS: Get here ASAP**

> **JUNE: Off the train, be there in 2**

> **JUNE: Everything okay?**

I smile to myself as I turn the corner onto our block. Lissie knows I've been emotionally fragile this month, so she's been extra protective—lots of check-in texts throughout the day, my favorite chocolates stocked in the cupboard, and an invitation to her mom's for Christmas so I'm not alone. Part of her hyperdiligent attention is because of the call from my grandma's nursing home. They informed me that she succumbed to her dementia at the beginning of November, passing away in her sleep. She was my grandmother, and she raised me, but she never really showed me love.

The guilt and sadness of the past still weighs me down. I find some kind of strange reassurance in knowing she's not in a constant state of confusion and pain. It's complicated, and I think it always will be. Thank goodness for therapy.

But the real reason I'm in the habit of crying myself to sleep is because of a guy I spent two weeks with who now couldn't care less about me. Who was supposed to be here today, actually. That familiar pang in my chest returns, and I take three slow breaths.

As hard as it's been to not pick up the phone and call him, Aidan made his goodbye clear. Cara and I talk or text most days, but I shouldn't overstep my bounds to ask her about him. I want to respect his space and his wishes for as long as he needs. Forever, even. I have to, no matter how much it hurts.

When I open the apartment door, Lissie faces the couch where Aidan's sitting.

Aidan.

I stumble into the living room and drop my bags of groceries with a thud. I channel every bit of restraint to not pounce on him. He's real. He's here. My heart jump ropes into my throat.

"Hi," I croak.

"Hi." His eyes look gentle, hopeful. "I, uh, had that flight, so I hope you don't mind me here."

"N-not at all."

Lis walks forward without a word and picks up the bags I've dropped. "Go get 'em tiger," she whispers before shrinking into the kitchen.

"Do you—do you want something to drink? Eat? You must be tired after traveling."

He shakes his head and paces by the couch. I can tell he's already run his hands through his hair plenty of times the way it's sticking out in multiple directions, but he does the motion again anyway. He's got his familiar scruff growing in and some dark circles. He looks jittery and nervous.

"I've been a wreck," he says, as if reading my mind. Even so, Aidan's the most handsome wreck I ever laid eyes on. "And I've missed you."

"I've missed you too. I messed up. Badly."

"Please, you—you've apologized so many times to me. And in multiple ways." He stops pacing. "I read the article."

"You did?"

"I did."

"I meant every word, Aidan. I do—"

Before I can finish, he rushes forward, his lips find mine, and all is right with the world. My breaths come easy again. His kiss reassembles me after getting ripped to shreds, and I think I could inhale him. When we pull apart, he thumbs away the tears from my cheeks.

"I'm glad you're here," I whisper.

He smiles and then presses his mouth against my cheek, my jawline, and my neck.

"I had to see you," he says. "Had to. That impulsive, erratic man who bought a plane ticket on a whim, that's me. It's who I am. It's who I want to be all the time, and not some man who's stuck living every day the same."

He pulls me in for another kiss, my cheeks smearing tears across his.

"I understand why you did what you did." He rests his forehead against mine. "The choices you had, they were imperfect. It was an impossible situation, and I'm sorry I was such an eejit over it." He kisses me again, and I could levitate through the roof. "But I'm ready to go all in. If you still want me, that is. I'm not too late, am I?"

"You're right on time," I say with a laugh. "And of course I want you. I've only been able to think about you." I rest my palms on his chest, confirming that he's not a figment of my imagination. "I promise to be honest with you, always. To not hide behind anything."

"Good. I like who you are. Too much."

We dissolve into another kiss, his hands sliding underneath my shirt as I hook my fingers into the waistband of his pants. I can't wait to get these off and—

"Ahem."

We turn our heads to see Lis emerge from the hallway. "Sorry to interrupt."

"It's fine," I say, wiping my mouth.

"Sooo..." She looks at me, her eyes asking *This guy's not here to destroy your heart, is he?*

When she's assessed the situation and sees us both smiling like fools, she claps her hands together. "Cool. I need to, uh, get my steps in and close those rings, so I'll be back later. Sometime." Lissie doesn't own a fitness watch. She hurries out the front door, flashing me two big thumbs up on her way out.

We're alone. Just us.

"I'm excited to show you the city," I say, wrapped up in him.

"Where to?"

"Your choice. There's the touristy spots. Statue of Liberty. Times Square. But also *my* New York. My favorite dumpling place. My go-to bar. My bedroom."

"Mm." He pretends to ponder the options, causing me to giggle. "Let's start there." He leans in, smiles, and whispers against my lips, "But I'll go anywhere with you."

Epilogue

Juniper

"Cuttin' it close there, June!" Mike rolls the words together in his beefy Brooklyn accent. As I set the champagne on the counter, he nods in recognition. "Glad you saw. Got those just for you."

"I always notice when these babies are in stock. Thanks for putting my fave on the shelf for the holidays."

Mike bags my wine, and I ask him what his children and wife are up to for the evening. An enormous smile blooms on his face, and he pulls out his phone.

"This was an hour ago." In the image, his oldest son snuggles his daughter on a polka-dotted couch, both of them passed out. "We let the kids stay up since it's a special night, but they never quite get to midnight. Maybe next year. And you? These ain't all yours?" He sets the packed bags on the counter. "'Cause this may make for a fun New Year's Eve, but I'd hate to see you tomorrow."

The bell on the door chimes, and in walks Aidan. Those green eyes look heart-stoppingly gorgeous coming in from a snowstorm. He shakes white flecks off his camera, and then off himself, onto the welcome mat.

"Mike, this is Aidan, my boyfriend." *Boyfriend.* I used to avoid that title at all costs. Instead, knowing we're together makes warmth swirl in my chest. It sparks an involuntary smile.

"Lovely to meet you," Aidan says.

"Same. June's told me lots about you. How's New York?"

Aidan appears dumbstruck by the word mashup coming from Mike. He lands on *grand* as a response. Mike then talks about a trip he took to Dublin with some buddies in the '80s, while tapping away at the keys of the cash register.

Bodega man? Aidan mouths to me, and I nod with a giggle. Luckily, the Times Square coverage on the television drowns me out.

"You two stay warm. And Happy New Year!" I turn back to catch Mike winking at me.

Most New York winters don't turn this brutal this early, but the wind, ice, and cold bite at our exposed skin. The poor weather made sightseeing the past few days a frantic dance of bundling into layers to walk to the train, sweating profusely underneath those layers in the subway, and then spending five minutes or more undressing at our destination.

At least the unbearable temperature, plus the threat of a December 31 snowstorm, convinced Cara that watching the ball drop in person would be an utter nightmare. We all would have happily put on every last article of clothing for her if that's what she wanted, but what a relief that those plans changed. We opted for a small party at my apartment instead.

"Hold on, stand right there." Aidan sets the bag of champagne on the ground and dares to pull off a glove, a brave move considering we've walked ten feet, and my face has already started to go numb. He raises the camera, and his mouth opens slightly while adjusting some settings with his forefinger.

"Where should I look?" I ask through chattering teeth. I still feel awkward in all the photos he takes of me, like my arms and hands are foreign objects. But he assures me I'm perfect.

"The lighting with all the snowflakes is incredible out here."

Aidan decided against grad school and followed his heart, rather than play by all the rules and expectations. In the past month, he landed a few solid assignments, which didn't surprise me. Work will only get busier for him after the holidays. Most of what he's working on keeps him local to Ireland, which is good since he still wants to stay close to his parents, especially with his mom going to grief counseling. He likes to be around if they need him. In the coming year, though, he has two trips lined up for work. I love seeing him in his element, walking around with his camera as an extension of himself. In a way, it's like getting to know him all over again and getting to know him deeper.

Plus, I have to admit, he's pretty sexy when he's working.

Once neither of us can bear the chill anymore, we scurry up to my apartment. The sound of jolly holiday music plays from the speakers, and I dig my keys out of my purse.

Aidan stops before opening the door, leaning over to kiss me. His lips alone warm my entire body. As his tongue meets mine, I think back to this morning in bed and where that tongue had been. Heat rushes to my cheeks.

"I love you," he says between kisses.

My body turns into a puddle. I won't ever tire of hearing him tell me that—the way it makes my heart shoot around my ribcage like a little ball in a pinball machine. I also can't get enough of saying it back.

"I love you, too."

When we walk in, Lis squeals. "Just in time!"

She enlists Aidan's help in taking a few photos of her and her date—a man she only met two weeks ago but who she is convinced will become her future husband. I grab the bag of wines and slide the bottles into the fridge.

"All extremities intact?" Yaz walks over with Cara right behind her.

"Think so. I'm regaining sensation in my face too, which is nice." I pass the last bottle to Cara, who immediately unwraps the foil. "You're not too bummed out about Times Square?"

"We'd have been miserable," Yaz says.

"Agreed." Cara points to the television, which is broadcasting live from Forty-Second Street. "Check out that sorry lot."

A huddling crowd shivers while a nearby reporter talks to the camera. His nose has a frozen snot icicle dangling off the tip.

"I'm here with my favorite people in the world," she smiles while offering me a fresh glass of sparkling wine. "Besides, we can plan that for next New Year's."

Whenever Cara talks about the experiences we'll have together in the future, her voice contains zero doubt. We aren't related by blood, but we've become closer than I suspect a lot of sisters are. She's one of my closest friends along with Lis, and seeing the two of them hit it off makes me feel like the luckiest woman alive.

"Bubbly?" Yaz holds up the bottle and walks over to fill glasses for everyone.

I savor this moment. Not because I worry it will slip through my fingers, but because it's mine to cherish. Because moments like these aren't finite like I used to think, or reserved only for certain people. I have plenty more like this in store, even if I don't know what next year's holiday season will be like. All I really need is an internet connection and a computer, and with Aidan's business taking off, he won't be tied to one place either. In fact, in a couple weeks, I'll join him on his assignment in Barcelona and work on some stories there. We've got other plans too—he'll come to New York in the spring, and I'll spend a few months in Ballygrá this summer. We're thinking about Thailand in the fall, just for fun. Although we can't live in the same country together permanently yet, that won't stop us from seeing each other while seeing the world.

I walk into the living room where Evvie and Roger plant a kiss on each of my cheeks.

"Thank you for hosting, love," Evvie says.

"It's a real New York experience," I say as I squeeze past her. "More crowded than any bar would be."

The apartment I share with Lis doesn't leave us much furniture for people to sit on or space to move around, but no one seems to mind. I make room by selflessly using Aidan's lap as my seat.

We're packed into my tiny third-floor walk-up, half watching the television as we talk and laugh. It's loud. It's cramped. And it's perfect.

"It's moving!" Cara claps her hands together as the countdown to a new year begins.

Aidan loops his arm around me and nuzzles his face into my neck. "Ready?"

"Yeah." I smile. "I am."

Three.

Two.

One.

Thank you for reading *The Half of It.* If you enjoyed this book, please consider leaving a review. Indie authors thrive with reviews from readers like you, so scan the QR code below to leave a review on Goodreads.

Newsletter

Want more spicy destination romance in your life? Sign up for Theresa's bi-weekly newsletter and receive her free novella, *Match Made in the Maldives*. Visit her website at theresachristine.com/subscribe or scan the QR code below to join the journey.

About *Match Made in the Maldives*:

Luna Moore holds herself to the highest standards, but no one knows how imperfect her life is right now. Her priority is ensuring her family has an amazing time on their vacation to the Maldives, though—not burdening them with news of her struggling graphic design business or her cheating ex-boyfriend. She'll put up a façade this week in paradise, and then she can go home to fix her mess of a life.

Finley Robertson needs to figure out what's next after selling his business, and a vacation is the perfect reset button. As the long-time best friend of Luna's older brother, Finn's practically a Moore and they've treated him better than his own family. Although the way he feels about Luna is anything but familial, especially after that kiss three years ago...not that she remembers that.

The more time Luna spends with Finley, the more she lets her walls down. But getting involved with Lou means Finn could risk losing the only genuine family he's ever known. When their chemistry becomes impossible to ignore, will they take a chance on love—or will the waves of reality crash down upon them?

Acknowledgements

Growing up, I was always very excited for St. Patrick's Day to roll around because I actually had Irish heritage—or at least I thought I did.

My maternal grandmother, Sheila, was raised in an Irish household, and my mother passed some of the traditions she grew up with to me and my siblings. As a young child, I only knew I was Irish. As I got older, I understood that my grandmother had been adopted, so that left me in a sort of ancestry limbo. Maybe I was Irish, maybe I wasn't.

In March of 2020, I went to Ireland with my husband for vacation, and we returned to the United States just before the world shut down due to the COVID-19 pandemic. My work as a travel journalist shriveled up overnight, and I suddenly had a lot of free time on my hands. With Ireland fresh on my mind, a wide open schedule, and a little inspiration from my grandmother's past, I began *The Half of It*.

Aside from writing something undeniably swoony, I wanted to represent Ireland in a respectful way. A huge thank you to Aimee Walker, who beta read for me, specifically examining Irish culture and language. Her notes were integral to making this world as honest and genuine as possible. Sinéad from TJC Writing Group, thank you for your "lol we don't do that" real advice that I needed. I know, I know, I still included mention of the famine, but hopefully the Gaelic football makes up for it.

Johnny Daly of Irish Folk Tours provided such wonderful insight into the tradition of Irish storytelling, and he gave me so many wonderful ideas to work into that scene upstairs at McCarthy's Pub. I struggled writing that part of the book, but after talking with Johnny, everything just fell into place. Thank you for sharing your time, knowledge, and culture with me. Thank you also to Alanna for sharing memories of sitting down with your grandmother for story time. I hope that some of the magic you felt as a child shows up in that scene.

Jeanne DeVita has given me some incredible guidance on this book, as well as invaluable advice for my entire career. June and Aidan's story would not exist without her wisdom and encouragement. Jeanne, you are an absolute legend—thank you! Sarah and Andrea, I will never forget how generous you both were to chat with me about authoring and the book industry. Our conversations encouraged me to go down this path, and I cannot thank you enough.

I love my crew at The Writer's Helm and our trusty captain, Gabby. It's such a lovely and safe space, and I have no lack of inspiration and support because of all of you. My critique partners, Danielle Amerian and Jess Walker: I respect you and value your input so deeply. I love our chats, and I love how you're both always encouraging me to become a better writer. Sarah, Anna, Maddi, Himani, Annie, and Ri, thank you for beta-reading my book. Fine-tuning *The Half of It* was a joy because of your notes.

I'm beyond pleased to have worked with my editor, Stephanie Fung, and proofreader Angela Garcia at Romance the Page LLC for the second time. The relief that I feel when my book is in your hands is like a deep tissue massage for my little brain, and both of you strengthen my story in a way I could never have anticipated. Thank you! Morgane Flodrops, my illustrator and cover designer, did such an incredible job taking all of my ideas and turning them into a living, breathing romance book cover. Thank you for being so patient with me and for creating something so beautiful.

To my Nasty Women Read Romance book clubbers, you were a bright spot during a dark time. Thank you for sharing my love of all things romance.

David M. Eagleman wrote that the third and final death of a person happens when their name is spoken for the last time. So, Sheila Terese Gazdziak, you live on a while longer. I may not have any memories of you, but I am thankful for you and your life. Thanks to my mom for sharing parts of her mom with me, including Irish culture. Thanks to my dad for all that ancestry research. I'll probably always feel a little bit Irish, despite what your findings revealed.

Ayesha, I'm forever glad that I took a chance and drove down to Santa Cruz to hang out with you. Suzanne, thank goodness the subject line of your first email to me didn't scare me off too badly. You two are the supportive friends a gal could only dream of, and you both bring so much light, confidence, and love into my life simply by being yourselves.

Matt, thank you for believing in me and for reminding me to eat lunch. Thank you for a million other things too, but I can't think of them right now because I'm too overwhelmed by how much I love you when I think about you.

And from the bottom of my heart, thank you to you, dear reader. I'm grateful that you picked up a book from a newbie author like myself, and honored that you're here and reading it until the very end. Thank you, thank you, thank you.

About the Author

Theresa Christine is a contemporary romance author who writes love stories that take people places. Inspired by her past work as a travel journalist, her heartfelt, steamy novels are set in spectacular locations around the world. She resides in Hamburg, Germany, with her husband and their two energetic cats.

www.theresachristine.com

@theresachristinewrites on TikTok

@theresachristinewrites on Instagram

www.ingramcontent.com/pod-product-compliance
Lightning Source LLC
Chambersburg PA
CBHW020006120726
47903CB00004B/1164